THE BLOOD STAINS

ALFRED NYAGAKA NYAMWANGE

COPYRIGHT

DISCLAIMER

This story is entirely a work of fiction. All the names, characters, places, locales, events and incidents are either the product of the author's imagination or used in a fictitious manner. Any resemblance to actual persons, living or dead, or actual events is purely coincidental.

ACKNOWLEDGMENT

I would like to acknowledge my family for their unwavering support and dedication to this novel, Caren, Sasha, Masha and Timon. My siblings Mwango, Orare, Wambui, Anyango, Marise, Kemunto and Brian with whom Dad David and Mom Dinah regaled and fed essences of serving humanity.

I also want to acknowledge my friends George Ochoti, Ruth Nyagucha, Lameck Mariera, Dorcas Nafula, Wekati Wafula, for reading the work in its nascent stages and giving their rich views. Were it not for them making me believe in myself and correcting my work, **The Blood Stains** would never have been completed.

I would not forget to acknowledge my Editors: John Owen and Margaret Wairimu for ensuring that my work was spotless

Finally, I would like to acknowledge the Almighty. His grace has been sufficient to me during my writing period.

DEDICATION

To all women in the trenches whose blood is spilt to water humanity

Don't we bleed when you cull us

For your deflowering debauchery?

When we pay nature's monthly tax,

When the nine months' bulge

Bursts blossoming in feeble bleats?

When defilers wreck our little rose buds,

When the shrine keepers disgorge

The cavity of its little finger?

And when our humanity

Spattered in blood stains is hoisted?

Why don't you cry with us?

Why don't you whine with us?

Enana Enuke (1989)

BOOK ONE

1

I hear the screams. Horrific, mouth-twisting calisthenics. My *goko*, dear baby, will be dying. The sound throbs at the core of my brain. She is writhing in pain as her weak limbs grow frail. There is a helpless trail of tears on her twisted face. Vega, the one who opened the way for the rest would be in real danger.

Suddenly, I wake up. The screams are part of me, *I've been screaming again, o Lord!* My body is enveloped in sweat. There are tears in my eyes. The bedclothes are in an ocean of wetness. I feel the dampness at the corner of my mouth—saliva. The pillow is wet too. How so real to be a dream!

I struggle to turn to my back but my legs cannot budge. The reality of my condition keeps striking me with fresh horrors each time. I run my fingers on the old scars and study the calluses. *This could not be me. Yes, this is a new born Nerina. No feelings. Numb.* Especially, my legs have lost it all.

I've long given up on that part of pitying myself. My new status is fully accepted. At the moment I just want to plunge back into my sleep. It numbs the past like a good sedative. To think of the past has again stolen dear sleep from my eyes.

I whisper a silent prayer. *"Good God, carry me in the wave of forgetfulness and plunge me into darkness."* It is therapeutic and desirable to sometimes smother one's thoughts and feelings. How I yearn for sleep!

But a different darkness like a chasm loom before me. It takes the shape of a monster, vast, amorphous and threatening. I open my eyes to stare at it. I can't see beyond my sockets but can feel it. I cannot also touch it.

My ears can pick sounds in the dark. A monotonous slap like ticking of the wall clock; a dull music of bed clothes as other sleepers make restless turns; a reverberating hollowness of the building, punctuated with foraging movements of bats, cockroaches, and even rats. Water is dripping somewhere; could it be raining?

I close my eyes but still can't sleep. I even see better with my closed eyes, and tears trickle their sockets. *No, I don't want to cry, LORD!* The globules of tears are slowly transforming into red. They take a horrifying dimension. They are stains of blood! Stains that litter my path of life.

There is a scream and thud. An endless pain. Yet, the one at the back, another scream that accompanies the final catharsis by the assailant, supersedes all the rest. A clank of the metallic rod landing on the floor and clattering along. The heinous work is over. Retreating steps. Closing doors. Sobbing sounds welling from me, then, darkness and a deep silence.

"Good angels wing me to slumber land. Oh, take me in your hands and bear me across the billows of life!" A song starts somewhere in me. Who stole my sleep? Suddenly the scream takes form, shape.

"No-! Nixon!"

The name of my husband. That jolts me awake.

I shake my head for clarity. Can I precisely place that? Was it on our wedding night while caught up with the excitement of staining my bridal garments? Yes, I paid a price to have that. No regrets. Or was it much later when the animal in my angelic Nixon came out, crawling, biting, and fighting to destroy my entity?

"No Nixon!"

"No-! Nixon!"

"Noooo, Noooo, Noooooo!" I scream like rings bursting in a placid pool.

I slowly drag myself over to the side of the bed. My entire abdomen is yet to adapt feelings and it might sound evil to resist deprived pleasures!

Am I not supposed to be a woman? Your type of shrink will call it martyrdom- a case of sour grapes, blah, blah. I call it premeditated murder.

He strode towards me in a rage and smashed his fist to the side of my half open mouth throwing me out of balance. I was completely shocked by this show of raw strength.

"Nixon, what is wrong?" I blubbered out, my tongue licking on my torn lips, soaking in the pain. The kick he lashed out hit me on the groin. I doubled over in excruciating pain.

"No Nixon!" I screamed and knocked my dizzy head on a piece of furniture as I tried to straighten up.

I heard the sounds of running feet. The children might have heard the commotion and were coming to check. The man was undeterred and breathing like a deranged bull, charging at me.

I saw the opening as he lifted his arms, something in his hands, and could have rushed him in self-defense and disabled him. But he was my husband of over twelve years and nothing like this had ever happened. I was determined to wait, and reason with him. Nursing a germ of hope.

A blow whacked my open palm and I felt something snap as pain shot all over my hand. I cringed in pain. In his hands he had a grey metal rod. The blow had been aimed at my head.

He swung it wildly around and rushed me before I could even master my survival tactics. The metal found the base of my spinal cord, with a hard-vicious blow that shook the core of my body. I fell, coiled, and writhed in pain as my bowels opened. A series of blows landed everywhere on my body as I kept screaming at him to stop.

The kids, whom I barely heard their voices add to mine as they beat at the locked door. I could not physically fight so I reached out with my voice, climbing over decibels, and as if the act was a threat to him, he responded by adding blow after blow, very savagely and barbarically.

"I've tried to kill you! I've tried to kill you!" Nixon was screaming as he made a pulpy mess of me.

3

I woke up to the beeping sounds and lines of red and yellow blinking on a screen. The room was congested with smells of morphine and laudanum.

There was an expanse of eye-punishing whiteness, like a searchlight driving its arrows of rays into my eyes. A wave of darkness hit the shores of awareness, dragging me under for a moment, rolling me over and over, with a burst of white foam. Riding the wave was a grinning face of a man, his eyes glittering with want, as he seemed to puff and huff away.

"No! No!" my protestations grew fainter each moment. There was an upended blob before me with bulging neck veins from whose punctured opening red bubbles dripped. One big bubble played hide-and-seek with me, moving upwards and downwards in a motion similar to the Adam's apple.

For a moment, I even imagined seeing the bubble ride higher through the vein, detaching itself from my body, levitating across the room, floating along the room, drifting along the white ceiling, coming lower, hovering above my nostrils in wheezing sounds. From far, throbs of pain ate me. I wanted to run but no part of me responded. A wished to drag myself away from the pain that had suddenly obsessed me. I stroked out but a giant wave dragged me below, my eyes and ears filled with noise.

My body felt unusually tired, gummy and disjointed. My groggy mind suddenly cleared and a murderous rod flashed before me. I began to squirm from its blows and cried out for help.

"Why did he have to do it?" I looked up and saw the creased face, toothless gums, pressed with concern.

"Saarange, my grandmother!" her eyes closed for a moment as she leant on her staff for support. The dry wrinkled face with hanging folds showed the ravages of aging on the woman. I saw whitish particles at the corners of her eyes mist with tears like rivulets coursing through a rugged terrain.

"Why did he have to do it? What did they feed him with to make him so mad?"

"Baba, grandma*"* I softly called out and saw her start. Opening her eyes, she leaned forward, one hand on the bed.

"You called? My *goko* called? My Nyabisio, the lucky one called?"
More shadows materialized. Faces peering at me as the old woman placed her face on my cheek, her tears flowing.
"She's talked! She's talked!"
She moved back with sudden strength. A leaner face moved closer. Those innocent eyes laden with concern. Vega, my first-born. I wanted to hold her, to give her a shoulder to lean on. Her scrawny, tall body with emergent telltale knots on her chest fell forward. She always was the subject of my dreams as if her delicacy in adolescence offered a panorama of my vulnerability during the same age and its painful experience. Was I reliving her life or mine? Somebody pulled her back as she sobbed uncontrollably.
I saw all those faces of friends and relatives, far away, out of the reach of my heavy hands. There was Gym my second born, a cool boy, standing rigid in a corner chewing something in his mouth. Omare, our last born, heavy eyed and sniffling every time he turned to face the gadgets attached to his poor mother. My sophisticated brother Erastus and his white American wife Pamela drawing heavy ahs and ohs all over the place. My elder brother Jones and Colista, his hypochondriac wife, and my sisters Jelita and Alice.
Even Truscilla the late brother of Nixon's wife, coiled like a serpent, with her 'bleeding eyes' ever bilious and spiteful in tango with Hortenzia my step-mother, she of neighing laughter and shrill tones hovering up there. The loyal and 'earthly' Peter, my father's farm hand in his trademark yellow boots and smell of cow dung to boot and his sidekick, Mongina, our perennial housekeeper, spoiling for tears as usual. Then Mr. Maina, 'my father' with a walking stick, a ghost of the once hefty giant, with bony appearance and clothes that ill flitted him, shuffling in. A family gathering indeed even in the absence of Luciana, our mother. Plus, a retinue of visitors and reporters to pick sensuous snippets of damning evidence to report.
"All men have evil blood." Female Rights enthusiasts said, bursting with gusto over this evident case of social human failure.
"No to violence!"
"Castrate the beasts!" Their NGO thirsty had to be satiated by the news of what had happened.

An abrupt, warm sensation engulfed me, soaring my feelings, and suddenly surging my emotions. I wanted to touch all of them, embrace them, walk with them, tell them how much I loved them and thank them. But I didn't have an iota of strength to move, and like a corpse waiting to be lowered to the ground, I saw them all through my tears, peering down at me, so near and yet so far.

The sight of Jemima, the Mvita policewoman galvanized me. We had not met for a period of almost six years and there she was still cute, agile and confident.

She touched my arm, her eyes on mine.

"We will make it girl." It was a whisper. Jemima was sharing in my pain as before, inviting me to be joint partners in the challenge ahead.

She might have looked round and seen my frail father, when she burst out.

"Maina!" her voice sounded so glad- "Bull of Auckland—it has caught up with you at long last eh!?"

"What?" My father swung around furiously.

During my wedding the two had almost come to blows and here they were spoiling for the same battle, and Jemima had sworn to shoot him next time. The root of their bad blood was still a mystery.

Several necks swung in amazement.

Maina lifted his stick and wanted to hit out but a vicious bout of coughing nearly toppled him over. He bent over and wheezed like a deflating tire.

"You can't even see that you are finished. That girl you once gave a lift, and 'the things girls desire most when at the threshold of adulthood' is here. You hooked her to *mbeca*, money, impregnated and threw her out!"

The sick man raised a weak hand in protest.

"But your wife had a better sense of the situation. She accommodated and nursed *her* daughter." She strode towards him and pursued relentlessly.

Time seemed to standstill for a moment.

"You wanted *her* to abort, didn't you? She kept the baby and gave birth; the rest is history."

The man at once straightened out as if awakened from a bad dream.

"Where did the child go?"

"Silly! The child, I gave it to your wife. RTS- return to sender."
"Oh God. Oh God!" The next thing I heard was a falling stick and a thud followed by rushing feet.
In dread I thought Jemima had finally fulfilled her last threat.
"Mr. Maina, next time you dare strike at me I'll shoot you good and proper!"
I swear I hadn't heard the shot if there was one. Instead, something like a fresh blow rose inside my brain, building up until I began gasping for air.
"Oh my! Oh my!" Jemima's hands were all over my face as she cried out.
The machine's bleeping intensified as something cold and hard knocked me out.

4

Mother, Luciana (in short Lucia) was a little sprightly woman who was ever cheerful with an abhorring sense of timidity in her approach to pertinent issues. I vividly recall her light oval and blotch less face.
On the other hand, was my father, big, black and sturdy like a gorilla. All hair had cleared from the center of his head, a feature which he effectively hid beneath a felt cap. He had shifty eyes, a booming voice and preferred brown full necked pullovers to cover his torso. He had built us a "palace", those days, a stone house with blue sheets roof, iron doors, big wide windows, beautiful bougainvillea and chrysanthemums curiously blossoming from its walls. Mum, to keep it clean, never allowed us into the lounge with our shoes or mud caked feet. She kept us in the other house until when some important people came to visit.
Father could drive the battered pick up from his business premises right up to the veranda, its defective exhaust pipe roaring like thunder. It always alerted everybody miles away of his homecoming and he fancied it. It didn't matter if the tires were muddy, the faithful us would clean up the mess immediately he got home. He would dash to inspect his zero-grazing unit, orchards and come pounding inside the palace, cow dung or dust clinging to his boots.

"Oh, when the saints go marching in" he liked whistling such a tune. All his family kept close by, ready to salute like Peter did every time he opened the compound gate for him.

"Where are your report cards? Exercise books?" the voice rattled the house.

Soon, a queue of squirming school children. Quaking to the bone would be formed behind his master seat with books, marked assignments and mark sheets. Nobody dared come close to his neat clothes.

"Dirt messy brats!" he dismissed the children with the indefinite phrase that showed his disgust.

He opened the window that gave him the view of the undulated land, trees, and endless greenery, and stood there for a while. Our eyes quietly followed his all the time. The house was spotlessly clean, polished and with bright seat covers. There was a picture I really loved, where father stood beside a timid Luciana, resplendent with her wedding garments, happiness written all over their faces.

He turned and saw us, winked and walked past us to the bathroom to wash. Fidgeting, we stood there listening, praying, and hoping. The water splashed a different tune of urgency over his sonorous baritone rendering a popular chorus.

He walked back, his slippers making a pat pat noise. At that moment, mum surfaced from an adjacent door rubbing her wet hands on a 'lesso' tied by her waist.

"How are you Luciana?"

"I am fine Daddy," Mum's voice was melodious. I've never known why she always addressed him as Daddy.

"Jones!" He said as he sunk into his seat.

"Yes sir!" the boy handed over his work. A nod of the head, a mumble, a wild look and then a sudden motion of hands grabbing Jones and bashing him against a book as the young man whimpered in protest like a dog.

"What do you mean; you can't get this fraction right?"

"I tried father."

"Not enough son. You do it! Life is harder than you think. You will work in the orchard for the whole of this week from 8 to 6 every day."

"Yes, sir."

It continued along the line of birth. Everybody got his or her share of chastisement and being asked to work in a place meant keeping time scheduled, pruning, spraying and weeding according to laid down procedures and standards. Daddy never fancied shortcuts or any monkeying. And we girls had no much grey stuff between our ears, always being closer to our mother, whom he usually dismissed as an idiot.

"You always incite them against decency and morality! Just let them give birth, or become prostitutes and I'll chase you from this compound to the harem!"

Luciana kept mum, stoically holding her head high against all odds. I felt that her quietness was her only defense for our 'waywardness' as he called it, and what do you think my elder sister had done to be pilloried? Just a normal lapse in English grammar, a wrong calculation, and we all became prostitutes!

There was a day when mum had dared offer Daddy some unsolicited advice on the sales of maize that season. The man without warning lashed at her, the blow throwing her off balance and as she whimpered fearfully sprawled on the floor he stepped on her body. We flinched and shrunk with fear, and scampered to safety. He proceeded to drag Luciana across the floor as if she was a dead *dik dik*.

"You always try to bring me down. You also incite your brats against me. Don't you know I unflinchingly took the cut?"

Mum only sobbed quietly as if she was afraid, we could join her to embarrass her husband and all this used to happen before Hortenzia, her co-wife who had joined our family.

When he was in a better mood, Daddy used a piece of rubber to instill discipline on all of us, Luciana inclusive. After cleansing our stupidity or waywardness, the high priest stomped about his heavy footfalls punctuating his points of admonition. We huddled in silence listening.

"Life is like a maize cob, hard and rough. I sweat myself out there to take you to school and put decent food on the table. There are families that don't enjoy any of these luxuries here. You drink milk and even bathe with milk. Jeffrey?"

"Yes, sir." Jeffrey was quick to blurt that out.

"If there is one child of mine who doesn't put on shoes let him or her stand up." There was not a single stir. Our heads hang guiltily. I looked at my Mother's featureless face. Even when she took us to the farm and made us do every chore, she had nothing to claim for herself. Daddy was ever absent from home yet things worked out due to his organizational skills and all credit went to him. We were his family and owed everything to him anyway.

It was stoic that mum was taking everything uncomplainingly in her stride until Hortenzia materialized out of the blue like a bullet.

5

Hortenzia, she of the shrilly and hilarious voice joined our family when I was in standard three. I had just come home and found my usually cheerful mother sulking in the shadows of the house, her eyes red with weeping.

"What is it?" I asked but she let out a jet of whitish spew in some direction.

Turning around a corner of the house was Daddy with a small and very dark girl almost the age of Jelita clinging to his arm. Mum dashed into the house like a scalded cat while the rest of her clan, Mongina, Alice dived towards the kitchen.

My father was rubbing his muddy boots on some rack as the girl looked around herself in a winded and fearful manner, alien to her surroundings.

Daddy, as if realizing Hortenzia's discomfiture, took her in his hefty hand and drew her to him passionately. Then hell broke loose when our docile mum decided to speak out.

"How shameful of you, Maina! Hugging a baby girl in front of your daughters is not good manners or is it?"

We all swung around like marionettes to look at Mama. She was talking fast as her chest heaved up and down.

"Mr. Maina, a respectful father you are! Full honors you grant your sacred marriage vows! Now that I am old, dirty and despicable, I have to be abandoned, Eh?" Tears freely streamed down her visage as she resumed waving her clenched fists in the air in an effort to drive her message home.

"Stop it! Nakusihi, I entreat you, stop it!"

The sight of Maina stamping his feet and producing guttural noises like an agitated King Kong left us little room to guess his line of action.

"How dare you abuse my husband" the attack took a wrong angle, the woman saying, in a high-pitched shrill voice that brought us out of our innocent cocoons.

"Husband!" my mother madly hollered back.

"Miss Beauty, husband? Where were you when this compound was bare, husband?"

At that point, my father like a crazy bull charged, his long strides dwarfing those of my mom. Edging sideways she kept her safe distance as she railed him with vitriol unknown to us before.

"How low can men stoop?"

There was a moment of consternation when he sped blindly after her, tripped on a log and barely secured his balance. Sensing danger mom turned around and raced out of the compound.

"I don't want ever to see you again woman!" his booming voice awakened us from the mesmerizing stupor inflicted on us by the unfolding drama.

"The nosiness, Pooh!" He muttered, only to see us huddled together like confused sheep quaking with fear.

"You can go and follow her, idiots!" Mongina beat it in the direction of the kitchen and we scrammed after her, except our eldest brother, Humphrey, who took the wrong side of advice and made two strides to go after mum only to be picked up like a young baboon, whirled into the air, made to kneel, and whacked twice across his bum. He sprinted, howling like a sick puppy, and shot past us into the bedroom where he remained for a long time. We couldn't stifle our laughter.

It was with such a kind of pomp that queen Hortenzia was installed on Mama's marriage throne. Her arrival so violently shook the Maina establishment that we had been used to, sowing seeds of discord that would haunt us for a long time in the future.

6

For up to a year that mom was away, our school going turned into a nightmare. We had to be up by five to milk and feed the animals, wash and clean the home besides preparing our breakfast and we assigned each of us a particular task under the guidance of Mongina and it was important that however young I was, I had to extricate myself from the warmth of the bed as early as possible to give a hand. The mornings could be extremely and punishingly chilly. Your fingers' blood seems to congeal as if frost-bitten and you needed to keep stretching and rubbing them to keep the blood flowing. The mist rose like smoke, energetically embracing the atmosphere and blurring the vision. However, the visionary farmers and other workers never missed their work. They had to sacrifice and be committed.

I think we all did this for Mama because we never wanted anything to go wrong in her absence. It made us committed to our course because it was our food that was to be laid on the table. Hortenzia who could never stoop to our low status allotted herself the envious role of a supervisor, and a real supervisor she was, one who did not accommodate anything below her own spotless standards of cleanliness, hard work and integrity. Her word became a rule and we never dared raise our eyebrows for she was the instrument of our father's bidding. We didn't want the risk of inviting dad's wrath on us either.

"What cleaning is this?" she could say, her shrill voice piercing the morning air. She would be pointing at the floor that Jelita or Alice had just mopped, her heel grinding along the moist patch, leaving some dirt splotches of her own.

"We can't allow some people to outgrow wisdom." The side remark meant that the girls had physically grown but little to show of it in the brains.

It is important to tell that Jelita and Alice had a unique childhood bond. They had been born 15 months apart and were like twins to most visitors who came to our home, since they were almost of the same height and complexion. Mom had 'accidentally" become pregnant when Jelita was about four months old. Three months later, the women in the know advised her against suckling Jelita claiming that this could affect her and the unborn baby. Somehow Jelita didn't become as strong as Alice who took what was meant for the former. The latter would swing into action to offer defense to her sister, as if the two had an unwritten pact to live for each other. Thus, the girls grew together, closely knit, bond by their strong cradle roots.

Therefore, when Hortenzia descended on one with words and fists the other hung about sizzling with emotions over the other. As the other was made to re-do a task the other remained close by merely fearing to assist because the wrath would be turned on both of them.

I once remember Saarange, our grandma telling Hortenzia off on the way she was being hard on us. Alice had just suffered an eye injury in her hands and the former's eye was swollen and red like pepper.

"You can bring forth your children and work on them with such barbarism. You can't go on punishing another woman's children as if she is extinct." The forthright lady was the only voice that was ever raised on our behalf in the village where everybody minded their business.

"Look here old bones, they either dance to my tune, or follow their mother wherever she is now. Which caring mother gives birth to uncultured puppies like these and neglects them?"

Saarange came out; boiling like a steam engine but Hortenzia had taken cover. The tongue lashing that flowed from the old woman was like the whips we could have loved to deliver on our tormentor.

"How can clueless lass dare call me old bones? Old bones could I be but not a witch! Old age? It comes unannounced on every being? Come out and today you will know what I am made of. The one who cleaned the bottom of your husband. And you dare?"

We loved her vibes and wished she could come out to square it out with old Saarange. From that time, we quietly began to call Hortenzia a witch. That evening, dad came and found his wife marooned in a safe corner of the room. The story she gave him made him mad such that he paraded all of us including the servile Peter and weepy Mongina and proceeded to randomly cane us for not protecting the queen from the old predator.

"This is your mother and she deserve all respect," he roared as we rubbed our sore backs. "Silence!" whack! The cane landed on me because I was still sobbing. "This is your boss in my absence." I was sure Hortenzia relished everything and knew she had gained a complete foothold in the affairs of this homestead. This marked the beginning of loathing anything associated with her. Even her voice disgusted me.

A few days later, Jelita and Alice decided to cause trouble. They woke up late and simply reported to school without touching a single chore at home. At lunch, they breezed into house and found Hortenzia waiting for them blind with rage.

They ignored her and proceeded to the kitchen and begun preparing lunch as if nothing was amiss. Hortenzia came looking for them and was about to box them when Alice grasped her from behind. Jelita pulled a burning piece of wood from the hearth and they continued to make a handwork of her. They thoroughly beat, kicked her and were it not for Peter and Mongina, they could have split her womb open (she was five months pregnant) with the kitchen knife. In our young enthusiasm, we cheered on, her screams had become music to our ears. Peter only freed Hortenzia from the grip of the furious girls who sped in the direction of Saarange's home, the girls in hot pursuit. Saarange came to the scene and Hortenzia had to duck behind her out of the girls reach, panting, bruised and full of soot and bloodied.

"Saarange, you have to help me. They are killing me, Saarange. They are after my blood."

"Listen girls," the old woman intervened. "You have done enough so the next thing is whether you bid your father's warning that you protect the boss."

"As for you I had asked you to go slow on these children. Respect is earned, not forced. I believe you could only be a couple of years older than these children. That is the problem."

Hortenzia piteously wept touching the painful parts as Saarange let her away. She ended up in hospital. That evening, Jelita and Alice joined mom in her home. Dad didn't raise a voice or remonstrate as we had expected.

A week later, we came to learn that he had gone for his stray flock. We could laugh in secret every time we remembered the scene, since we were careful not to bring up the topic at home.

7

You could imagine that Jelita and Alice's action led to an automatic celebration because mom was back with us. We feared that dad in his humiliation was looking for an excuse to bash our heads for going against his personal convictions. We all the time felt that a malevolent force was spying on us. You couldn't even be free around the weepy Mongina and servile Peter.

It was until Alice narrated to us (of course at school) the plans they had come up with, with our furious maternal uncles threatening to beat him up.

"He started by berating us for not going to school. But those uncles sat him down and read a list of evils perpetrated on us, thereby silencing him. He appeared shocked."

"How would you tell he wasn't acting?"

"What he said later. 'Your mother will go with you to take care of you. Surely another woman can't take good care of children who are not hers. Jelita and Alice, I am ready to take you back to your mother.' He was pleading though we feared that maybe he wasn't being truthful. Mother just sat in a corner sulking demanding that the evil woman should get out of her compound. Our uncles reasoned with her and she simply stood up, picked a few things belonging to her, looked at the two of us, smiled to the consternation of those present, and got into the vehicle. We might have been too hasty in trusting him, but it was a victory. Mom's seven months of exile were finally over. It wouldn't matter how many times we would be beaten as long as she was with us. It's   like he had kept his part of the bargain not to harass us."

My mother's homecoming would have been the last act Hortenzia, now heavy with a child, could approve. Jelita and Alice's lesson were not forgotten by her and her voice could be heard boisterously cursing some imaginary enemies who had made it difficult for her to enjoy life around, something she could go on doing until she grew breathless and lost her voice. However, to us, it was an invitation for physical attack until we wondered what would happen if we hit her protruding belly.

But so long as the two women who shared a husband continued living under one roof, the conflict would still continue. Hortenzia later gave birth to a bouncing baby boy who she named after our late grandpa, thus securing a niche within the larger family setup. Not long after, she began to flex and wax for a fight and we inadvertently began to suffer evil eyes from her whenever we were in the wrong and alone with her in the house. Mom tried as much to ignore our complaints as if she didn't care what happened to us.

One day, Hortenzia sent me to collect her milk from a nearby kiosk. Of late, I had been down with a flu that had prevented me from going to school and I delayed running her errand. Hortenzia found me along the corridor dragging my feet. Her fingers got hold of me by the neck until I couldn't breathe, and as I tried to recover my breath, she pushed me and my head hit the wall. The pain shot through my body and I let out a loud cry that attracted mom from the other room. The spot suddenly swelled into an ugly lump.

"Hortenzia!"

"Luciana!"

"It wasn't anything mom," I tried to lie.

"Your daughters are too rude Luciana!"

"That's how I bring them up Hortenzia, to stand up for their rights. Besides you have given birth to an obedient son. Get him up and push him around, understand?"

"I don't expect such remarks to come from a Christian mother like you Luciana. You…"

"Shut up! My Christianity has nothing to do with your impudence my dear co-wife." Mother spat to her left. She began rubbing my painful lump. This was followed by a sarcastic laugh before adding. "You even snatched a father from them by playing the harlot…"

Hortenzia laughed in turn. "I truly came to eat some fat that was about to make you a pig. We could be having a round-to-round thing that wouldn't be walking around by now."

"Don't dare me gal…"

Hortenzia stood before mom, her full chest puffed up, her eyes glittering and her hands ready for battle.

My mother pushed her out of the way and Hortenzia hands flew out smacking mom across the face. And before one could say eureka the two bitter women like eternity were locked in a physical confrontation that silently involved pushing and weighing each other's strength, scratching, punching and biting until a sudden burst of screaming escaped Hortenzia's lips. Mom had always possessed a latent energy that if provoked would bring even Jones down in a blow. It was for this reason that we quietly called her 'Daudi mdogo," little David, and father … you guessed right. We never at any time contemplated a physical fight between the two, since mother was such a lousy fighter, owing to the way he openly smacked her around.

"Uuuiii uuuiii! They are killing me! Saarange, help!"

God was my witness for I was completely shocked at the sudden turn of events and therefore I had no hand in fighting her. I could swear that the two women were a match and could have even walked away without anybody knowing what had happened. The first people to arrive on the scene naturally were Jelita and Alice and at their sight Hortenzia panicked and dashed out of the house as Mongina and Peter were arriving on the scene. The latter could construe the scene which wasn't the true picture.

"It's my beauty that they hate. They want to fry me up and eat me and my child." Hortenzia sobbed the words out to the whole village, her folly being unleashed without limit. The child might have realized and charged up the atmosphere for it woke up and burst into an endless cry.

Dad came home and found a piteous sight of Hortenzia who had pulled at her hair and torn her clothes and cried continuously. In a flood of tears, the shriveled queen explained her woes. Mr. Maina hit the roof and summoned "all bitches" to the sitting room and ordered us all to go flat on our stomachs.

"Mr. Maina got the facts right before you," mom's words were cut midair with a blow to her belly that hurled her across the room where she crushed and passed water. The enraged man lounged at the wounded woman and literally stamped her body with his boots. It was another time I was witnessing this. Jelita and Alice slipped away so easily but I wasn't that lucky. The man snatched a nearby walking stick and swung it at me. It got into contact with my arm with a whack that saw it split as my arm broke into an excruciating pain that paralyzed me as I swooned to the ground in a dead faint. I could see surprise in his eyes as he went to gather me to himself.

When I came to, I was in my father's hands as he tried to stifle tears, trying to stem the blood from the wound. "You're the cause of this big head."

I got my first booking in hospital to fix my broken bones. It was also my first taste of male brutality at another level. The hand remained in a plaster for four months. Mother was the first one to be discharged as she had also broken a bone. When I came home, I found Dad had already bought building materials so that he could put up a separate house for Hortenzia.

Mom remained in a sullen silence while Jelita and Alice kept their distance from Dad and Hortenzia. It was   like closeness to our step-mother would inflict them with a deadly disease. I was like a savior who had carried their burden of sin. Reflecting back, I couldn't see the reason why I had to break an arm for being an eye witness. I wanted to get a chance and explain the situation. I had been unfairly condemned and I could see that Mr. Maina was avoiding a scenario where he would have to explain his acts. Deep in my heart, I knew he was remorseful but couldn't bring himself to tell me. I kept turning the words he had uttered "all bitches" and "big head" that evening over and over in my mind. Was there any bitchiness or big headedness in me?

8

Big Head was a term used in school to refer to a boy who appeared to be well endowed with this part of body; what teachers sometimes mockingly called Headmaster. In our formative years one to three in school, we were left on our own most of the time to run up and down in the field, playing, and fighting. A few minutes to lunch we would be gathered next to a hillock with a wooden structure from which a vehicle wheel rim was hanged. The rim was our school other bell or gong that could be hit by respective time keepers especially in the morning to announce the start of school time. The sound vibrated across the hills and valleys and made us make it to school on time. It was also used from calling us to assemblies within the school.

Our meetings were spent in story telling sessions that produced stars like Big Head who could render stories that left teachers and pupils in stitches with ease. Indeed, Big Head used his head in ways that surprised us, as if he knew some of his exaggerated moves would produce the required effect.

Sometimes, we were allowed to carry food to school. I preferred the sour millet porridge that mom usually packed for me. I had been running around when I discovered it had poured in the paper bag and the lid unfastened. I was distraught at the loss.

"Snotty nose!" Big Head said, out of the blues. Part of the gruel had messed up my dress and I was actually sniffling at the smudge. I wiped my nose with my hand thinking it might have been the problem.

"Not so sophisticated eh? A hand to your nose? Whom do you think will eat with you again?" the boy taunted me.

I was enraged and hit him with the paper bag. The gruel splashed out into his whole body. Before the tongue-tied boy could even utter a word, the other kids were jumping up and down, excitedly chanting.

"She's smeared him with porridge."

"She's smeared him with porridge."

Taken aback, I   fearfully slipped away and ran all the way to Jelita's class. Luckily there was no teacher in their class and clung to her and really cried.

"What is it baby?" she wrapped her hands on my head protectively. Some of the other pupils burst into laughter as she shepherded me into the verandah. Just then we met a girl whom I had just made friends with called Catherine looking for me. She was the one who gave Jelita the whole story as I shook with fear. In my mind, I had messed up someone's child and I was going to be beaten to death for it.

"I'll stand by you Nerina. I saw him provoke you." The firm words made me turn to Catherine. I hadn't known it was possible to defend my actions before the teachers whom I associated with caning.

Jelita then squeezed my hand and said warmly.

"You see, Nerina. Tell the truth to the teacher. O.K?" I nodded in agreement and Catherine took my hand, walked me to the rest of the pupils. Our colleagues were gathering around the bell and Madam Jane and Mr. Mobisa were trying to calm them. We joined them. My frantic looks around did not spot Big Head yet.

"Who is the owner of this container?" Mobisa was holding something in the air. It was my tin. A cold shiver ran up my spinal cord.

"Mine, Sir," Catherine shot up to my relief and went to get it. For the few days I had been around, Mobisa's physical features and voice scared me. He was a swarthy man who was bald at the center of his head, mean, with red eyes and a twitching moustache that some pupils had nicknamed Meow because it looked like a cat's whiskers. Every time he would use his long supple canes, he made sure it swished in the air before it hit the mark. Therefore, to have Catherine get the container from him was a sacrifice since she was going to get herself in trouble for my sake.

"Where is Master Porridge?" There was a loud laughter from the pupils as the fellow referred to stood up. It was Big Head, still wet from the porridge splash.

"Tell us a story." My mind went into a wandering rampage before it nudged to what Big Head had been saying.

"The lion with all his chutzpa was spoiling for a fight when he met the wily hare. "I am going to shame you man." "Ha ha-ha. You're too tiny for that." "One. Run away." "Silly jokes are not my type of menu young woman." "Then, wait for me." "Warning, the first blow will bring out your liver." "Nonsense. You're wasting my time." Roaarrrr! Pah! The first gourd broke on the lion's belly and some substances like blood and flesh dropped out.

"If you advance a step your brain will come out." The lion looked at the mess but since he was so annoyed, he advanced. Pah! The second gourd broke just between his eyes. "The brains are now out!" the lion seriously studied the blood and white mess all over him. *Jesus, the hare couldn't be joking*. "A mere step forward and out comes your heart!" The hare cautioned. The other animals were very quiet now. Pah! And out looped a piece of the flesh blood and flesh, the size of the heart. "The heart! The heart! The heart!" shouted the hare triumphantly. All the animals began the sickening chorus. The lion shot off like a rocket quaking with fear to the marrow. The hare had won this fight again."

There was instant cheering as Big Head stood there stealing the show, his head at a cockish angle nodding slightly in appreciation. It suddenly dawned on me he was referring to the porridge incident. Who did he think he was fooling? The uproar had not died when Madam Jane asked for another story. My hand shot up.

"Yes, the young girl with braided hair."
I was shoved to the front. I had no inkling of a story as I stood before the sea of excited faces, my jaws opening and closing spontaneously. All the stories I had heard before from Saarange, mom and even my sisters simply evaporated. I remembered Big head's story had been referring to me. The faces before me were getting impatient and some two or three giggles had begun.
"The stupid lion had on that day over eaten. He couldn't run as fast until the hare released another gourd full of bees on his back. The tutored bees knew their work well. The lion moved like lightning yelping in pain and shame."
My coup had been deftly delivered.
"It's my story!!!" Big Head was up protesting.
"What did you say?" Mobisa swung around livid with anger, his lips shaking and one or two beads of sweat glistening on his baldhead.
"She is destroying my story!"
"Destroying or building it?" it was Madam Jane's turn to wonder. The kids laughed. I slipped away cursing my mouth and hand.
'Where is the girl so that we know the moral of her story?" Mobisa couldn't find me. "She is here! She is here!" the other kids were pushing and pulling me up.
I began to cry and refused to budge even an inch. I felt sick and embarrassed. Catherine was holding me down too.
"This is notorious. Big head…?"
"Notorious! Notorious!" the pupils picked on the new word and sung it out. They might have loved its articulation. As Mobisa remonstrated with Big Head on the evils of being selfish. The young minds seethed with the word and at the end of the day, a nickname had been born, Notorious Nerina.

9

The fact that only Maina's daughters, unlike his sons, learned in local day schools showed how Dad valued women. In fact, while our brothers joined boarding school at standard three, we girls were left in the village with the common rabble.

For one to be admitted in standard one those days, your hand had to pass overhead and touch the opposite ear. Our school was an old one with rusty iron sheets. It consisted of three long blocks of mud housing of over fourteen classes and several offices. The windows were places on the wall that had not been filled with mud. The floors were perpetually dusty and you had to sprinkle water on them before you swept. This also meant constant smearing of the floors with a mixture of clay and cow dung to parry jigger attacks and give it a new look.

On such days, pupils came with containers of clay and cow dung from their homes. A whole day could be spent fetching extra clay while the bigger pupils did the smearing. The work was thoroughly done, overseen by the tall hawkish and wirily prefects. They also wielded long canes that they used unsparingly. Anything that reached the teachers had most definitely reached the disciplinarian Mr. Rioba.

"Come close and witness a donkey is disciplined…!" he would make the announcement as he bounced on his toes and strutted before the quaking culprit like a god of death. He was heavily built like a bull, short, fat and very dark, a darkness which seemed to grow with his anger. He caned using a wire cable, and occasionally added fists and kicks at the slightest sign of resistance.

'Our system allows only teachers and the police to cane, maim and kill. The Bible advocates that denying a child a cane is destroying him." He could say. The huge boys, some of them who were bearded, would tremble at these pronouncements that easily materialized into action.

"Here the system works and you are either in or out. Obedient disciplined pupils pass exams. What are the school rules?" he said, and the whole school, like puppets, would recite the rules like Sunday school kids reciting the Ten Commandments. Woe to you if you found yourself on the wrong side of the rules. The moment you were in a mistake the standard question was "which rule have you broken?"

I had already known all these happenings before I had even started seeking for admission. Perhaps the good side of school life was more attractive than finding yourself on the wrong side of the law.

There were the new things that expanded our horizons beyond the obvious and these were the brainy competitions; the nit grit of passing exams, the prize of being a winner, and its reward of claps, books and pencils. There were the juicy stories, the games, the friendships that home never accorded, and yes, the freedom of freely lounging about. It inspired the desire to yearn for school and once there, I had no reason to leave. My mother would wake me up before seven and assist me to clean and dress myself and dispatch me on time. I had noticed the kind and loving nature of Madam Jane who would hug us, lift us up, sing songs to us, dance with us and tell us stories.

"What did you eat last night?"

"Er, an egg."

"There is a piece of beef stuck in your teeth." I would blush as I covered my mouth.

"Nerry, I was only guessing." She would add laughing. She made me feel at ease. I loved the moments when the whole class would be flashing hands in the air shouting "Teacher! Teacher!" rhythmically like flapping wings of birds, all wanting to answer a question. When Big Head knew an answer, he could leave us to sweat while he sat grinning like a contented vampire. This boy had what it takes to annoy one, and an air of pride. "I am special, so why don't you treat me like one." These were the same characteristics that Maina exuded at home whenever he wanted people to know he was a special human being, a man.

"Remember I am circumcised. It was done in the cold of the morning and by one touch of the knife." Who could dare a man who had been hardened by the simple chivalry in the hands of a ghost-scaring circumciser? He repeated it every time until it was too boring as if he wanted us to limit our view of him to his carved phallic symbol above what he was to us. It was meant to belittle us and create him a room for respect, his virtues as a father, our provider, and our moral barometer notwithstanding.

"It has long legs."

"A giraffe."

"The rain," that would be Big Head doing it cockishly. The teacher led in the clapping. The jolly good rain and its long legs stretching from the sky to the ground, to my upturned face, soaking it, fresh and cold. It made me imagine what could have eaten crooked Big Head's feet? They were crooked and faced sideways, especially the little toes. The jiggers? They were every child's little nightmare. Teachers could cure such with acerbic juices of wild fruits squeezed into the spots they had dug out the parasites with pins. The victim found difficulties walking in grass and sand afterwards unless he healed.

Big Head also possessed this habit of letting some brownish solid mucus stream down his nostrils down to his upper lip. He was fond of sniffling through his nose, a game he had perfected until some teachers called him 'smoker.' Gosh, one who smoked mucus!

Another time he was arguing that at my home we washed our hands with milk because we were rich. I glared at him and he started flagging explaining he meant we had plenty. I couldn't say we didn't have enough as children of Maina, since we were provided with everything as a family whose father was an astute businessman.

"Those are rat's tales." Catherine dismissed his arguments. Big Head punched her. The next thing was Big Head sprawled inside the desks screaming for help, Catherine hitting and biting him. Madam Jane was the first one to arrive at the scene as the two separated. Catherine was all tears when she was given a chance to explain herself.

"He did it first."

"I'm sorry…" Big Head said and Madam rapped his head with her knuckles so loudly. How I loved Madam for that simple tap to the culprit's head! She didn't rush the matter to Rioba whose wrath was uncontrollable. I felt that what my father needed was the same tap to shed off his chauvinistic behavior.

For the first time, I saw Madam Jane's protecting hand; firm, brave and decisive hover over us like a guardian angel. While my sisters, the duo of Jelita and Alice had a youthful zest, energy and rash strength, she offered me something solid, the sure and confident feminine assurance of someone in control of her surroundings.

Mama had not prepared me for some things that I would meet later in life. Even with her sprightly cheerful nature, her laid-back nature was perhaps her greatest inhibitor.

Not even Nyakerario's, the circumciser, the expert in nicking of the grubby things between our legs, whose mere nicking was assumed to shove a girl into the threshold of womanhood had prepared me for the future encounters.

As for Nyakerario, it was an anticlimax for far from the excruciating pain I had anticipated knifing through me as I writhed in pain. It came to me as an abrupt keen, some smarting and the blood dripping a line on the ground as I wadded along, but it didn't prepare me for the mental anguish of being unable to feel my womanly potential every time I lay into the night smarting. The pain that never hit me during the cut would every time open up in a smarting ache that killed all waves of erotic desire pumping into me with feelings of unknown fear. It was both a physical and a psychological scar that would haunt me forever.

"You are of age," a neighbor had hinted.

"We are soon to take your tea," another woman added.

"You are about to wipe the *enkene*, a tapeworm, from the top of the cooking stone."

I was in the dark until they explained to me that I was about to be circumcised. This would prepare me for another level as a woman, make me wiser and hand me a different perspective of life. Through these couched implications, the society wanted to make me a real woman but at the price of robbing me the clitoris which they would feed the ants with (they made me feel it was the offending stuff in my body and getting rid of it would leave me clean and pure). From that time, I had an agenda to convince my mother because I wanted to be full like her, like other older girls. My actions indeed converted mum to my new religion.

I still see the 'real" women bubbling with excitement like a pot of ripe beer, leaping, gamboling, and ululating happily as they did their sex-dance. What do you call a dance where the bottom is stuck out provocatively, gyrated, in mock sex that scares men from the path ways? Then the ribald tunes, the slapping of those bottoms, the act of giving it more prominence as if woman is all bottom.

Okunire ontone	She's touched the grub
Okunire ontone	She's touched the grub
Kuna Moyare baba	Touch Moyare, mother
Kuna	Touch!

(By the way, while Moyare can be somebody's name, it also refers to the farthest place from my village). They sing themselves hoarse, punctuating the silent interludes with coquettish laughter with resounding uuhs at the end. There is always the small girl in even the oldest woman, something   childish that never dies whenever they are together as company. Their faces were decorated with a variety of colors as rivulets of sweat furrowed streaks along them, giving them the ghostly look. Their bodies were entwined with creepers and leaves so that they resembled moving thickets. Lessos, shawls, lassoed their waists so as to give their bums a hardy protruding impression. This was basically a woman's do.

Once every lad's wife
She is a wife of men.

They excitedly chorused. Wife of men or thing for men, my foot! Small and young as I was? After teasing and dancing my mother sore, as they escorted me and some village novices to the hut where we would live in seclusion until we were healed. They sat to gobble food in large quantities to compensate for their exertion. All this dancing was generously rewarded, for they could not depart until the tea, *mandazi* and meat flowed.

My mother took up the challenge, dashed around ululating and flashing the cooking stick all over the place. I thought she had lost her head. Some of our guests, during such an occasion where everybody was welcome, induced vomiting to start all over again for the hostess had to be punished somehow for being too clever. These are the ones who were said to have the appetite, "the uvula to swallow" and the host just played along, no reprisals or reprimanding for this was an occasion for happiness. Circumcision of a child graduated a mother from being a mere fellow to a woman of class. Why then should you complain of your newly acquired status which others begrudged you?

My colleagues and I stayed away from the outside world tending to a fire. The fire was never to die all the time as this would bring us a curse of death, infertility or something worse. With our hawkish attendants, we kept it blazing all the time, night and day, choking on its stinging smoke since the stumps were usually damp. Our fire burned on and, in the end, we celebrated our successful graduation to the next level. We were taught a few things on motherhood but not enough to launch me to wifely duties.

Mother, perhaps like all mothers before, you abandoned me to my own womanly whims. Did you ever tell me that I would pay the monthly tax with my blood, those awkward nasty discomforting moments that I've failed to get used to all my adult life? Did you teach me how to excite my man and take him to heights, when to avoid him, when to welcome him to my doors, even when my body felt repulsive? Oh gosh! I am yet to teach anything to my own Vega? What will I teach her? What will I teach my baby? It's with shock, dread and tears I remember your presence, yet you were absent to handle issues about my womanhood. And when I most needed you, *you* disappeared leaving me in the hands of the ravenous wolves called men? I was a mere toddler in this forest of life, fumbling, bumbling, and tottering around. Did anyone expect me to find the path home? Are things any better for my Vega now that I am alive? I promise as a mother to make a difference. It is perhaps the only reason why I am alive.

They only robbed me of my little finger and made me feel important. LOL. How mistaken for with my little finger gone cold, I've never had a total grip of my femininity, my sacredness, my individuality as a woman entitled to wholesome happiness

11

The moment mum disappeared, the gap in my life was soon taken over by Daddy who wanted to stamp his presence in my life. His behavior to me was greatly endearing and encouraging both in school and at home. I was still too shaken perhaps to worry over this overnight change of behavior towards me.

One day, he brought me a colorful body-hugging outfit. My other sisters were livid with jealousy.

"Wow, you look gorgeous in that!" Daddy expressed his admiration. To see myself standing in better light than all the rest in the family filled me with pride. As he tugged at the hem to straighten the creases, I felt flattered. For the first time I warmed up to Daddy.

I sensed he wanted me to dress well and I began to preen myself and expect his pecks on my cheek. In the absence of mama, I had assumed a strange new role in my family that my eldest sisters Jelita and Alice could not even dream of. Not even Humphrey attracted the same treatment. The earlier admonitions on my shoddy work were forgotten. Was Daddy spoiling me? Was he making up for his past cruelty to me?

I didn't read any hypocrisy in the man; that was for the experts. I am sure even Hortenzia's hostility doubled towards me with this queenly handling by Dad. I was the least worried now that I was the apple of my father's eye. Could have the sudden disappearance of Luciana left a yawning gulf in my life that needed to be filled?

One evening, Dad came home and announced that he was taking me with him to collect some kitchenware consignments for his wholesale from Kotu city. I was so excited and looked forward to the new experience with a sense of exhilaration.

On the material day the ride in the front seat beside him in the pick-up was thrilling. It was the longest journey I had ever made outside home and every scenery captivated me.

"Here, people don't fence homes like at home. They cultivate pineapple and sweet potatoes. This is Aroba, where the rice we eat at home is cultivated…" My father updated me on the strange places we came across.

The sight of magnificent and tall buildings left me agape. He took me to see Lake Nyancha and the vast stretch of grayish waters on which canoes zigzagged was so attractive. I could have loved to ride in one but for Dad's busy purchasing schedule. I listened to his shrewd business talk with his Asian suppliers and wondered whether I'II ever manage the haggling and bargaining involved.

By the time we did our final purchases, it was getting dark. We were only able to make it up to Bongo town.

 "I don't think it wise to travel at night, Nerry."

I was slightly surprised at his use of an abbreviation of my name. He parked at a hotel where we had our supper. After watching TV, Dad showed me to a room he had booked, two adjacent boarding rooms each for either of us. I left him watching TV with a couple of hilarious revelers and flung myself to bed too tired to switch one inside my room. The day had been hectic and soon I deep asleep.

At some time into the night I was awakened by a loud noise. I was about to blurt out my sister's name thinking I was back home when the lights flooded the room. Standing there and closing the door behind him, was daddy, a towel tucked around his waist. He had a beer bottle from which he was swigging, his hairy chest reminding of a gorilla in a zoo.

The first thought in my mind was that he had lost his way to his room. My eyes were adjusting to the light when he staggered across and sunk to a nearby seat and might have realized I was awake. A partial glance at my wrist watch showed it was approaching a few minutes past 2.

"Oh, my darling you are not yet asleep." He poured himself a bubbling stuff of brown into a tilted glass. "You know I failed to sleep until I shared this secret gnawing my soul with you."

He laughed warmly and emptied the glass in one gulp.

"I have always wondered how my family disintegrated. You see, your brothers were accusing your step mother, but did your mother ever tell you where she was going?"

I was now wide awake.

"I know she wouldn't," he said mischievously emitting a guffaw. "I know she was really hurt by my betrayal. In the heydays of our marriage I kept promising her that I'll never leave her for anybody. But then she grew sick and never wanted me near her…I don't know how to say it. It was painful, and I had to fill the gap. She kept saying things would be alright but I couldn't wait forever. I had more fire in my blood– you see. I had to salvage the family, my ego, so I took on Hortenzia. But it was a mistake…"

In my groggily state I couldn't believe what I was hearing. Why was I being told this stuff? A trail of tears stole along his temples and it made me utterly uncomfortable.

"Besides, babe, I have always yearned to tell you about your origins. Believe me, we picked you from a dustbin. A mite thing with ants crawling out of your mouth. We thought you wouldn't make it, but with faith and drive to do something positive, you made it. The scrawny, wasted thing is now a ripened being of all the time. Luciana prayed a lot indeed."

A cold shiver ran through my body. I didn't want to believe him. Was he drunk?

"Your mother had wanted me to take on another wife but your adoption seemed to recover her sickness. Somehow in my mind I had seen the other possibility. I had the money and means so I went ahead and did it anyway. Why don't you say something?"

The words had made me tremble. I was in a mental paralysis and I couldn't speak. He was now drinking from the bottle.

"Now you are the good girl, the best thing that came out of your mother's care. I've sought for an opportunity to tell you the truth. Your mother ran away because she had lost her dreams. But I haven't lost mine: to hold you, to make you feel one of mine to empower you with the gift, prepared and ready for consumption."

I coiled voluntarily as his fingers dug into the bed clothes.

"Don't ever run away from me Nerry. You-- you are a smart-brained, smart-assed baby…" He chuckled and emptied the bottle which he put aside.

"The angels are my witnesses! Who will ignore your physical beauty, the compactness of your body, your twin gazelles, and your shining eyes? Out there, there are wolves-- yes-- I mean men dying for you? I don't want them to ever touch you,"

He stood up and staggered towards the bed almost half crawling his long hands brushing roughly on top of me and his eyes glittering strangely.

"Mr. Maina, it's a mistake!" I sat upright and even the vehemence of my voice shocked me.

"What? Look, you don't even call me by name ha ha. Not the "Baba", "Dad" stuff. Resourcefulness. How pleasant!"

He simply pawed me the similar way a lion does a gazelle.

"You are sick!" My shout was a feeble protest.

"No, I'm normal babe. I- I love you and nobody will ever take you from me. No Man. No god. Not even Satan."

He yanked me out of bed, blankets and sheets falling all over the place as my half naked figure coiled with shock and bore me around the room like a sacrifice to the gods as he sung drunken praises at me, to his ingenuity and prized catch, a move his evil mind had schemed step by step. I tried to wriggle myself out of his powerful hands as his beer smelling breath stifled mine, almost suffocating me. I realized with pain and shock that there was no chance in a million for my salvation from such a hungry monster as him. It was night and, in a lodging, where many maidens screamed, it was a norm and couldn't attract any attention. The queenly pampering, the praises, the hugs were a calculated bait. I had now swallowed it- hook, line and sinker. He hurled me hard back to the bed.

12

I slammed the door shut behind me with a force that shook the room to its foundations. The image of the man's ruffled face, sprawled on the floor, a malevolent mocking glint in his eyes haunting me.

The door was flung open again. I walked on not bothering to check.

"Nerry," he called out. "Nerry, please?"

I turned around. The act brought pain riding inside my joints. He stood at the door awkwardly tugging at his chin, peering from his guilt-laden face like a mouse. A heavyset hotel worker peered from a corner and eyed us suspiciously.

"One of those naughty *hotties*, sir," the man muttered accusingly. Perhaps he was used to young girls being lodged here all the time and it was his turn to wonder what had gone wrong with the bargain.

I cast a diabolical glance at him. An urge to curse him crossed my mind but I could barely control myself. I spat and dragged myself from the scene. There was a vicious urge in me to widen the gap between me and all ugly men like Maina. What could you make of a man whose shape was rotund, bald headed and filled out like an avocado? Even the monsters in hell were better than idols of your doting that turned against that trust and hurt it. Where could I ever hide my pock marked face, enveloped by guilt blushes and a pricked conscience? Could I ever stand aloft and announce that Dad kissed me, scooped me in his loving paternal hands and smothered me, and stained the hotel bed with my blood? The image of stains on the white clothes dancing before my eyes like mocking demons, with silent voices that cried out, "Your blood! Your blood!" O my! Was there a way to get myself an amplifier in order to proclaim to the whole world his heinous act?

I cried and cried. What do you do when your little bouquet has been crushed? When your most treasured gift has been soiled? And soiled by your own trusted Dad whom you thought was your security? I had no more tears to spill.

Suddenly, my soul would well up with a loathing like a volcanic magma riding up my throat threatening to choke me. I hated my afflicter with all the wrath I could master. I hated his face with the whole of my soul and could have enjoyed destroying him if given the opportunity. I desired to avenge myself in totality.

Yet I felt hopeless and I realized I couldn't do anything, so I tumbled into a deep pit of self-pity of my helplessness and inability to reverse anything. My inability to take control of my faculties loomed big like a dark cloud of monstrosity before me. This left me with a deep sense of dread that filled me with the wish to die and free myself loose from the dirt besmirch of the wickedness that was assailing my soul. *Suppose I jumped before the wheels of any vehicle, couldn't it end all the shame and agony?*

"You?" I confusedly looked around and saw a policeman with a whip under his armpit, approaching. I had no business with grim-faced policemen and I was sure he was mistaken. They were all men with hidden agenda: to maul young girls and start the blood flowing. I edged next to the road, closed my eyes and ground my teeth waiting for the right moment to do it. A vehicle revved up the street coming at a steady pace.

"You?" he was now a few yards in front of me. He might have read my intentions. He might have discovered my sin-stained mind. A group of women jabbering excitedly moved between us. Here was an opportunity. I ducked behind them and made a dash towards the opposite street. I heard somebody shout but I didn't wait to look if someone was giving me a chase. The pain pursued me, grinding my joints but I had to do it.

The pain was now unbearable and my lungs were burning with exertion so I stopped to check my bearings. I ducked into another lane and was about to lean on the wall to rest when I saw mean looking *chokoras*, street boys stir up to welcome me. I stepped back to the street trembling with trepidation and got down to my knees. Some familiar people were approaching- Irene, my church colleague and her mother. I knew them closely so I fell into their arms and continuously blubbered.

"Hide me! Hide me, Irene, mother, please."

They hesitated but were quick to drag me along with them leading to another street and I remember we clambered up some stairs before entering some busy hotel. My mind was in turmoil and I was certain I was fast running mad.

"Calm down, dear," Irene's mother led me to a seat as Irene brought me some cold soda. I don't know for how long, but I was trembling, my limbs immobilized.

"Talk," they urged me.

I cleared my throat. However, no words materialized out of my heavy tongue. We were by then attracting a curious crowd.

"My little baby, how could I hurt you so? I'm sorry. Forgive me, Nerry…"

How could I stoop to that lowly level of forgiving the abominable act of betrayal? Was forgiving a zoo ticket that you acquired once you showed at the gate and paid? At least at the zoo you paid but not like the on-off button that you fondled with at will.

Instead of sound, a low keen like of a sick dog and tears took over. The reservoir emitted big blobs without fail.

Irene's mother wrapped a *lesso* around my head and faithfully wiped the tears as she held me to herself. She assisted me to blow my nose.

I envisioned myself in the arms of Luciana. God! Luciana- the runaway! I hated her for everything. She had presided over my darkness and execution by creating room for it. Wasn't she my mother? *How could a mother run from her children? Was I the reason why she abandoned us? Oh God! How could I know?*

The bait had been dangled before me ever since she left and the nice clothes and compliments nicely hurled in.

"Wow, you look gorgeous in that!" Dressing well made my dad proud, earning me a journey to Kotu, a treat meant only for the queen, dad's favorite baby.

"I don't think it is wise to travel at night, Nerry." he said and booked me a room… The vista unchained itself before me like a film reel, like a calculated unwinding clock.

Irene shoved the cold soda between my teeth. I took a sip. It tasted strange. She also took a sip and passed it to me. The gesture at least showed that some people cared. They were here to support me. I slowly began opening up, casting a few hints of my plight. I was so ashamed even to tell what had happened. Dad's ignominy knew no language of expression.

They paid and holding my hand, led me to the streets. The *lesso* concealed my face and body so I wasn't worried anymore about the police or anybody else. Irene's arm fondly supported me and wondered what I would have done without them. They were godsend to provide me what I needed most, a place of refuge.

13

Words could have gone that I had also disappeared the same way Luciana did. On the other hand, my revelations had extremely shocked Mama Irene and though she allowed me to stay in her house, she feared she could be accused of child abduction.

Mama Irene was a widow, a nice gentle soul who had worked with mom in the joint church functions involving Women Ministries (The a few days that I had stayed with her she regaled me with mom's focused and devoted Christianity). She made sure I regained my composure through her prayers, uplifting words, and her kindness.

"Your mother couldn't just vanish like that without even telling me. This story doesn't add up, daughter," she whispered as she held me to her bosom. For so long, I longed for the days when mom would do the same when my body stung from the grass scratches following an evening bath. Well, here was one soul who trusted mom and could not take crap for what had happened. A soul who had believed my story and taken me in. But inside her, she feared my dad's reaction if he discovered I was housed in her place.

However, to assuage her fears of my Dad's temper, I proposed she contact Madam Jane who could know what to do. As a result, one evening Jelita walked falteringly into my abode. Her large eyes had tell-tale rings of copious weeping and sleepless nights.

"Dad claims that you simply ran away. How could you do this to us, Nerry?"

We hugged and cried together as could babies when abandoned by their mother at a public park. She had been furtively informed where to find me by Madam Jane. Dad had made some spirited efforts to search for me, and inform the locals claiming that his daughter had escaped from home.

"Daughter? How old?"

"Twelve."

They had laughed, patting one another's backs stupidly, believing such a girl had eloped to marry. Where on earth did a girl of twelve just willingly get married off just like that?

"If we hear anything, we will inform you." They promised thinking the next news would be someone coming to confirm their silly fantasies.

I would have been at loss on what to tell Jelita in face of Dad's remarkable theory- but Irene helped me out. Jelita just gawped, paralyzed for long. She swore not to go back home.

"How could he do it? Nerry, girl, I'm sorry to imagine you ran on us. Our own father? Oh God!"

I had purposely withheld the information from anyone that I was not even his daughter. Having grown up not knowing any other family, I couldn't that easily float the fact that I was parentless. I was still shocked by the truth but that was adequate justification for being away from the man and his home anyway.

Jelita was finally convinced that her going back was for my own good.

"I'm going to report this."

"Will they believe you? All men seem to be there for the sake of other men. They will protect him. His reputation." Mama Irene who had approached some authorities in vain explained.

"The police, the administration, even the teachers…"

"Oh…" Jelita's jaws dropped as she clung to me and cried.

"Oh my God, my God, why have you forsaken our family? Mother, why did you have to go?"

I could no longer stand that so I tore myself away from her and ran into the house and buried myself in bed and sobbed endlessly. I was healing well. Yes, Irene's Mom had done her best. I was always in despair, crying myself to sleep, had mood swings and disturbing memories, and above all, was asking myself why it had to be me, and I believed that maybe I was star crossed.

During these moments, Irene also brought up songs we had done together in church. She was a gifted singer and we together could sing the children's choir, duets and most of the time, the songs brought tears to our eyes. Our pastor had awarded us with Christian magazines and small bibles. Irene's sultry quality would blend with mine, helping me to forget the darkest moments in my life, and it was a good move.

Our singing reminded me of an incident when Madam Jane had asked me what I wanted to become in future, and as I hesitated, the effervescent Catherine said she wanted to become a musician before an answer had even formed in my mind. Everybody laughed but Catherine always struggled to lead in songs. We responded since none of us wanted to frustrate her efforts. Her mixture of high and low notes and sudden voice breaks and untimely breathing never discouraged her and she improved with time. Female music models weren't many and the industry hadn't even become lucrative.

I lay there for some time sobbing into the pillow. A soft hand gently touched my head. It was Irene.

"She said Saarange or Madam Jane will visit soon."

I guessed Jelita had parted. Yes. I had all this time forgotten about the old woman, Saarange. Here was my key to the many questions about my origins. It was like my parched throat had scaled a gob of cold water. I looked forward to meeting her, to fall into her warm but rough hands and look into her wrinkled face to read the message as I listened to her part of the story. Was Maina's story faked so as to vindicate his heinous action? I was ready to pour my heart out to her.

14

If Teacher Mobisa's pronouncements of doom on petty subjects such as 'red knickers' and 'empty coconuts' were a prophecy come true, then my condition was its manifestation. I was holed here putting school behind me and actually had lost any taste for learning, thereby becoming a real empty coconut.

I was still mulling over my nosedived prospects when Hortenzia gallantly surfaced in Irene's home and shrilly ordered that I accompany her home.

"I am not going anywhere unless you want a corpse!"

'You only show me haughtiness forgetting who I am to you Nerina. This campaign to spoil your father's name is meaningless!"

Campaign? Which one? So, they had also known about it? Something hard choked me. Was I campaigning or simply stating the facts?

"That child's sensibilities should not be hurt any further. Tread softly,' Mama Irene observed quietly.

"Tread softly, eh? You think we don't know your objective to destroy my family, Mama Irene? Who doesn't know your nosing nature?"

That did it. I saw Irene's mother walk briskly towards Hortenzia who backed off. She somehow halted and pointed at the gate, a gesture that brooked no resistance.

"This is my home Mrs. Maina and I entertain no nonsense. Get off and don't ever step here not even when you think you can invite yourself!"

Hortenzia left in a huff, her shrill voice exploding in a number of accusations that echoed all over the usually calm countryside. We only heard something like the police- but Mama Irene's unshakeable resoluteness was worth admiration. "Let them dare," was what she only said.

The next visitor was the local chief. In spite of his official regalia and a halo of authority, he wore contagious airs of bonhomie about him, young and friendly as he was. As he listened to Mama Irene, he punctuated the silence with the word sorry.

"The girl needs education all the same. It is the only way she will emancipate and empower herself. Please of all things, let her go to school." There was a concern all over his face as he concluded his visit. I believed him.

"Sir, kindly I want to talk to my grandmother first. Please, let her come and visit me."

As he left, we knew he would pass on the message. Here was one good man who was sensible in what he said. In his opinion, without medical tests a crime against my violator was void and a mere character assassination. I could have done better had I walked straight to the doctor on the material day prior to washing and taken the tests.

Three days later Saarange came, in the company of Catherine. She was her usual benign receptacle of traditional lore and matriarchal dignity. In her hands was a letter supposedly written by her errant son, Mr. Maina begging for forgiveness, enough evidence to incriminate him. What could you say of a statement like "I ask you to forgive me 1 million times?"

He was careful not to say for what reasons.

"Come and live with your sisters."

"Whose child am I Saarange?" I had taken a blunt approach with an objective of arousing her from her elderly slumber. The old woman surveyed me, the white particles in the corners of her eyes and her skin folds making her look piteous.

"It pains me to discover that I've been living a sham… With my past dismantled, my wish to live is gone…"

She snorted and grabbed me intimately, a stale smell of sweat lingering in her clothes.

"*Goko*, dear, a skunk's smell, however, disgusting does not kill."

Catherine broke into laughter and I thought the two had conspired to confound me with puzzles. The old woman went on.

"Look at me in the eye. You see these tears. They are for my own seed. It grew wild and neighbors wanted to cut it down. I gently bent its shoots and branches and tied them together. It's loose…" The woman's shoulders shook and her skeletal long fingers rapped the end of the table. Her body was wracked momentarily by sobs as tears spilled from her eyes. I shook my head uncomprehendingly. Mama Irene nodded her head in the affirmative.

"Tell me grandma, please. I want to know who I am!" It was a cry from the soul, dreading that I could be left to grope in further darkness.

"Yes and no. There was bad blood between him and your mother. They were fighting day and night-like a dog and a cat. Then one day I found you and brought you home; somebody might have put you there for me. Luciana took to the task of tending to you. He came in one evening and I waited to hear the cat and dog snarling, clawing, growling but it was all quiet, nay, only your child decibels bent at naughtiness. You brought them together. They soon had begun to spoil you. I remonstrated with them. You have always been my child but they were only your keepers."

The room was so quiet that you could hear a pin drop.

"Yes, a baby wrapped up in newspapers, flies and insects making a circus in your mouth and nostrils. I thought you were dead. I took you home, cleaned, warmed you and wrapped you in my old blanket waiting for your mother but nobody came to claim you and neither was there any report of a lost child. I knew you were lucky because you could have ended in some quack's basin, or a pit latrine, or a dog's mouth and that's how I called you Nyabisio, fortune. I was old and couldn't take good care of you properly. I gave you to Luciana, a gift from the ancestors. They never let me down.

I've watched you closely. I've loved to see your father adore you over the rest and always thanked my ancestors. Little did I know the dog… the dog was buying time. That wild seed whose branches....I've hitched up my skirts above my knees and sworn that he will die like one."

"No!" Mama Irene slapped the old woman errant hand downwards. "Don't curse your own blood!"

"Nobody sticks a finger up my cornea and lives to celebrate. The dog has been evasive of late, telling me this and that about you. My question has been, where did he bear you from? Which part of his body did he drop you from? What does he know about you? Nobody hurts my Nyabisio and lives in peace. Oh me…" she clung to me as if I was going to vanish into thin air again.

Her tears flowed as her old body shook in agitation than the conviction of her revelation. I remembered her story of Mr. Hyena and for a moment I couldn't tell the difference between this cunning, conniving and salivating tormentor and the little baby, me and the savior. Grandma was my savior and nothing could be a sweeter perfume to me than the musty smell of her ageless clothes.

"I'll hound and haunt him out of town, Mama Irene, at least."

That was when Catherine began to cry a strident moan until she collapsed into the hands of Mama Irene. She fainted.

15

I could envision her toothy smile, wrinkled face, folds of flesh hanging about her neck and arms, the colorful bangles on her hands, and her gruffly voice.

To reach grandma's place, one walked up a gulley of an eroded path. Her house stood like a lone sentry at the far end of a compound surrounded by a clove of trees, a structure with rusty iron sheets and clay walls that was peeling off, leaving the wooden parts sticking out like naughty toes. A hedge of overgrown flowers hid part of the ungainly sections of this wall.

I still remember the idyllic picture of columns of smoke coiling upwards over a burning smell of overcooked *ugali,* which would be taken with sour milk, a condiment for this food. At no time did I miss that grey choking smoke probably emitted by wet firewood or some mysticism I associated with grandma. In her house, food, and talk, there was a sense of wild adventurism associated with canoodling and capering youthful energy.

"It should not break your bladder," the old woman would say in reference to the troublesome smoke streaming my eyes and nostrils as she drew me to her in a bear hug. The smell of animal dung and urine emitting from her uneven floor had that rustic village air that made you part of the lifestyle no matter how far you climbed the human ladder.

"Why don't you house them in a kraal?" I often wondered.

"For my age that is like donating them to the eager hands of animal thieves. Who will monitor them at night? Let them break this door, at least I'll be able to show them a bit of my little bones." At least she would repulse thieves in her house by calling for help.

"What if the jiggers cripple you?"

"They don't find animal urine conducive to thrive." I had at least learned something from her.

I studied her strong hands like those of my father, hunched shoulders, brown teeth and a dress that parachuted around her hips, sagged and with many patches. She was of the philosophy that pumpkin, black nightshade, spider flower leaves made one's body strong and firm against diseases. Some of these bitter vegetables cooked in blood and milk were a relishing accompaniment for eating ugali with.

It was here that whenever I had the opportunity, I learned my community's folklore; the narratives, songs, dances, and culture. Her way of telling these was captivating and mystifying, and I longed for the time when others would also come to drink from my fountain. I yearned to be knowledgeable just like her.

There was something about her humility that was worth mentioning. The door to her room had cow dung and black wattles weaving contraption hung at an angle that could confound architectural experts, yet she was a mother to sons and daughters of means who could have put up a more decent home for her. However, she never complained or seemed in need of improvements to her status. One day while I sat on a two feet high log, she pulled a low-lying folding chair and gave the Mr. Hyena's story.

"Mr. Hyena was on his evening stroll when he came across a deserted baby girl inside a basket crying incessantly.

"Oh mucus! Oh dirt! Pity they left you to die! I'll all the same take you home and see what my wife will make of you! Poor child!"

He gathered the child wrapped her up nicely and pushed her into his bag and zipped the top closed.

As it was his habit, he walked to Mama Sabina's to spend nice time with other elders in catching village gossip. He handed his luggage over to the friendly Mama Sabina for safe keeping as he proceeded to buy himself a round of drinks which he enjoyed with others.

"The moment Mama carried the bag to her sanctuary, the bedroom, she sensed something was wrong. The weak cries of a baby disturbed her. Her motherly instinct forced her to be a bit nosy and inside was a wet, weak, dirty child. She first kept her visitors happy as she thought of a plan.

"Later, she called on the kings of birds, Engocho, the king of music and coached him on how to cry like a baby and shoved in a rock with the equivalent weight of the baby. Later when Mr. Hyena staggered home, his philanthropic mission had been clouded with appetite.

"If humans cannot take care of their own, who am I to bother?" He looked forward to a juicy supper and salivated openly. The baby's cries were the only assurance that his catch was intact.

"I can even throw a feast for the clan." His drunken mind goaded him. As he approached the vicinity of his homestead, he started announcing the great news. Instantly a clay cauldron full of water was set up on an open fire and a crowd that was eager to feast danced around it awaiting the meal.

Mr. Hyena arrived in style, with his catch shoulder high, saliva dribbling the sides of his mouth such that everybody was salivating too. The crowd paved the way and he made a jig and swung the bag over the cauldron from which hot steams of boiling water rose. *Chwaraa!* Unzipped the bag. *Ntimbu!* The rock dropped breaking the pot at once unleashing a deadly splash all over.

"*Ngo! Ngo! Mwakaga nkende!* Pity! Pity! You expected much!" The *engocho* mocked the dying crowds as he flew away. Mr. Hyena was the first of the casualties."

I had a long enervating laughter, tears freely flowing down my eyes. The old woman joined with rib-cracking ripples.

"Laugh child, laugh child. You have missed it."

She held my head, patting it tenderly.

Why was I laughing with the possibility of many hyenas hemming in, stifling a girl's life? Why was I laughing?

After her delicious food, correctly seasoned with herbs and cooked tenderly I walked home. I was coming on into the lounge when I spotted Peter stomp out of the house with Mongina. The two looked agitated as if they had been quarreling. Mongina's big eyes were suffused in tears but when they saw me, they all stopped in their tracks. There was some déjà vu effect that was happening again like several years back, the cast being Mr. Maina and Luciana.

"Maina, what again? The way you talk about that girl is like she is an outsider." Luciana's voice carried on. "Think of your obligations…"
He moved about sulking like a naughty mate spoiling for a fight.
"I think you are spoiling her. She needs spanking like everybody- real proper spanking like all my children." He saw me and cut off so abruptly I was embarrassed by my intrusion. I didn't know who the girl in question was until the hotel incident and the fact that Mobisa had told Dad that I was sleeping over my lessons. But ever since, I came to discover that dad was unusually uncomfortable in my presence, as if he feared to face me in the presence of Lucia. All the time I didn't see anything wrong, although I could sense something unnerving in his attitude.
It took Lucia's mysterious absence from him to start building the bridges towards me. He was better relaxed and with the vacuum created by the absence, I gave him room in my heart. This was dad and he meant nothing bad to me.
"Nerina?" Peter and Mongina called out at the same time. I got more confused, before they burst into laughter and pulled me along into the house. The two were bond by some affinity I was yet to interpret.

BOOK TWO

1

My homecoming was as dramatic as it was earthshaking. True to Saarange's words, Mr. Maina was made to move Hortenzia to Moza where he had a farm (in a bid to protect her baby, Nyabisio) and would only visit the way a thief also invades a home. It was as if he had signed up a new contract with the old woman on how I should be treated and what distance he was to keep between himself and I. Apart from Catherine, Irene, and her mother, nobody knew about our little coup. Not even Madam Jane, Jelita or Alice.

Once Catherine had been revived from her convulsion, her story was as gory as mine.

"He had asked me to go wash utensils in his staff residences. I used the single key he had given to me and I opened the window to let in light when I heard footfalls behind me. Turning around, it was him…

'Oh sorry. Get me the class register in the bedroom,' he said as he busied himself with his shoelaces. I stupidly walked into the lion's den and the door was instantly shut behind me and I was unknowingly hurled into the hard bed. I had no time to scream or protest. I was done."

The narration brought fresh tears into my eyes, the stains of blood dancing between my tears. Why were these blood stains playing the ridiculous carouse with my mind, as if they had the permanent contract to play with my femininity? Could this masculine nastiness be relived without opening fresh wounds from a hurt heart? Hadn't the same opening up drawn a reaction on Catherine with a sisterly concern?

"Have you reported that?" Saarange asked, her voice quivering with apparent anger.

"Not yet. Who will listen to my word? Afterwards he er-- he actually read me the riot act. One, he said I was in the teachers' compound illegally. Two, he was a respected teacher, married and a Christian too. Three, he was ready to assist me both financially and academically if I did not mention anything about what had happened…" I saw the fear of what had happened to her in her eyes.

"No girl. Leave that devil to me. What did you say was his name?"

"Mr. Mobisa." Mmm the old woman pondered. The name locally meant the enemy.

Yes, maybe he was. What of his common reference to the "red knickers" and 'empty coconuts' for those who failed his subjects? He who once tweaked my bum! He had all the potential of a violator! Catherine tried to entreat us not to tell anyone as it would lead to further punishment and grave consequences. What would happen when a trusted mentor became a predator, when a chicken ate its own egg? For such a hen locally, the beak was blunted by being burned?

Saarange came to school even without the consent of Catherine's parents shortly after hounding and haunting Mr Maina out of town. She walked up to the office leaning heavily on her staff.

"How can I help you mom?" Rioba asked, smiling.

"No sir. It is Mr. Mobisa that I need." She responded demurely. "I'll handle him."

The head teacher laughed thinking the old woman was joking and called for Mr Mobisa. The latter walked in and seeing the old woman, he screwed up his face. He was known for not wasting time with old people who according to him were smelly old witches. Saarange waved him to the space beside her on the bench by the main office. The man sat at a good distance from the old woman, twirling his moustache and waving a nonchalant hand over his nostrils as if she carried an airborne infection.

"Son, here I have your forms. I don't know how to read but I can recognize a good signature. This parcel," She pulled out of her folds of clothing a neatly wrapped paper bag, "contains Catherine's pants that you had torn the other day."

The young man swallowed hard, blinked severally and opened his mouth speechless.

"You like the red colors and if you don't take them now, I'll break my old bones on your young body!" Her voice dramatically rose, in a whisper close to his ear.

"I'll eat you up for our next Sabbath if you insist to stay around- you know that we are witches. I'll poke your dead eye with my chopstick and munch it for disobeying my orders to transfer from this school." Saarange was only playing with his fantasies.

"And remember this old man. You are old enough to be the girls' father and if you keep sticking that old root up young girls, you will not honorably retire from this job. Your own daughters will have old roots stuck up in themselves. Listen, eh? Are you signing?"

Mobisa shot off like a rocket with the forms and within a week he had transferred from the school. This was the condensed version of what I got from Madam Jane and the old woman herself. Saarange had taken up the crusade for silly girls like us, I mean easily cheated, fooled, nay baited, and singly scared off two violators out of town. Her tactics and resourcefulness baffled both the learned and illiterate and even was heard far and wide. Soon, many girls were coming to her for advice and help.

Grandma's actions sincerely gave me a new lease of life. Being my final year in primary school, I was determined to pass my exams, despite the recent slurs in my life, bury the past and start a new leaf. I was determined to prove to all and sundry that I was not a mere empty coconut.

The support I received from both home and school was tremendous. My sisters were also very positive. Not only had Jelita and Alice passed well and joined a prestigious school, but they were also my beacons. Maina had accepted to pay their school fees for boarding, thanks to Saarange's new found authority over her son. Erastus was preparing to fly to America for a course in Computer Engineering while Jones had joined the University of Nairobi and was doing a degree in Business Administration. Jeffrey was also in form one in a reputable high school. At school, Madam Jane egged me on pointing to my family members as pacesetters worth emulation. She egged me on, and provided a shoulder on which I laid my burdens.

I had embarked on my academic work with enthusiasm. Even a subject like Mathematics which gave me hurdles was dealt with head-on. The teacher was a non-nonsense type of Carey Francis Math School and not only demanded a neat work, but also working out the formulas as opposed to only giving answers. His long swishing canes stung on our backs, his swift demand for mental sums and exercise books for marking kept us awake. (You see, corporal punishment hadn't been banned from schools.)

Later, my own critical assessment failed to show the adornment that had inspired a normal man as Maina to paw me. This convinced me that out there, were so many sick men who thought that when God created them, he also gave them a divine mission to open all female legs. This was before my physical body would entangle me with men, when feelings of lust would threaten to overthrow my resolve to avoid further stains in my character and mind. I was just growing with big ambitions and big dreams. Dreams I wanted to fulfill.

2

At the end of February, I joined Prestige School which was located on top of a hill fourteen kilometers from home. The place was quite windy and perennially cold even during the hottest of days. It was a confetto of red roofs and brown brick blocks wherein were the classrooms, the administration block and other offices, the dining hall, the kitchen and store, the sick bay, and the dorms. Inside, the walls were painted cream with a strip of black. The desks were big and smooth unlike the ones I had used in primary.

The blocks were hedged by flower beds of red, violet, purple and white. Small wooden fences enviously guarded them from animals and human interference. The neatly trimmed lawns between blocks sported beautiful trees and thorn less cacti. A network of slab laid paths linked all the houses against the 'keep off grass' signs fixed strategically. Woe to you if you were spotted walking on the grass apart from play time. To the south, were a few blocks of houses with blue roofs that were home to a good number of our teachers.

The principal's house, a one-story building of green and cream lay separated from the rest with a kie-apple hedge that was always trimmed to the waist level. It was believed the principal had one top window from which she observed the going-on in the school compound since nothing ever escaped her attention, whatever the time was, and whoever was involved.

To the further west was a huge Cathedral with long glass windows with a maze of green, red and yellow color that spelt medieval Christian symbols. The interior was a sight to behold, with Christian saints' images, and the impaled savior's cross pinned on the wall behind the podium. A large piano rest besides the cherubic altar connected to speakers which were imperceptibly placed in the innards of the auditorium to render any church service the ambience of awe and sacred mysticism. The church served the school and the surrounding villages, and this center of worship formed the foundation of the school rules.

A student only came here with the permission of the head teacher, her deputy or master on duty and was not to mix with strangers, save the students and staff. You were not allowed to talk, leave alone smile at even your own mother in case she happened to have attended the service.

I joined the school almost two weeks late because Maina had misplaced the money order. On the evening of my second day, I was looking for a free space on the line to air my clothes when a girl, built like a barrel and dark like soot confronted me.

"What is your name, bush girl?" I thought she wasn't addressing me and continued moving around my clothes that were dripping with water.

"Hey Baby face? What is your name, bush girl?' A girl, with a Goliathan stature; tall and sturdy, breathed the question, and stood in front of me, stopping me on my tracks.

"Nerry. Nerry Maina." I said fearfully. By now, a group of senior girls had made a circle around me, their eyes scanning me like an animal in a zoo. The water from the clothes continued dripping. I was about to place them on the line when she restrained my hand with a firm grip.

"You don't air such rags here, Nail." She screwed up her face in disgust as if I had broken an immutable law of nature.

The rest laughed hilariously. My name had been smartly corrupted by the bully.

"Lots of grass for monos' underwear," someone else said, "Or don't you even know that your stained panties can turn us blind in case..., eh?"

As I flinched in confusion, the whole company's faces were scowled at a possible spectacle. I looked at the grass, then to the unoccupied line. Mono? Yes, that meant a form one.

"Well, I can do anything if it pleases you." The words came out effortlessly. A heavy slap whacked my left cheek. I had heard of bullying in schools from my brothers and thought it was only a specialty of boys' schools.

"A mono is a pregnant gecko," the barrel body said slowly like a cop reading me a riot act, spewing out the words one by one as my wet hand rubbed away the pain on my cheek. "Living on the shores of lake Nyancha, only to be seen and not to be heard, understand?"

Hot tears shot out of my eyes and I hastily dropped the clothes and raced to the principal's office. She was just coming out when I confronted her with the tale of my woes. She immediately followed me. The place was deserted, save for the sight of my dirtied clothes.

"Do you remember any face?" the head teacher, Sister Favour inquired as her lips trembled in anger. I tried as much as possible to give the description of my assailants.

I was rewashing my clothes when I was called to the office where I positively identified my attackers who were so innocent-faced that you could think they were saints marching into New Jerusalem. They were heavily reprimanded and were to have certain privileges withdrawn for a period of one week. They were asked never to dare touch any form one. As the devils left, I squirmed with fear as I felt like a heroine.

I was negotiating a corner that led to my dorm when I heard several footsteps behind me. At the same instant, several seniors were running up my path from the other side. I ducked against the wall to give them way but I had miscalculated their intentions. They hit me, all at once, sprawling me to the ground like a drunk who had lost his balance. When I rose up, there wasn't a single person either way. I rubbed the dirt from my clothes and stretched my limbs. Nothing was broken. I then let out an intentional guffaw as if I had enjoyed their joke. I knew it would infuriate them and make them more determined to hurt me.

I went back to my washing. The clothes had been dirtied even more with what I thought were feaces. I carefully placed them in the sink and opened the tap full blast.

"Oh, young girl, we don't waste water here as if we live next to the lake."

I looked up and towering before me was a prefect, telling from the red blazer and tie that she was wearing. She turned off the tap and scooped me by the collar and shepherded me along as if I was a rat being carried to a cat feast.

"Water is precious here and rare and we wash using basins or buckets."

"I didn't know," I protested weakly. There was a chorus of laughter from groups of senior girls. Immediately, I learned that my attacker was not a real prefect.

"Then take me to the principal, now." I said, not caring anymore. Her grip slackened and the sham prefect melted into the crowd. I walked back to my washing now quite agitated. I didn't know how long I was to put up with this disgusting behavior.

Barrel body and Goliath were waiting for me.

"Take off your underwear girl. We want to see whether you are cut." Murderous rage filled me as my feet refused to budge.

"Get out of my way. I want to wash!"

"Wash? Ha ha ha ha! You don't have to soil your clothes as if..." Goliath lifted a skirt belonging to me. It was plastered with human waste. I swallowed hard as raw rage blinded me.

"What you need mono are napkins not water, Nail baby. We, being our sisters' keepers and good Christians have decided to do it for you. Your underpants!" she said, her hand stretched out menacingly as her tone was. A group of emboldened seniors were gathering around. I knew the odds were against me and a wave of dread attacked me with a sense of helplessness. *I can't beat them. The principal too can't manage this evil force.* I was thinking on how to beat it when something like rushing air swept by me and in a twinkling of an eye Goliath and Barrel body were down on the wet ground crying with pain and surprise. My savior was dressed in green tracksuits and had felled my assailants with precise chops and blows. No sooner were the two on their feet than they scrambled for safety amidst the shouts of "Karate! Karateka!"

There was a general pandemonium as groups of new girls kept swelling and the seniors had to give way. The tracksuit turned to me and to my relief and shock before me was Catherine. The picture of this clumsy grown-up body hadn't been erased from my mind. I didn't know she had joined Prestige and ahead of me. This was the second time she was intervening, the first incident being when she had attacked Big head. Her brave fight had given all the new girls a new lease of life.

Apparently, I was more shocked by her act of fighting than her rescue. After their help with the clothes, we decided to put them under the bed to dry but to my utter disgust my mattress was already soaked wet with water. Catherine simply slipped into a uniform and asked us to do likewise and carrying the mattress we stormed   the boarding mistress' office and at the sound of the commotion, several teachers came out as Catherine boldly presented the form one case. We didn't mind her rustic mixing of 'ls' and 'rs' provided justice was done.

"Rachel Kerry, Stella Bajar and company cannot make us miss our sleep. Can't make us miss our academic heart beats. It is either you permit us to go away in peace to schools where civilization is the order of the day, where such brutes are not condoned by the society." Somebody almost clapped. It was total admiration for my former schoolmate and we coalesced around her. The accusation infuriated the teachers so much that the culprits were suspended after a thorough spanking in turns from the teachers. The rift between the juniors (form ones and twos) and seniors (form threes and fours) was so intense for some time that it required the spiritual services and acumen of Father Mika, the parish padre, to defuse it and teach us on the essence of co-existing with sisterly love.

3

In spite of her run-in with Mobisa, Catherine was one big girl who because of academic weakness was suspected to cull academic favors from 'other' male teachers. Over time, I had gotten used to keeping a good distance from her such that you could rightly describe our relationship as lukewarm. Any good grades that she scored she made sure everyone knew about them which was quickly dismissed as a collusion with her many male admirers. We ignored her loud mouth. I even sometimes wondered whether grandma hadn't wasted her time to send Mobisa away when the benefactor of her ingenuity was so morally sloppy and reckless.

But in the environment, everything was forgotten as every form one and two dotted her, worshipping her every move. And she enjoyed this crowning moment judging from her continuous emissions of saucy laughter. On my part, I was determined to find out how she had learned karate.

The chance came two evenings later when the two of us were alone. "Nerry," she rolled her eyes in a nice way, conspiratorially said, "My brothers are adept sportsmen. Remember that teacher who had taken advantage of me?"

I nodded. How could I forget Mobisa? "I never wanted it to happen again; someone creeping behind me. Anyway, they thought I was a joker but when they found I was so flexible and teachable, they got down into serious business. The rest is history. This was purely for self-defense and not hurting any soul. It gave me the confidence. I become in charge of my destiny." I looked at her in the eye and would see the fire of confidence in them. Her hand was so tender I wondered where she found the muscle to face Barrel body and Goliath. Still, something was not clear.

"Cathy, you mean you never left Mobisa?" she studied her fingers, a tinge of sadness clouding her face. I was starting to get unease and blamed my loose tongue when she bizarrely quipped.

"Goddammit!" her breath came out in gasps. "My violator had still such a hold on me, an enslaving power over my will; I don't know how to actually put it. One day I found him with another girl in bed and I went down on my knees and begged him to take me back. I seemed to shadow him everywhere. He gloated over me like a deity whose mission was to open other new buds to spite me. I still don't know what I should do. In his presence I am hypnotized. I've always asked whether it is he that took me to bed or I am the one who forced it to happen. The line between what happened and what I feel is so thin that I don't …" her voice had reduced into a bare whisper as if she was paying homage to some shrine.

To my consternation, I felt that our heroine would go to bed with Mobisa even right away. The thought shocked me because of its truism. I instinctively felt it inside my guts. The silence between us was tormenting. An inexplicable feeling rose down my bosom soaring to my throat like a sticky yellow phlegm. What happens when your violator metamorphoses into an object of admiration like a ritual totem?

"Cathy, please," a girl called Rhoda was pleading. "You're our teacher. The others are waiting." The girls had continuously pestered her to train them some martial arts. She appeared disinterested until the request had turned into an obsessive demand rather than a request. The girls hang around her every time they were free. Catherine had taken them through the ritual of swearing to tough dos and don'ts in a way, maybe to dissuade them but this had increased their curiosity. Every one of them wanted to be a Catherine. She finally consented but demanded that self-discipline was the paramount rule to everything. The girls agreed to supplement her diet after a spell of rigorous training. They all wanted to move swiftly. Down the Barrel bodies and Goliaths in their lives. The craze was contagious and I found myself carried along.

When we walked to the hall, Mr. Mote, our English teacher, tall and slender in his oversized tracksuit stood leaning on the doorway as if to balance his delicate body frame. He was popularly known as 'mosquito.'

"Oh, my dear queen, why should we wait?" Catherine smiled and shook his thin hand. Whispers were already doing rounds that he was going to be the Karate club patron. In an iron fisted administration, a teacher's conduct was supposed to be above reproach. But this man got away with everything however outrageous it was. He staggered to the compound, made some drunken noises, missed lessons, used uncouth language and questioned the logic of having the nuns' lord over married couples. Sister Favour, our principal, a typical disciple and student of the Spartan and puritanical sisterhood furrowed her face, boiled over, suffered bouts of high blood pressure but did nothing. When the man was sober, he worked like a donkey and produced unbeatable results. Many schools were waiting for her to surrender him, a fact he knew.

Teachers were parents and not incestuous pimps whose duties stretched beyond the formal, to teach and cause learning; full stop.

Teachers were supposed to be cultivated in honorable speech, angels who enhanced hues of purity in the task of raising future straightforward citizenry.

"Yes, my wives," Mr. Mote would address the school before sister Favour and she would grimace and gesticulate like she had taken some dose of bitter quinine tablets.

"Mo. Mo. Mo." The students would chant and enjoy a long laugh. Whether the abbreviated mo., either stood for mosquito or Mote nobody cared.

> *"When you hold sweet dreams of our concupiscence*
> *When you accept our primal seed of conscience*
> *You will be delivered in colors of success*
> *And to golden castles find access."*

The whole school could be clapping, not that we understood the message but for the love of the music of the words volubly spoken. Sister Favour would open her eyes and real tears would spill out. Maybe the outrageous act of Mote tickled her Christian roots, shaking her holy conviction of hell-bound humanity, or in the words some moral comeuppance. Mr. Mote's soul represented the irreparable Purgatorial clients whose intimacy with *keroro*, a local ethanol brew, was unforgivable. Why else could she cry? She never said it expressively but we read it in her gestures, and we her beloved daughters stood equally condemned at appreciating the serpent's speech.

This was Mote who when he began the training regimen by Catherine cut a comical figure. I still envision his tiny long arms and legs slashing the air as we sweated out the whole bit. More students, even from senior forms enlisted in the club. The Mosquito's antics and Catherine's magic wand were irresistible. The stories in the dorms on how the training was going on filled our nights with laughter. That was when hell broke loose in the form of Madam Jennifer.

4

Jennifer, our games mistress and Religious Education teacher, was a huge, plump, tall, round and robust in a way I fail to describe. She was always towering about everybody in argument, laughter, and 'dishing' as we called eating, and if Sis Favour thought Mote was a potential client for alcoholism, then Madam Jennifer was an appropriate one for the sin of debauchery and her tendency to give birth every season although unmarried. All the four years we were around she took several maternity leaves.

There was something cantankerous and some sadistic pleasure she derived whenever her subject of malice stewed in her own juices, while she directed the act behind the scenes. Even petty issues like a petticoat sneaking below a girl's skirt; a girl consulting a male teacher were her right to report to the admin. We later came to learn teachers called her *Senior*, not senior because of rank in school administration which was held by Juma, but because of her snooping behavior, a chief senior 'mole'. We students had our fashions like Jezebel, the biblical conniver and General for her hawkish demeanor, and Catherine later calling her, in-law.

Now the vibrancy of an authorized karate club in the school compound was to her the final straw in the camel's back.

"The girls will grow wild. They will strike and beat the hell out of the administration. They will burn us. Tell me whether we have a parallel games department because as the in-charge I have not commissioned anybody to do the work for me." This was an apparent attack at Mr. Mote who was practicing with the students. I think the administration could have chosen to ignore her because of the drastic transformation the club had wrought on the drunken teacher. He had begun to change his drinking habits, courtesy of his training schedule and had grown more responsible in other areas. His cynical perspective of the school management was toning down. The club miraculously survived various onslaughts even from other jealousy members of staff. This irked Jennifer to the marrow since nobody acted on her warning. She was still determined to condemn us to her own form of Dante's hell. Definitely, this called for a change of tactic.

5

Next to the Southern part and in a valley was a Modest urban center, almost built along the tarmacked road. A feeder murram road going to my home passed by the main school gate on the East. Just a few kilometers on the West was Embambaru Mixed Secondary School.

It   was from this school Catherine had acquired a boyfriend called Jomo in one of our many sports outings. Sometimes, Jomo would sneak into a dale behind our school where there was a clamp of trees with a cool shade and screening passersby. It was during these escapades which Catherine dragged me along when I also met Felix.

He was tall, light complexioned and with a lithe body pulsating with athletic muscles. With the congenial face, good big eyes and a heavy lipped mouth, my heart couldn't help flutter at his sight, and when he talked to me, my whole body melted and my head went muzzy.

I would not have known what a prize catch I had landed on until my dorm mates in the confinement of the blankets would extol the physical virtues of my boyfriend. I felt if I ever messed by abandoning him, they were ready to snatch him from me. I jealously guarded my catch and every time looked forward to meeting him. I hadn't seen anything wrong with that because all girls seemed to love such moments during games. And since our school field was small and there were other surrounding schools using it, the rest of us who were not serious with games would sneak out to meet our boyfriends.

Jomo and Felix were day scholars and so getting out of school never poised a real problem to them. We selected days when we would meet them to talk, hold hands and allow youthful fires to take the better of us.

Catherine could allow Jomo's hand to ride up her skirt as she huffed and moaned in ecstasy. However, from my past nasty experience with men, I refused such exploits. Furthermore, I had been so embarrassed by my first menses. I really messed myself up but luckily, it happened at home. I was so shocked that I ran to grandma thinking I had seriously fallen sick. She cackled like a hen, and after trashing the fire that was grumbling in the hearth, turned to me beaming.

"You're now super ripe." I eyed her with confusion. "It is a sign you can get pregnant if you sleep around." However, that had never helped me stop myself from messing up. Even the later biology lessons did not assure me about sex. I was as ignorant as the next girl in the neighborhood about my sexuality.

Therefore, so long as we held hands with Felix and he kept it away from my skirt, and promised each other a fruitful future with grandchildren, there was no problem. But I could see his eyes and actions were drawing excitement from what Jomo and Catherine did and I knew given a chance, he couldn't hesitate to do the same.

It was on a Wednesday evening when we sneaked into the comfort of our tête-à-tête rendezvous. Catherine's voice excitedly rode over the cowed whispers in her wild yap yapping. Madam Jennifer had a few days back warned girls who went looking for boys of dire consequences.

"If I catch you, believe me you, I'll twist your neck until you see the North Pole." The whole assembly broke into an uproarious laughter and it was like this chided her. She lost her cool and swore to get us, even if we did it in rat holes, and to squeeze our little selves into pulp and destroy any excitement of ever looking at a man again. The laughter died when we saw her in such a foul mood, since her whole body trembled with anger. "I know what some of you are thinking, what can such a woman tell us? Mark my words. You are kids and there is a long promising life ahead of you and you need to preserve yourselves."

That evening we sneaked to our popular rendezvous shortly to inform our lovers of the dangers such meetings poised to our existence, but once we set eyes on one another, everything about Jennifer was pushed to the background.

The grass batch under me had a velvety feel having been mowed recently. Felix's hand and eyes rested on mine as his fingertips were tracing a tender map along my face. A sudden spasm vibrated through my body without a warning.

"What is it?" he teasingly said, with sweet words like pure honey.

"I don't know," I confessed, quite sincerely as I tried to catch my breath. My breast was full of an upshot of excitement.

"Look here, Nerry. You're the only star on my inky sky. I reach to your twinkling light, your blaze to worship you, to offer my sacrifice. And then to feel your tenderness…" His voice broke into a whine. A cold shiver crawled all the way up my body as the words of a poem I had read somewhere burst forth in my mind.

To shine like stars
To smile like an angel
How flees unsightly mars
Hearts that sing that lie
Of my love that shall never die.

His penetrating gaze breaks open the core of my cranium, imparting rays of cascading luminaries that scatter and fall like meteors. I can no longer look straight for I swear I am getting blinded and so I close my eyes, and my heart misses a beat. A wave of excitement hits the shores of my mind with excited joy. A voice is querying "Are you sure you're alright?' My lips shake, my hands and legs too. I feel so weak. The tears begin to roll.

To shed blood for tears
To clothe thy skin with scales
And curse awake the seers
To a life of dubs and hell tales
For my love shall never die.

His fingers are engrossed in my hair. Something transcendental is unfolding inside me. Something that surpasses pain, injury, miracle even transition.

To never feel my being-ness
To ride on a horde of dreams
And share with you all sweetness
For my love shall never die

In the shadows of tomorrow, beyond promise looms a large shapeless being, its centrality commingled in a love nest; its essence immersed in a pure pot of emotions. It was when we were lost in our dream when a voice larger than life burst in our ears like a thunderclap.

"Hello, ladies and gentlemen." We all swung around like well-oiled cogs and there was instant cessation to our dreams. There was a post haste taste, a suspension of things like the unfinished combustion of engine oil. Hovering over our mortal sin was His Holiness Reverend Father Mika accompanied with Sis Favour, the deputy principal, the chief security officer, two mean looking guards and Madam Jennifer whose eyes were shining with glee. 'I said I'll get you girls in a compromising situation.' Her threats had been ignored and now you see.

Father gave us one withering look before the security swung to action. We were all nabbed (about eight of us) and no one, even Catherine was there to save us. Sis Favour clicked and shook her head in petrified disgust and we could imagine a tear was stealing around the corner of her eye.

"Father forgive us. We know we are terrible sinners," Catherine just blubbered. I wished somebody could put an end to this. A new rope was produced to yank our hands together and we joined in her blubbering at its sight. We were led single file, the ropes biting into our hands. Someone had already informed the school girls and they cheered and jeered from a safe distance as we were pushed to the main road. My vision was numbed with paralysis as I only envisioned expulsion. The fact that Felix had offered his hands to be tied with a smile churned me over. He wanted to prove to the whole world that I was his.

"To the police station!" the grim-faced Father ordered. Some villagers besides the road jeered at the sight. The matatus stopped business to watch the free show. Jennifer towered from the rear enjoying her handwork. At the sight of the captives, some villagers nodded in consent with the padre's action and accusingly mumbled.

*"Watoto wa siku hizi ni malaya, T*oday's children are whores."

Already the public had condemned us without knowing our side of the story. This being the route to my home, I felt doubly condemned because I was sure any villager commuting would spot me and spread the news. I don't even understand how my jelly legs carried me along because I was visibly trembling. As we descended the dust rough murram road to Modest town, a pick up matatu with a board made of tarpaulin was incongruously protesting spitting a cloud up the hilly batch spitting bluish smoke around its excess human passengers' heads sticking out of it like pineapple leaves.

"Take them to work in a pub madam," a mischievous tout taking a ride on the roof of the matatu shouted winking wickedly.

A blanket of dust that trailed the vehicle engulfed all of us as the same time a group of men timing the vehicle to complete its ascent of the hill running along threw us off balance. As we reeled crazily about, Jomo swung into action like a mad stag and before Omoyo brought his police skills, the end of the ropes was left in his hands while the former scampered to safety. Just then, Felix brought the other surprised guards' heads clashing together with a sickening thud and the two collapsed to the ground like rotten fruit and he too was gone. Father Mika stood there bemused studying his security detail.

Efforts by Madam Jennifer to chase them came to naught when she missed her step and slipped on a stone and almost broke her leg. We quietly triumphed for her mishap as she sat on the road and it took Omoyo's frantic aid to bring her to her feet. Her fury was unstoppable and were it not for the presence of Father, she would have murdered us with her bare hands.

Father and the principal's change of heart to take us back to school didn't improve things for her. She excused herself on the pretext of going to check on her doctor and left in a huff. Our hands were loosened and we walked back to school in mournful silence. Our names were entered into the scary Black Book and we went down for the whacking punishment, an occasion where you bit your lips and felt as if the cane penetrated your whole body. While still sore and limping, the assembly was called in the dark and various confessions openly extracted from us and we promised never to repeat the mistake. For the next whole week, we scrubbed the administration blocks where everyone could not miss to notice our plight.

For the next two or more weeks the school was hilarious over the incident and talked while Barrel body and Goliath in their final year commissioned cartoons that portrayed us in awkward positions under ugly looking ogres. Catherine withdrew from all games and joined the drama club. I was not sure which way to go but I was certain the shining stars here at Prestige had been dimmed for the time being. I couldn't perhaps religiously seek love while in that compound again.

6

The nasty escapade with the school administration did not however deter Felix from looking for all sorts of ways to get me. According to the letters sneaked into the school compound by some of the girls and the support staff, he talked of his undying love for me. "I live in your shadow watching your every angelic step and smile with a laugh and enthrallment." I hid these notes from my colleagues fearing they would spark another discussion and lead to humiliation. That didn't mean girls were not cleverly devising ways of reaching out to boys but keeping it under folds and carrying animated discussions on their cavorting and trysts that left most of us envious. Girls will always be girls. But I had learned to add some dignity to my deportment.

For instance, a trip to a boy's school was not an all-academic affair. It was a full-blown adventure where girls wanted to smother their lovers with the unforgettable. The daring ones even hang in the cubicles, though this was not a possibility for risk of mass rape. The most popular days were during the games and drama when the events ran into late hours and boys and girls hung on each other's arms and read the stars in the sky together.

Every hidden part of the landscape was ideal for crooked moves and it got exploited well as if girls were so hot that they couldn't keep their pants on. The girls' nightmare then was a pregnancy, not an STD because it would be cured with the right dose of penicillin or some herbs. Even with our Christian roots, the question of moral aptitude had been relegated into the back of our minds. These were the stages when hormones, as someone had put it, wanted to overthrow uprightness.

However, we had our moral police in the name of Jennifer who had been nicknamed General, and if you heard whispers that the general is presenting the arms, you knew she had her antennae directed at you.

"Gluttons don't love heavy eaters," Catherine would walk around shouting to the amusement of everybody, a thing that Jennifer couldn't imagine referred to her indirectly.

"This is sheer jealousy. You can't prevent other curious flower pickers from plucking them if you had picked one with a bee and got stung." The girls who knew her private life like the palm of their hands could always parade it out of her earshot.

The relationship between a teacher and student wasn't so good. Catherine had been suspended severally through the instigation of Jennifer until out of the regular visits by one of her brothers to present their sister's case, a relationship with her had started, a fact that Catherine referred to in-law. This actually involved Catherine since her every move was sure to get into the ears of her parents and relatives. In the course of her suspension, they always made hell for her. When Jennifer caught her knocking about with her Jomo she had been suspended with letters from her local headman and sub-chief where she could be reporting thrice a week to plead her law-abiding behavior. At least, as she claimed, she had the honor of being escorted right to their home with the school van. When she came back, she had some fake woman who presented her as competently as a sister in-law until she was almost turning the tables against her accusers. Nothing could stop the girl from trying the system with her ingenuity and craftiness.

I had become a good volleyball player which placed me in the first seven. Jennifer, who was our coach, made sure we vigorously trained each day to compensate for the packet of milk and half a loaf we each received from the school thrice a week. She kept us in the fields during odd hours to drill and exercise, to learn new moves and this paid off since we terrorized the teams in the whole province. This also subjected us to publicity but Jennifer's hawkish stunt could not allow us any room for little mischief. Our team came to dread the games day's and preferred other kinds of outings for that was when we could also relax and romp about.

There is a particular game I still relish. It was the provincial championships against Clarion girls and the whole field palpitated with tension and expectancy. They had narrowly trashed us during the qualifying matches and everybody had predicted that in the finals we could give them a run for their money. We were set for the feat, our small hearts quietly pulsating against our ribcages as we studied our able opponents.

"Girls, you know what? You have nothing to lose because you' aren't yet Champs. Play with your hearts and heads and go for it. Being second position is being a loser. You only win when you're number one. That's your position." Our coach had encouraged us.

My eyes surveyed the sea of excitable faces. There was this boy next to Jeffrey (their school was presented in some indoor games and he was in form six) who had introduced himself as Nixon. He was slender, tall and of a light complexion. He was unusually quiet, almost introverted, the type that only talked when talked to. One curious habit was his knack to ignore jokes that made everybody break out into laughter. He chose to laugh on his own, a long-drawn laughter that made him look nuts. His hair was strange, dark, silky and curled and matted as if he had treated it at a saloon. His gait was elegant and straight, never stealing backward glances as if whatever he left behind him was for others to savor. His hands were tender and unsoiled with long fingers.

I was really interested to know his background and when I learned he was from peasant roots; it further heightened my curiosity. However, he seemed not to notice the little sister to his friend as he wore a bored and aloof expression which made one wonder what he had come to do in the field if he held the going-ons in such a disdain.

It was until the whistle blew and the game started when something true about him came out. The flying, the lifting, the punching, the volleying, the serving, the tottering, the rolling, the racing, the ducking before the jeering and hissing crowds, the cheering and egging on supporters. I saw Nixon up in the air, his school blazer swinging up and down, his mouth wide open as he hollered "Queens, you make my day! Queens you make me happy!" Jeffrey was beside him but he couldn't match the former's exuberance. I thought for an infinitesimal second that he was cheering our opponents until I delivered a killer punch and saw he was actually my supporter, our supporter.

The supporters of each team were dancing on the either half of the pitch waving twigs, dressed funnily with either pullovers tied around their heads or waists. Their feet pound the place threatening to lay it bare of grass. Nixon was in the lead of our fans and I became jealous of my school mates who were swinging their bums around him. Catherine had found a radio system and it was yodeling Marley's number that had enthusiastic responses: Stand up, stand up. Fight for your rights.

It was intensely hot and I felt stifled in the heat and very thirsty. Nixon and Madam Jennifer had joined the Catherine's group and they were all urging us on with the song. Hadn't we been dismissed by our opponents as ordinary folks? We trashed them and they fled the field in tears with their coach. We were crowned the new Provincial queens and for the first time, I saw Jennifer as a kind soul. The celebrations vibrated in the school for weeks to come. The scintillating giant trophy was touched by every girl nay kissed and the girls carried Jennifer and all of us in three laps of honor around the field. These were strong fellows indeed capable of any feat.

Madam Jennifer lumbered around the field singing herself hoarse. She had a library of curious songs that we excitedly sang along. I was lifted quite high and up there exposed to the world I felt a heroine. I felt invincible. Jeffrey was waiting for me with open arms and hugged me. I smiled sheepishly and the hug from Nixon give me strange feelings that I had never experienced before. I wished it had gone on longer and I moved aside later quickly and was left smiling sheepishly. Catherine came and also hugged them. I felt some uneasiness creep into me. Was I jealous and yet the man hadn't even seduced me? What was wrong with me?

Back at school, the usual humdrum was back and it was then that a surprise parcel arrived from Felix. It was a packet of perfumed expensive pads and two hundred shillings. It made me feel cheap and I was determined to send them back hadn't Catherine and others restrained me.

"We always receive this and we have never complained."

Catherine put it later curiously. "Nerry, I sometimes wonder where your silly pride can take you. You say you have enough. Let's take a personal assessment of you. A thirty-bob digital watch, sixty bob brassiere, skirts and blouses barely costing four hundred, two hundred bob shoes and twenty bob socks! You're sickeningly cheap, Nerina. Phew and you say you don't need two hundred bob from an admirer!"

I let her have the money and whenever she bought bread, she could call me to share it.

"Your fifth ninth shilling going down the drain!" I felt like puking and avoided her company like leprosy for some time.

As we broke for the April holiday, Sis Favour underscored the importance of a fruitful and progressive holiday during the closing assembly. I knew a lot of things were lined for my colleagues and I fleetingly thought of Felix and Nixon. They were like distance shadows and I wasn't surprised.

"Girls come back in one piece and not pieces." The principal remonstrated and we resonated with laughter. As we sung the last line of "God be with you till we meet again," Catherine asked me to accompany her to Modest town from where we would take a vehicle home. After the prayers we moved out of the compound. My bag was not as heavy because I had carried what I only needed for the holidays.

I remembered that I had received a note from Nixon. "Queen of queens, your playing was superb. I've gone to the doctor to diagnose my disease and I am sure the cure lies in you. I'll tell you once I learn. Bye. Love. Nix."

I'd proudly shown the girls this note and I was sure it was somewhere in the box well preserved. I often read it at night under the cover of the blanket as I let my imagination guide me. I looked forward to meeting him and hear him talk and cheer me up.

My response to him was a bit funny. How do you respond to a senior guy in an upper form? We produced a Thesaurus and sat down to author an appropriate reply. Several notes were written and torn up. We enjoyed the big words that some girls had difficult pronouncing. However, the words remained hollow and dull to us. We decided to keep it simple, nearly word for word.

"King of cheerers? We have learned that all doctors are sick from the same affliction and will refuse their diagnosis. The queen of queens. Nerry.

7

I don't know what came to me because by the time we were at Modest central terminus I had managed to dodge the unsuspecting Catherine. I looked forward to be at home pronto.

The vehicle took long to fill. I was wondering what had become of Irene as she had had a problem brought about by my brother Jeffrey. The thought of Irene reminded me of many nice things about our church upbringing. Together with one Flora, we had kept close to the church before the turmoils of life started overthrowing our zeal to different ways. I can say the devil was a calculating vicious enemy. I don't know how, but I suspect myself because Irene used to pay visits to my home since the day, they had rescued me with her mother. Unknown to me, they started something with Jeffrey and fell into the haunches of sin, never to rise again. One day, we met the once jovial and lively girl. She had lost her sheen.

"What is wrong, baby?"

"Surely!" she snapped as if embittered with my curiosity and roved to my face.

"I've got it," she answered vaguely. "I was expelled from my school for being pregnant." A cold shiver ran down my spine. I had seen the plump in her tummy and suspected she was eating well. Something like a spear hit my head, chilling my blood but I was afraid to ask.

"I'd thought I was clever."

"Does he know?"

"He told me not to worry."

I looked around the homestead as if to confirm there were means available to support the baby. The two corrugated houses showed signs of aging. A calf mooed from one of the animal structures. I held her reassuringly, really afraid. While she languished at home, Sir Jeffrey went on with his education as if nothing wrong had happened. It was as if all girls were compelled to zip up or meet the devastating fate. Even in church, it wasn't any better for the girl. They had her name expunged from the church register while the oat planter survived the axe in the faceless societal niche, waiting to continue with his wild planting on the unsuspecting sisters. *And the sower went forth and sisters zip your pants or else…*

During these difficult times, her mother's resilience helped. She stoically lit the darkened path with words of hope.

"I want that baby, here," she pointed at her lap. "Don't imagine I'll allow a silly thing such as abortion. Tell the father that I'll bring it up so long as he will take up responsibility at the end of his schooling. Right?"

However, Irene's uncles who paid the school fees had different ideas. They arrested Jeffrey and made him suffer the humiliation and committed him in writing to support his child in future. The poor guy had no options in front of a team that included a battery of lawyers. He had a mortal fear for Maina and I was sure he wanted everything hushed before he could hear of it.

"I hope this guy doesn't take after his father," Saarange expressed his fears to me. I however learned was that he truly loved Irene in spite of the accident.

Grinning up at me was Catherine, Jomo and Felix.

"Rina, we are going home in the evening. You haven't even had your lunch child." She glared at me in a funny hooded way as if she was telling me '*stop being childish.*'

"A meal is over that corner," Felix imploringly added. I didn't want to look like a kid and I nodded in agreement.

My bag was taken off the matatu as they easily shepherded me away. My mind had misgivings, something like a gear shift inside me. It wrought images of a girl that was drugged and gang raped then left for dead. Felix maintained a reassuring chatter but every word did not inspire any iota of confidence in me.

Jomo's family owned a prime wholesale and I was sure a treat wasn't a problem. We entered one of the most extravagant hotels. My reservations for hotels was well known. Roast chicken, ugali, chips, fruit desserts, washed down with a glass of milk or mango juice was their ala carte. Nothing went down my body as I merely glossed over everything. My heart was quietly living the ugly images I had conceived and it was as if it was an alert of what they were up to and I had to stop it.

The trio tried so much to dissuade me from rushing home earlier by walking around the backstreets and taking me to video shows. I had already taken off my school uniform and avoiding the public was one way of avoiding meeting the wrong company. I was surprised that dusk came so fast and I deliberated on going home without the bag, which I couldn't tell where it had been kept.

"Let's go for it," Felix said, engrossed watching some Kungfu film extricated himself with difficulty. I wasn't enjoying anything and I felt relieved at his acceptance. We walked up the stairs to a three-story building. Girls younger than me in skimpy clothing hung around some macho looking guys in dreadlocks chewing kat, smoking or drinking some brown stuff from a bottle or glasses in strategic corners. A big hi-fi system rattled the place, the ground shaking vibrations to which the revelers swayed unobtrusively.

The real time for leg shaking was yet to begin and the earlier starters had not finished. Some technicians were on a podium testing some strobe lights that burst in a motley of red, blue and orange that revolted dizzily around. Just at the entrance, the words 'THE PARADISE restaurant and Bar open 24 hours' shook me to the core. What was Felix up to? Was he taking me to a lodging?

Felix, half dragging me along might have read my mind as he held me closely as we inched slowly through the milling humanity. The upper floor was full of patrons some of them familiar school girls and boys drinking, playing snooker, smoking and chatting excitedly while others swayed to the music uninhibitedly. Everyone seemed to be minding their own business.

We came to a balcony overlooking the town center. This could have been the tallest building around where we had a bird's view of the humble town's activities. The rusty roofs, the cajoling hawkers milling about with their ware, the noisy touts ushering passengers into vehicles traveling different routes: it gave the impression of a variety of insects crawling all over on a moldy food. In a nearby corner, a *short* woman with buttocks that jutted out of her jeans was clinging to a male companion. That was when I saw Nixon prodding around like a bird whose wing had been broken and involuntarily coiled.

"What is wrong?"

"My brother." I lied, my heart fluttering like a dynamo. Where Nixon could be found also was Jeffrey. Quickly, Felix steered me past a woman with numerous bracelets around her wrists, coppery hair and earrings to a back door while I clung to him hiding my face into his body. What was Nixon doing here? Where was Jeffrey? Were they looking for me? Had the doctor discovered his ailment? The last one almost made me laugh.

"Where is my bag?"

He walked by a table at a corner. Jomo and Catherine were engrossed in a corner and she was drinking from a bottle. He hastily pushed me aside and picked something from Jomo and then led me down through the fire escape into the back streets. It was getting late and what I needed now was my bag and catch a vehicle home. As for Catherine, she appeared to have her own different plans.

My mind remembered the vows that had been extracted from Jeffrey the other day and he had agreed to be the one responsible for Irene's pregnancy. He was as good as married. What was he doing in this house of sin? Why couldn't he be at home taking care of her pregnancy? Was he after another skirt and mischief? The church members had huffed and puffed in livid anger at their angelic girl who had stained the altar of God. She had begged for their mercy in vain.

"The only option remaining for you is to be re-baptized or forget about this book." The church elder had advised. The punishment was aimed at the woman, the seed of the wandering Eve that had gotten to the fruit before Adam. She had sworn never to step in the church until she was sure.

"If I sin again, they will humiliate me and strike me off." I relived the experience of my sister condemned to hell. If any of those leaders spotted me loitering in these backstreets at these hours, I was certain my goose too would be cooked.

Felix led me into a compound that had a wall and rental units on either side with bluish doors. He walked into the fifth door and opened it with a single key he dug from his pockets. I stood there waiting him to shove my bag into my hands.

"Hey, Nerry, you want to become a painter!" He mocked as I stood there studying the houses. A man walked from one of the rooms and looked at me. *He might recognize me.* I dived into the typical bed-sitter that contained three stools, a small table, and a rack on a chair with a variety of utensils and cutlery, and a bed over which hang a blue curtain. Felix was bent under the bed and was busy dragging out something.

He straightened up and switched on the lights and the walls of the room become alive with nude and semi-nude wallpapers of Western women celebrities. My mouth dropped open at the extent of this kind of show.

"Where is it?" I was growing impatient and wanted by all means to zoom out of this place and catch a vehicle home. He didn't answer but turned to the door and fitted the slot. A look of triumph creased his face shone in his eyes. This was not the Felix of my dreams. I had made a mistake and actually brought myself into the lion's lair.

His hands were all over me fumbling with my clothes so frantically. I feared he could tear them apart. My body was paralyzed and didn't react to his touches. He quickly pulled off my blouse and shoes as I stood there dumbfounded.

"Can I pee?" I caught his ear. He hesitated.

"There could be a tin under the bed." He muttered and dived for it. His breath was coming out in loud whistles. I had been waiting for this and three steps were enough to get me to the door and pull the slot off.

I could see his fury as he swung around to restrain me but I threw the door behind me with a force. In my haste I didn't lock it but dashed blindly out to the veranda, towards an opening, shined a low wall and leapt to some street. My blouse was flapping around me and curious spectators were eyeing me suspiciously. As I edged into a dark section with the smell of waste water, I heard Felix calling out and warning me of my stupid act. I only wanted to create even more distance from my predator.

I ducked by a mound of stinking rubbish and squatted so as to take control of my senses. My feet were sore and there was pain on my shin were a trickle of blood was coming out. Would the street lead me to the bus stage? I didn't care if I had left my bag so long as I arrived home safely. I didn't want to see Felix and the treacherous Catherine again. That was when several hands gripped me wildly and as I tried to look up, several ugly faces were bearing themselves down on me with wicked grins.

My scream was stifled by a piece of dirt cloth shoved into my mouth. I was choking and as I fought off my captors, I found myself in the air. I kept on struggling and realized they were going to kill me. Had Felix resorted to this? What was happening? I squirmed helplessly as I was dragged into some dark end by passing some scrubs deeper into the bowels of evil. I was dropped onto a hard ground and pinned down and in pain and shame the bouquet bequeathed to me was grabbed by force. I only produced muffled cries. At some moment it was as if Nixon's face flashed above me.

"Mama, oh mama, don't do it!" Nixon?

8

I lay there for a long time stoically soaking in the pain, not stirring. A distant clock's tick tock filtered over and I began to time the pain spasms with the beats.

I opened my eyes slowly and saw Catherine at the foot of the narrow bed wriggling her hands and dancing, a face of worry. The source of light was a candle placed on some upturned gallon, casting some faint long shadows all over the room. My head was groggy, as if under the influence of drugs.

"Jesus! Jesus!" Catherine uttered the name in a quiet prayer as if addressing the darkness. A dog barked nearby and a car's sound traveling at high speed could be heard too. I was sure this place was close to the road.

I turned over to check whether any bone was broken and the bed gave a loud creaky protest.

"Nerina baby!" Catherine came running to the bed and just then an adjacent door opened and a gruffly voice inquired,

"Is she conscious?"

Despite the pain, I turned to face them. Catherine was all over me with bear hugs. Every bit of my body was sore as it had taken a thorough prolonged flogging.

"What happened?" I asked in panic, a vague picture of what had occurred flicking.

"You were done…" said a huge woman with a masculine body dressed like a man who confirmed my worst fears.

"We found you in a ditch, dirty bloodied…" Catherine pulled me closer, her eyes in tears. "I am sorry Nerry…terribly sorry. I led you to this mess, baby…"

There was a long silence.

"Forgive me, Nerina." There was a panicky timbre in her voice. "Promise you will do it. *Gaki,* please." She sounded so desperate.

I would have told them what had happened, but deep inside me there was a nasty feeling that they would not believe me. I would have thrown it to their incredulous faces, that it took several men to hold me down, to smother my coiling young energy, to spread-eagle me, to rape me on the coarse ground. Tearing, crawling at my womanhood, prising me open, desiring more and more of me as I fought the whole dirt battalion of hot, sickly excited beings trying to prove their masculine ego against my will, my feeble protests exciting them the more as they goo-ed their seed all over inside me. I was also to be blamed for lack of a strong resolve in my decisions, yes. So, I had allowed myself to be cornered by putting myself in the way of the firing squad like one running from one flying spear into another. I had stewed myself in my own juice!

Sorrow embraced my soul, unspoken and deep like a well. What if I fell sick or became pregnant? Why was this happening to me again? Was my life jinxed? How many guys had done it? How on earth could I run around naked in a world of full-blooded men? I wept in characteristic denouement over a heroine fallen from glory to goriness. Felix?

"Did Felix organize this?" the question was out before I would even think. A loud masculine click rounded in the room. Through my tears I saw Felix shaking his head.

"F… you Nerina. F…you! I am the most hurt person –my ego. You left me holding the feathers and went to party on the streets."

"Who is hurt here fool?" that was Catherine in her fury.

"Nerina is physically and emotionally hurt –and you parade your small man around just because you didn't have the pleasure to dip it in her and you talk of hurt my foot! Men and their small brains!"

Felix eyed Catherine with a long murderous glimmer I thought they would bounce on one another and destroy what remained of their sanity. The other woman chuckled and waved wildly.

"There is more to this Cathy. Mom is at home waiting for my future wife and we are holed in this ramshackle like robbers –and indeed if the police get wind of it all of us will regret. 'Felix boy,' she will ask 'where is the star you had promised to bring me?' I will stretch my hand and say, 'Don't hurry things. Wait for Thursday mum.' 'It's a promise son.' And come the day you get grabbed by *chokoras*, street boys, and you don't know how much I've done to have you pieced up- and you think I organized this."

The tears spilled from his eyes.

"This business of the only son should cease…" He blew his nose on his jacket. "So long Nerina." He stormed out despite protests from the woman and Catherine.

The woman turned to us and explained that Felix was the only son and was under pressure to marry as quickly as he could. His father worked in Mvita and the lonely mother had had her daughters married off.

I was utterly shocked by the revelation because at no time had Felix hinted about his grand plans to me. How dare he think I was that cheap to be married like a brainless girl? Was this the brand of love promised in his verses? Was true love so lopsided? How could he imagine living with me without my cooperation?

"Will he commit suicide" Catherine wondered.

"Suicide?" I gasped.

"Then let me go for my money in case he does it." The woman made for the door rather quickly.

"Why not stop him?" Catherine expressed my concern.

She turned by the door. "How can you stop a man thinking of marriage from fulfilling his decision?" The woman's attitude astounded me.

Suicide? Between me and Felix who could be justified at it. I recalled how once I had wanted to hurl myself before a vehicle. What if Felix died? I found myself unaffected by such a possibility. Wasn't he the one who had undressed me in order to rape me? And rapists deserve worse than that. If all of them committed suicide, the world would be a clean place to live in. I reflected on his triumphant voice: "You can do it in a tin" as he dived over to get something from under the bed. I had been utterly foolish and either way I had paid the price. Man, the inventor, the phallic fetishist, wham in the head at the sight of a female crotch and thighs, no matter what age. Even into a two days old he would insert himself, shove himself up, tearing it so long as the wham head hit the imaginary mark, boiling over, puking all over, damn it, going flabby, whether he killed doing it, for he had to sickeningly prove something, his only head functioning being the one beneath the belt. Phew!

"What if I get sick—er?"

The woman, who was called Mary, explained that she had injected me with antibiotics and should not be worried. I could not help wonder about her credentials as even quacks came in different shades, those solidified in their illegal experience.

"The great bend girl is not how high you bounce when you hit the ground but whether your mind will heal."

The tears will not stop flowing, not today, not so soon. I cover myself with the only tiny blanket on the small bed to suppress my woes. *Oh, King of the universe, is there a way you could fly Saarange or Luciana to me, during this hour of need to comfort me, to assure me of the stolen future?* Some things I would never have learned, even on the lap of my mother, whoever she had been. How come life has been this bad to me, every step becomes a misstep, a move into the jaws of suffering? What was the purpose of being born only to live a miserable, checkered life to be a victim of rape, and now dear God, was I reliving my unknown mother's life? Catherine could have cuddled me until I slipped into a deep sleep.

I saw a man with humorous eyes peering into my eyes, his presence pulling me to him. His presence wounding around my weak mortal heart. I raced into his waiting arms, smelling his masculinity, my eyes never abandoning his, the whole of me enwrapped about him. He promised to love me to death. "I met you and you stole my heart and I'll report to the police you told me…." A pensive giggle. "This is the truth, God one, the heavens are my witness." *Who am I to listen to cheap talk and trust cheap men whose only desire was my crotch? I hate them. I hate you men, who have taken advantage of me, those who are conspiring to do it to me.* I wake up with a start and there is something heavy holding my chest down. The room is bright. Catherine's hand is on my chest as she snuggles up to me like a puppy. She stirs up and sits up abruptly.

"In fact, I swear I've just seen your cousin Rodgers."

Rodgers, my uncle's son, was another Felix. He was shrewd, glib-tongued like the serpent, full of taste like a world sailor, a dandy and a plain liar. Even Saarange often referred to him as young Satan, for he could make his ends meet at whatever cost even if it meant stealing from the old woman. He even conned her a whole tea bonus money on the pretext of bringing home his white wife to settle for good. Grandma had always dreamt of grandchildren who would play on her laps. Even the tearful story he gave three and half years earlier about him getting locked in Kami Maximum security all the while couldn't really sway grandma.

"I want to scrub." I rose agonizingly slowly and had to get the water after a long wait. As I cleaned thoroughly, all my stains, the words of Sis Favour to behave well at home rung guiltily inside my dulled and sickened mind.

Jennifer's coup on me materialized when I least expected it. She had waited for so long to fix her spiteful eye on me and when it came, it was only a few guys who really knew what hit me. It wasn't the Felix mishap but a mere miscalculation on judgment.

At Prestige, senior students were exempted from games since they were supposed to give academics more time so as to excel and land into lucrative college careers. Efforts to improve the school's mean grade were concerted efforts whose foundation began being in form three, hence girls were supposed to ease off from strenuous co-curricular activities such as drama and sports. My enviable position as a volleyball skipper had to cease but Jennifer didn't want our reign in the field to end so soon and therefore flouted the rules to accommodate me, as long as her winning streak gave her a chance to bask in more glory.

I wasn't keen to play since I also wanted to be away from the General's eye. My brother Jeffrey and Nixon were out of school waiting for their A-level exams and had more time to relax and attend sporting activities where Prestige was featuring as our loyal fan base. I could sense the later wanted to share with me his issue about the doctor and diagnosis and I was looking forward to it.

After a relaxed playing and coaching, our girls were doing fine and I wanted to relax with *jamaas*, company.

"Let us go to the changing room girls," Jennifer spoke behind us as we mixed freely with guys from other schools in celebration. This made me conscious of the smell of sweat on my uniform and body.

"Meet my brother, madam?

I made introductions but Jennifer just looked away and as if not bothered remarked accusingly.

"Don't be cheeky, Nerina. Your brother?"

Jeffrey beamed on the face and uttered dryly.

"She is my follower, Madam."

"You know the regulations, brother!" she hurled the words with contempt while she tugged at my arm in a bid to take me away. I yanked my arm away from her hold and glared up at her.

"Madam, I won't go with you and I cannot ever play any volleyball here again. Don't forget I am a senior girl. If you find it hard, go ahead and report me to the principal."

"Okay! Okay!" She muttered briskly, anger clouding her face.

"Have it headstrong but Maina, you will regret this."

"We are sorry to be the cause of the bad blood, madam" Jeffrey civilly apologized. "But it would have been easy if the parties concerned developed some common ground. We are not new to you madam and making an attempt to greet my sister is not spoiling her... All the same, we are really sorry."

Jennifer clicked and walked away in a fury.

"She is a little hot in this type of sun." Nixon put it jokingly drawing loud laughter from the students present.

A sudden whirlpool sprung in a shallow dusty ditch hurling dry earth and pieces of dry vegetation athwart. I stared at it and found Nixon doing the same thing. He had not said anything to me at all this time and I didn't want to start it either. I thought he was trying to find the right words or was simply gutless. In the meantime, the wind was eddying very fast towards the nearby shops. People on its path waved their kerchiefs or simply covered their faces with hands. Two elderly men who were moving in opposite directions but watching the progress of the wind collided. I laughed. Nixon who had seen it clearly didn't. The now lightening air was made tense by his humorless silence. I felt like running after Jennifer and confessing I had made a mistake I would play more volleyball than waste my time with this mad guy.

I was yet to learn of his diagnosis and I knew he was spineless and regretted to push it.

"I read your letter and I really laughed to tears. From that day I promised never to laugh. It was my last laugh." He looked bizarre with his glossy hair shining.

"What was there to laugh at?" My voice had a smack of arrogance.

"It was the discovery that a woman will always be a woman."

Favour had once congratulated me for being a steady woman. In his unflattering tone he was singing the same tune. *Was he right?* It was my turn to wonder.

Still, something remote, something unreachable in him hung between us as a heavy invisible fog dividing us into different worlds. Our wills braced against each other as I stood my ground. I was no longer scared by his seniority.

"We used to talk and walk and stood watching the streams of vapor ascend before our gaze along the gurgling waters. How I wished the vapor of human elements rose and intermingled us! I thought you could be dawned with reality. I wrote…er…," he stammered as I tried to look for the right word to fight the soliloquy.

"Scrawled?" I said and looked down.

"Yes, scrawled to tell you I was sick. You advised me to take things with ease as every doc was a potential competitor and liar to my situation. Tell me earnestly what should I do?"

He cast his eyes boldly on me, across the chasm that divided us. Our eyes met. Two balls blazing with desire. We left them that way for a grip moment and then hastily looked away guiltily.

"You're a dreamer." I spoke as I bit each word. "Until you stop that I'll never stand beside you. You have no chance with me."

"All of us dream in one way or the other. And dreams live to become realities. I promise to pursue mine and make it a reality."

I remembered Jennifer and the thought of her trumpet blowing filled me with uneasiness.

"I am going to them," I muttered extending my hand to his.

"But they haven't called you." His eyes popped in surprised mockery.

"I am their student. But if you want a girl to live in your wool-headed fantasy I can link you with one, can't I?" I offered and I saw his head shake in what I thought was in the affirmative. Inside me, I was fearful I was losing this thread: this curious guy who I was growing to admire. He lowered his voice and in that flowed like a waterfall muttered.

"It's you I want, you and you alone."

"I've said no and forget it."

I placed a contemptuous tone on my no. Jeffrey who was canoodling with some girl at a distance might have overheard me since they looked in our direction.

"I'm sorry," I apologized to them and turned to go, and then I swung.

"I am very sorry, Nix," I rolled my tongue around the coinage. "I hope you understand. My teacher is going to give me a roasting and you won't be there to share in it."

Jeffrey stepped forward and gave me some money and thanked me for the company. Nixon too came over and gave a warm shake and it had me think I was obstinate for nothing. The girls stood jealously eyeing me but Nixon's face didn't betray whatever was brewing in his inner mind. Amidst the shouts of bye and well wishes, I walked into the rest room proud to have withstood Nixon's encroachment.

That evening as we drove back, Jennifer was boisterously jovial and freely cracked vulgar jokes. She might have succeeded. In her celebratory mood, she even allowed a few songs to be sung in my praise. Little did I know she was giving me a rope on which to hang myself.

The following morning, I was summoned into Favour's office. She continued working until I thought I was an intruder to the peaceful existence and serious ambience of the office. She looked up and said.

"You've been a good girl, Maina until success got into your head. Pride comes before a fall. It is true that your teachers tell you what is the best for you. They are the beacon to be followed. I'm astonished after your wonderful lead you wanted to hold your games trainer and beat some sense into her."

She took a plain piece of paper and wrote something on it as she continued to talk.

"Although things can be exaggerated, I have in my heart the survival of this institution. A smack on the coach's face is a fatal blow to us, and she is the one that makes Prestige what it is. We have not stooped too low at least to allow our students' gang lout boys against our teachers."

She continued writing in continuous wavy strokes. Fear clamped my heart like a mouse trap.

"Here take this one. You're hereby suspended from our school for the next two weeks. We need you to come back with your parent on the date of…"

My legs collapsed under me as a dizzying feeling enveloped me. I could be the first Maina to be expelled from school and to drag the man here was a dreadful feat than death.

When Jeffrey read the reasons cited for my suspension that evening, he was extremely amused. They were attempting to fight the coach, inciting the girls and hanging along with strangers against the school's policy. He pricked holes on every accusation in logical and reasoned arguments and I wished he could be the one to accompany me. At least I was happy I had an ally who had witnessed it all, but how could you convince Maina that this was exaggerated and based on some vendetta or beef with a teacher? Which parent of that generation believed in such a nonsense? That's how Jennifer had had her revenge and could be celebrating wherever she was.

"You modern kids are out to damn me and slap at my moral authority." I could even imagine him shouting at the wind. Was he a better father or some role model to imitate? As Saarange had once worried, *were we following his footsteps to depravity?* Soon, everybody in the village knew I was out of school and were talking about it. Some exaggerated that I had been expelled for falling pregnant. It didn't affect me at all since I knew the plain truth and I didn't want to be carried away by the fancies of my enemies. It was then that Jones who was married and working invited me to the city perhaps to hammer into me some sense of direction.

10

My journey to the city started in the morning and concluded in the evening. I was tired and sleepy because the previous evening had been spent trying to imagine what the new experience would be like. I had even incessantly kept asking information from the adults around, Peter and Mongina but they were the wrong clients because I even knew our local Modest better than the two combined.

I learned that the first time Peter had passed by Modest, he stood there awed by everything. According to him, every person who looked his direction was either a suspect pick pocket or some private detective nosing on who drank local illicit brews. He excitedly regaled us with his discovery of stories. He was only safe in the home-bound vehicles and very comfortable in the home perimeter, where he knew the best brewer, whose cow had calved, which wife had been battered etc.

Mongina was limited to the outside world due to her menial duties of housekeeping. She had children to take care of, with a husband who had abrogated his duties in his drinking escapades that lasted from dawn to midnight. She had inadvertently become the bread winner. She always agreed to what Peter said or nodded her head in confused amazement about what the world outside her cocoon had offered her in her struggle to put food on the table. Thank God, for there was plenty of food in our home and the two were their own supervisors. So, you couldn't expect her vamoosed, making that perennial *mwananchi,* citizen appeal: *"Twaomba serikali iingilie kati!* We plead with the government to intervene." However, how much was the alcoholic husband a government problem?

I did not blink all through the journey. I drunk in all the sights, the landscapes, the strange vegetation, and the farming activities which was a variety presented by our beautiful land. There were an expanse green tea plantation lining the road, running for kilometers like play fields. In the plantations were workers in green and yellow outfits with baskets on their backs doing the plucking. There were the wooded valleys and slopes, the savannah shrubs and fields of thistles and thorns harboring the zebra and giraffes, the wheat farms on the rich red volcanic soils. This was the case of the low lying Guru with its flat plains and gusty winds; the dull shiny waters of the Elam and Guru lakes; the chalky atmosphere of limestone mining along the rocky Gila up-setters. There was this upper Guru encrusted with bush and the jetting geysers and irrigation pumps spraying foamy white jets into the air amidst yellow stemmed acacia, the fog-laden hillocks and farms and tree groves encroaching the roads.

The first signs of the city were the high rise buildings lining the road, some hidden by clusters of tall trees. The road traffic dwindled into a snail's pace as tall buildings like giants with raised arms sprawled into the skyline. It was concrete and more concrete, like toothed mounds, like the strata of enormous blocks atop each other in cyclical progression, giving the impression that there were many eyes watching human activities.

Breathless touts shouting the routes and fare. The revving vehicles straying to the pavements in order to sneak through a blocking juggernaut of fazed drivers fighting for passengers enjoined by hawkers expertly displaying their wares as their hawk eyes watched out for the city council *askaris,* law enforcers, and customers simultaneously, ready to run away if anything. Woe unto you if you had not received your change when it happened. Woe unto you if you did not watch what item was wrapped, since you might discover at home that the trousers you bought were only two arms sleeves.

The street comedians, preachers, con men, pick pockets, hustlers, tarmacking graduates, whores, and everybody else completed this landscape of the city in the sun. I absorbed everything, as if I wanted to determine every creatures' profession until my eyes were sore.

Jones was waiting for me by the bus stage, the final destination of my country ride. We stuffed the ample country produce that Peter and Mongina had generously packed into his car. It was the best means to get such generous amounts of bananas, sweet potatoes, maize, vegetables, pumpkins and so forth to his estate resident. We snaked through blinking billboards and cone-like buildings lunging into the sky till I lost count of what else was happening. The vehicle was inching forward in a slowly due to the famed city traffic. We took hours and hours on the road with intermittent breaks that saw us move a few paces before hitting another gridlock. There were more people and vehicles around as if everyone had moved from their home the city in the sun!

"In normal circumstances, the ride should take less than fifteen minutes," Jones tried to assuage my frustration. I had the impression the vehicle was lurching forward and then sidling backwards.

As we approached the residential quarters, the drive was mostly smooth. He stopped on a huge red gate before houses that closely resembled that it was difficult to sort them out. He hooted and the gate slipped open. We drove into the parking and as we came out, Jones said to my relief.

"Little sis, welcome home."

The family mobbed me with the eldest daughter Madge shouting "daddy!" and "auntie" over and over. I held her, lifted her and we instantly became friends. She pulled down and was leading me into the house when a heavily-set lady came out and extended her hands in a cordial welcome. This was Colista and she had put on weight compared to when I last saw her. Her younger son, called Maina junior, hang by her skirts fearing the unfamiliar face. He hid his face behind her skirt when I tried to reach to him but took the sweet, I gave him. He was slowly looking for ways to familiarize himself with the stranger called auntie.

I bathed and felt refreshed. Madge was exuberant, trying to show me her books, (she was in baby class) and her expertise at operating the numerous entertainment gadgets in the living room. She was so adept for a child her age, confident, and sure of herself even by the way she used her words. After the pleasantries and catching the latest gossip at home, which I eagerly expressed since I was the able student of Mongina and Peter, I excused myself and retired to bed. I was exhausted and Madge insisted to sleep with auntie. Maina also threw similar tantrums, until I promised him his turn would be the following day. We crawled into the warm sheets and the girl told bubbly stories of her own world, but was soon snoring until eight in the morning when I woke up. Though I had hated the town at first encounter, the estate life wasn't that bad.

I was slowly learning the ways of the city and its nature. Colista was a charming host who took me to visit the parks, the orphanages, and the tree resorts whenever she was free, and it kept me busy. She even took me to the university where she and Jones had studied and that inspired me. I loved these sights, grasped the details and knew that my story would never be the same. I also discovered that Colista never did any of the house work since she had employed two house helps. She remonstrated with me when I tried to help with the washing and the general cleaning. I could laugh her off and tell her it was my everyday work at home.

"I want you to raise your scales higher, Nerry. Why think of doing a work other human beings can do at a pay? Are you planning to become a man's housewife, miserably waiting for him to drop you some change? You have the opportunity while in school to change your destiny. Work hard, eh?" I had heard similar words spoken by Sis Favour, that girls who failed academically became family padlocks, remained at home as housekeepers while their husbands worked out there.

"If you refuse to wake up earlier now, dear daughters, you'll compensate later in life, waking up at cock crow to make ends meet. To hustle with menial life, rushing to green goods market that opens at 3am. Ever known how those who excelled and are the bosses, 'chew life' by waking up when the sun is high… Work hard and you'll never regret!" That was the characteristic Sis Favour, urging us to make hay when we had the opportunity. And yet I was out of school on suspension!

It explained the weight Colista was putting good eating and little manual work. The outcome was perpetual complaints of disease and pain and it's like every night she had to take medicine. I guessed Colista's problem but didn't know how to put it to her. At the same time, she was my inspiration, and tipped me generously, and at the bottom of my heart, I knew I would surprise the girls back in school. I would also afford bread from the canteen and breathe down on them about how rich my family was.

I was yearning to go back to the lackadaisical pace of country life and the hopscotch school life. I also wanted to earn my own money and be independent on how I spent it. I would build myself a home, purchase a long car, the best entertainment and become a local tourist. The dream was within reach- in my final exams a few months ahead, and of course, after squaring the suspension. Jones and Colista advised me never to despise my teachers no matter what the circumstances were, whether they were on the wrong. I had to write a letter and apologize to Madam Jennifer, they advised.

When I came back, Peter and Mongina's ignorance about the city both surprised and amused me.

"I understand there you sit down and switch on a gadget that cooks, feeds and washes for you." Mongina wanted to know.

I really laughed and explained it was hundred percent human labor.

"Then you didn't visit the other places where all that happens. My cousin has been telling me about it. What of the walking stairs where you only stand and they do the walking for you?" I thought he was referring to the elevators.

"The town never goes to sleep. It is like daylight and people are ever working." I nodded in agreement. There were so many things to describe to the two. Humphrey had since moved in with one of our maternal uncles from where he took his studies from, since he had joined a bad company at home.

11

School life was back to normal, with preparations towards the national examinations. Time, to me, had flown so fast that I could not remember even the events from my high school. I saw life at Prestige to be another summary, a verse of few lines that was scattered in my memory. I only remembered the reporting date, the tearful days, and very few moments of triumph. Otherwise, Prestige had given me momentous occasions that would shape my perspective about life for a lifetime after what had happened to me. Jennifer had preened at my letter of apology like an angel who knew what was right for me. I had written and rewritten it, torn it until I came up with something that simply requested her forgiveness.

On the other hand, the inscrutable Nixon had written to me, harping about our last moments together. He painted the romantic scenery– he had a way to make them alive on paper, as poetically and picturesquely as possible. He had passed his A-level exams and joined university. Jeffrey had managed to secure an admission in an American university. He and Irene were still blowing strong despite the murky baby issue in their smooth romp. There had been the uneasy moments of denial and reprisals but Jeffrey had stood by her. Even in their long silences the flame of love burned, smouldered, and soldiered on. Jelita had been married to the Central part of the country. Daddy was a vibrant business man in Mozo and doing fine. Hortenzia was now filled up, huge, a sign of peace and good eating. Erastus was now doing an advanced degree in software programming. The photos he sent us showed a huge round comfortable man who changed cars like shirts.

Catherine, this session was unusually quiet and everybody welcomed it because with exams approaching at the end of the year, all we needed was fervent bookwork. She sat at a locker that was in front of me and this made me notice something uncanny was cooking. This certainly had nothing to do with exams but I failed to figure it out.

One evening, I walked her to the center of the field and sat her down.

"I know you want to ask me what is wrong with me. Nerry, I am pregnant, and you're the only person I've told. So, don't betray me."

I sat there digesting her words. The revelation was hard hitting.

"Do you know who the father is?"

"I surely don't know who is responsible but someone is going to believe he is."

"Does your family know about this?"

"I couldn't be alive if they knew."

"How old is it?"

"I missed my periods about five months ago. But I've had irregular periods… Er…I can't exactly pin it."

I feasted my eyes on her. Her body had nothing physical to show for it. However, her face had some pimples and dark rings around them as if she spent lots of time weeping, and I guessed it was possibly at night. My mind traversed back to the time when the fear of pregnancy had devastated me, leaving me sour and dejected. I remembered Irene and her fate.

"What will you do?"

"Do?" her eyes flickered with irritation and looked away. "I am yet to decide, Nerry."   Deep inside me I knew this was an outright lie.

"Don't try anything stupid"

"Stupid, numskull? Stop nosing! I know my fate and I beg for nobody's hand to carry this cross." She hesitated and looked at me, and confidently added. "Nerry, I repeat, don't tell anybody about our little secret and you will be my lifeline."

I wondered whether she could manage not being discovered until she had done the national examinations. The school invited the health personnel every term to carry out tests and weed out pregnant girls who would go home until they had given birth. From what I knew of Catherine, she was capable of surviving such an ordeal since some girls took the test and turned negative until they surprised everybody when the labor pains struck. They could keep their tummies flat by tying them with bands underneath their normal clothes. Since this was a possibility, I was counting on it until it was reported that Catherine had mysteriously vanished from the school compound.

An intensive search in all the crannies and nooks of Prestige grounds did not reveal anything. Even the chief security officer Omoyo, an ex-police sergeant, didn't have even the slightest clue. As members of her class, we tried to trace her last moves in vain. The only probability was that she sneaked out during the morning prayers that were always conducted at the cathedral.

The dark cloud of uncertainty hovering over the school forced the administration to dispatch me to her home. I arrived in the compound at around 9 o'clock in the morning. The first person I encountered was her mother carrying a hoe and a tin of beans that she was going to plant. The moment she saw me, she stood still like a statue until I reached her. Behind her stood two huts, one with an old rusty iron sheet and the other grass thatched with a lean cow tethered to a huge avocado tree. As I was wondering what to tell her in the course of shaking her hand, she made the first inquiry.

"Is it about Catherine?"

I stood there in confusion. I immediately understood that Catherine wasn't here.

"No, Mrs Keronche. She is missing from school."

"How can that happen? The school owes an explanation if anything terrible happens to her. I have had nasty dreams about that girl of late."

"That is why I am here."

"Daughter of Maina," I was surprised she knew me. "You don't understand the pain of motherhood, or do you?"

Maybe I understood another different pain. The pain of losing a mother at a young age or better being picked from the roadside. The pain of… I stood there like a fool trying to mutter an apology. It was then that a male voice, possibly overhearing our conversation, asked behind us, "Where could a girl like that run to?" The speaker was a wizened old man in a ragged shirt and over-washed patched-up trousers.

"Catherine is a naughty girl. She might have eloped for fear of exams." This was said by a middle-aged man in a brown *kaunda* suit whom I guessed might be one of her brothers.

"Catherine is your sister!" The old woman who had now placed the hoe and beans on the ground yelled back clouded with anger. "I know you don't care what happens to her but she is your sister."

"I'm sorry, mum," the man apologized. "I was only pointing at the possibility." He shook my hand and promised they would investigate the matter as he was to travel to Modest town over the lunch hour.

"Treat it as a matter of urgency, son." The father cautioned.

"Go back and tell them she is still missing." Catherine's mother said, her hand resting on her cheeks, cutting a forlorn miserable picture.

I caught a *matatu* back to school with the grave news. We again tried to unsuccessfully piece together evidence that would give us a clue to her whereabouts. There wasn't anything in her locker or box to show she had planned to run away.

That evening, matron took me aside and brought up the topic I had thought was a well-kept secret.

"I had told her she had only four months to the exam and if she were smart girl, she would have been patient. Where does one get the patience to get a child only to lose it when it's this vital?" I only looked at her wondering what game she was up to. Did she suspect I knew her whereabouts or she wanted to alert me about her present status?

"Do you know any friend close by who might have sneaked her out or may be accommodating her? We are about to let the police handle the matter. We may find she is in good hands and on her own volition and therefore would love to let the sleeping dogs lie."

I listened to her diatribe, only nodding. She could have interpreted it as rudeness but her words were challenging. I wasn't also used to people who just disappeared and had their secrets shared by others. A fleeting picture of a man making it off in a dash reared in my mind. There was Felix, now a police officer and then Jomo. Could it be possible Catherine had moved to the latter's place? Then there was that woman, heavily dressed in woolen clothes who claimed to be a nurse and in a backstreet room, where I had received the worst medication ever. What was her name, Mary or Maria? *What if Catherine had decided to abort? No.*

"What is it?" I felt dizzy and I could have fallen hadn't she held me in time and sat me down. She let me relax and gently plodded me to remember anything. I kept my fears to me, afraid to share them lest I would be accused of being a traitor.

"If you recall something let me know and I'll be of assistance. Our school's reputation is at stake, and so is the life of your friend."

I could barely sleep that night. I was very restless, on and off like a faulty electronic appliance. It was as if I was sleeping inside a culvert where weird tarantulas were clawing on my skin, snapping large macabre jaws at one another, then breaking into a song;

We seek to choose, to choose, to choose.

We seek to choose, to choose, to choose.

A very good girl.

Whom do you think we can have, we can have?

Whom do you think we can have, we can have?

If not Nerina?

As if in a tandem, their flanks closed on me so that I could hear and feel their breath and creepy touches. I abruptly opened my eyes to stare into the inky darkness full of human snores. The security lights cast streaks of light outside and on some beds. The rest of the night was spent coiled up in apprehension, and a long one it was. At a time, I felt like dashing into the matron's house and waking her up so that we could search for Catherine. I tried to formulate how I would express my feelings to her in vain. A strong premonition that something terrible was happening saddled the centre of my mind.

The following morning before breakfast, I was at the matron's place. She allowed me yap on and when I finished, she implied she would permit me to check since the place wasn't that far. I went back feeling like a fool. I even wondered if this was how Catherine would have loved me to keep her silly… secrets.

I took a *matatu* and alighted at Modest town's principal bus stage. My fingers were stiff with the stinging morning cold. A few people were in the back streets as I descended the stairs leading to a familiar quarter. I quivered to imagine there was risk of again running into a gang of 'street rapists'.

I walked briskly like a person on a noble mission. There was a narrow lane between the houses and a maternity home. A shallow trench carried a stinking greasy water that had pooled next to an electric pole where a heap of garbage was threatening to become a hillock. I negotiated my way around it and ran up another lane and crept through a low creaky gate hanging delicately on one hinge into a compound fenced with old iron sheets blackened by soot and brown rust at intervals. When I reached the shabby houses, I counted the number of doors weighing down on memory to get it right. Most of the doors were latched, a sign that the occupants were either away on their menial callings or still asleep. One or two doors hung half way open but I hurried to a specific door. My memory did not let me down. The place looked the same, like it was two years back.

I pushed the door. It gave way and I got in. I squinted as my eyes adjusted to the faint light inside. A muffled groan came from one of the rooms, as if by a divine act (I had whispered a prayer.) There was something instantly familiar about the same room. I surged forward like being propelled by an invisible force of urgency. The room was the same and, on the bed, lay the prone figure of Catherine emitting intermittent groans, uncovered and stretched out full length, her pale hands knotted around the bed clothes as her body arched in strange angles as if she wanted to crawl down the other end of the bed crabwise.

I rushed to the bed as she groaned again, foam spilling from her clenched mouth, dragging herself weakly along the bed and then back as if she was afraid, she would slide off the edge. Her face was contorted as great waves of pain rode inside her in constant spasms.

The bed was a mess of excreta, blood and other mess. I held her, calling her, wanting her to speak to me, to turn to me and tell me that all was right, but there was no response. I wanted to feel her heartbeat. I couldn't tell whether there was life in her and I was horrified at the imminence of death of my friend on the very bed I had been resuscitated. I had to do something frantic and since I didn't know what kind of first aid to give, I rushed out of the room, made some turns, and made it to the nearby hospital.

The watchmen stared at me as if I were a ghost, listened to my story as if they were part of the gate posts. I yelled, explained and struggled to reach whoever was on duty for assistance. A man in a white coat walked over and when he listened to my story, he examined me as if trying to determine my sanity.

"We usually treat patients here in hospital young woman." He looked at my uniform for a wee bit. "Nyakundi, go and check out." One of the watchmen who had been leaning on the wall reluctantly extricated himself from the noble duty of taking care of the hospital duties.

Once in the streets, he moved at a brisker pace as if he had contracted my panic. I led to the place and entered inside. The sight in bed made him falter but he courageously reached out for her pulse.

"So little life in her. Quickly! Get hold of her as I remove the mattress for carrying her."

She was too heavy for me but he assisted as he fixed the tiny mattress on the floor. We laid her on it amidst groans and in a rush, we were carrying her to the hospital, stumbling back and forth. Nothing had ever been heavier to me than Catherine. I didn't know where the strength came from but some good Samaritans joined the stampede to the hospital. We met the curious matron on the way, she had promised to come along later and assist. She also gave hand and soon Catherine was wheeled into the hospital's best facilities. A team of medics soon gathered around her but we were kept out of the room. "She has lost a lot of blood." One of them muttered. I hung about praying to God to spare her life

One nurse walked to us. "She requires an immediate transfer to our mother hospital where we have the ICU. Who is meeting the expenses?" My mind was blank. "The ambulance is on the way."

The matron nodded, took my hand and guided me outside the hospital. She sat me on a bench. I stood up when madam Principal,

Father Mika, a coterie of teachers and the man I thought was her brother walked towards the entrance led by the matron. They waved at me and trooped into the hospital. Soon after, they came out. At the sight of Sis Favour wiping tears and sniffling into a handkerchief, I knew it was all over. The talk about the ambulance had been a gimmick to make me feel something was being done and that my friend was going to be alright.

I sat there for a long time, finding it hard to believe that Catherine my mentor, my defender at times of torture was no more. I wasn't prepared to swallow such a bitter truth because it was unpalatable. I abruptly rose up and trudged to the room where my seniors had formed a ring around the body. The body had been prepared so that it would be transferred to the morgue. A tag with a name had already been fastened to her toe. I walked to my still friend and touched her flesh and felt her congealing blood. There was no hope.

I thought it was a mistake. I wanted to hold her to myself, to perform a unique miracle such as calling out her name and she wakes up and smiles to everybody's consternation. But I knew this was impossible. *What could her old parents say? How could the students react to the news? Catherine? No!* I remembered the mother's meeting and premonition on the day she was to plant beans and her ragged father. Humble souls who expected the best for their daughter! As the trolley moved to the morgue, I rushed forward to restrain it. I was held back and Sis Favour who was in no better shape herself gathered me to herself. I emptied myself on her bosom as she continued invoking God's name.

After the message had sunk, we drove back to school, being bearers of the sad news. The school was thrown into disarray, for, who didn't know the *kareteka* and defender of humble souls? Her cause of death had been confirmed and it had to be put to us firmly and openly: complications related to abortion. Matron also cleverly explained my involvement in the search that a message from an unknown source had reached her and being her home mate, the two of us had gone to check it out and stumbled on her dying form. I was devastated more so by the premonition in the dream and the words of the old woman the day she saw me in their home. Was there a force that always announced our beloved's destinies, preparing us for the unforeseen eventuality that we didn't understand?

However, there was a missing link in the tragic story. Was Jomo involved? Who had been the father of Catherine's baby? What was the role of the nurse woman who I only knew as big and dressed in wooly things with a name like Mary? Who were the occupants of that room and how did Catherine end up there? Who gave this concoction of herbs and tablets and tried to pull out the baby with some crude tools? Not even her funeral could provide these answers. The police had a role to provide us with the right answers.

The burial became an open seminar to educate us girls on the folly of opening our legs to men and proceeding to abort the precious babies inside us. Scripture after scripture were read condemning abortion and fornication until they sounded like the same thing.

"Girls, your bodies are as delicate as eggs. Handle yourselves more carefully if you don't want to break them."

Nothing spoke the truth of who Catherine really was than our tears. She was a real friend, the ubiquitous ever cheerful, magnanimous and loud-mouthed creature. We were going to really miss her. Even Jennifer, the one who had no love for her also had fond memories to say about the late Catherine. Nobody would afford to continue making enemies with the dead. We went back to school after we had laid wreaths of different colors that expressed our true love for her on the mound of earth that was now the final resting place of our friend.

The coming month was a hectic one to form fours as we prepared for the District mock exams. The desk in front of me was a stark reminder of the missing occupant. The mock results were not so good for me and I could at least point the blame at the disturbance occasioned by Catherine's death. However, we all as a class vowed to work harder, putting the prerequisite final touches, working closely with the teachers, not ignoring anything in the memory of Catherine.

However, an absent occupant of the seat before me her spirit was always present. It was there urging us on, laughing boisterously at our silly mistakes, flailing around in the ring, letting out some chops, jabs, hooks, still telling us to go on, and add an extra mile. Ninety percent of the time was occupied by bookwork with little time to play. We did it for Catherine and the exam did not seriously scare us into silence. One could notice the effervescence accompanying every paper, the excited bubble around the dining hall on the final day of the exams. As we parted company, we carried our valediction notebooks bearing one another's physical home and contact addresses and words of wisdom, favorite music, dishes, pet peeves and memorable moments at Prestige. We hopefully looked forward to excellence. As the December festiveness approached, I was certain college life was beckoning me, the eagerness in me overwhelming.

BOOK THREE

1

There is something symmetrical and handsome and lithe in a horse compared to a donkey. The former's hair and skin permeate harmony, style and beauty. Then, there is the donkey, ugly, un-proportional, dull, and awkward featurelessness. Maybe it's because I've witnessed how hard a donkey can kick and how it can foolishly wallow in dust. While in primary we had big boy in school who used to enjoy 'crushing girls' which was pulling them to his breast in a bear hug with his foul mouth oozing bad breath.

The teachers called him "donkey," and thus he came to be known. He didn't go beyond standard seven and the other day I met him, he was a miserable village lout known for heavy drinking and doing menial jobs for a few coins. His wife could not stand the miserly of hunger and depravity so she left him for another man. Sammy was his real name. He used to exude a wrong form of confidence on unsuspecting girls unlike the staggering wreck at the moment. He had become the beast of burden as his nickname foretold his fate.

Sadly, it was the same attributes I came to discover Rodgers and Peter possessed as I knew them better. Whatever their positions in life, you could not trust them with anything in a skirt even if it was a two days-old girl child.

Take for example Rodgers, my cousin, the young Satan according to Saarange. He was an 'ozone guy' because his demeanor placed him above anything terrestrial and urbanized. He was a Sheng champion- a lingua that was a mixture of Kiswahili, English and local languages- and a refined gentleman who knew how to make a woman feel wanted in words. He was also, though surreptitiously, a heavy drinker and smoker.

He one day came home and lured me to his cage, some forsaken hut in the neighborhood, where he feigned to be keeping a gift for grandma and once there, he wanted to rape me. We are yet to lower the banner and intermarry in our community among relatives including paternal cousins. But there he was, slurping and salivating like Mr. Hyena. His mission was not to drink in a woman's beauty and symmetry but to lunge his hand into her pocket and yank out her treasures. He wouldn't even mind to tear her dress in the process. It was sad to discover that my smart urbanized cousin was a rotten individual of no character and substance. Maybe, a man's measure and refined character, I came to learn was basically on how he behaved before the vulnerable female characters whatever the circumstances.

Donkeys like Rodgers do not admire or recognise beauty, I swear. They only see what every woman hides from their view. They don't feel, or fantasize that tenderness or softness womenfolk are naturally endowed with. All they desire is to satisfy their animal lust and furnish their deprived egos. Like Donkey of yore, they want to 'crush' and defile beauty. They want to destroy albeit what is good, treasured, vulnerable and debase it to their low animal instincts. They are not 'horses', lofty beautiful kings in character and judgment. They are base devils, accursed beasts of burden. Forgive my indulgence in things I little understand. It's my stupid opinion informed by my stupid relating with men.

I could see Rodgers' eyes glittering with the morning dew on grass- a topic of their love items. The glitter that would fade momentarily once the mission was accomplished and which most of my sisters mistook for love. He was a beast bearing his own lust, ambitions, frustrations, anxieties and confusion all in one thought. Arced like an angler's rod and swollen like a cobra's venom, he edged towards me, drooping sweet names like Babe, Love and even sung a sweet melody.

I kicked him. He honked, brayed and began to rough me up. I screamed and Peter, his comrade in crime, as I came to learn later, who had been promised that it would be a smooth execution, lay, and was waiting nearby rushed in and knocked broad daylights out of Rodgers. The script was the same in history, a would be saviour, with pretended chivalry. He could have murdered him, were it not for some of my cousins and I who yanked him from the helpless prostrated figure. Peter and I escorted him close to his home as he kept saying drunkenly, "I will and I must… one day. I will and I must…"

As we walked back, Peter dominated the talk.

"He can never touch you. I know his type… You're a good girl…someone worth the pain …." He swallowed his saliva loudly with his hands in his pockets. The dark was catching up.

"Listen, Nerry, Rodgers is such a bad boy. He does not know how to show respect to women. He should worship your feet. Not just dreaming about and coming to...to…" He inadvertently crashed to me as he hurried ahead of me. Our bodies didn't welcome the touching but Peter knew better. He suddenly stopped and it was my turn to collide on him.

"Ugh!" I cried out for full effect. His hands reached out to steady me, one brushing across my left breast. In the dying evening light, his eyes had picked the same glitter I had seen in Rodgers, his breath strenuous. He blushed shyly as I peered intensely into his pupils and led the way.

"Who would not give everything for a good girl like you? Ask me and I'll tell you who can…"

I could guess the answer. Why ask when it's Peter blowing the trumpet, his ego rioting over mine. All the same, I asked.

"It's God's angel!" I was taken aback. I sought clarification.

"Angels are innocent beings. They faithfully work for their masters without any complain. They take care of the home, land, children, everything…."

Yes, this Peter had been an angel to us. In fact, my father's faithful servant for years. I could see him vividly opening the gate and giving his loyal salute unmatched anywhere.

We could see our home looming a dark silhouette against the gathering darkness.

"Look there, Nerry," his hand was pointing at some birds swooping on insects, then the stars. "They are beautiful things. Our souls are tied with them."

I wondered how he had imagined that. Peter had little formal education but sounded so romantic than the educated Rodgers. He at least possessed a sense of romance than the young Satan's approach.

"You know all that Peter?"

"Yes," his face beamed at the compliment. "I know that you are also lonely. You need guidance before you get out of that compound. You need a learned and a clever gentleman to un-bottle the beautiful pleasures inside you. That man is… is …" his voice quaked and measly trailed off.

What an angel! There was a long sickening silence whereby I recalled Sis Favour's lecture on the quality of being a strong woman capable of standing your ground and saying no, so strongly you left no doubts or buts in your listeners. Once Peter in his juicy stories had confessed that he loathed the mousy-squeaky type of women who left you guessing what they really meant. I envisioned Maina looming over me, forcing himself on me. No, it was those boys at the back street prying me open, terrorizing me apart and my head was going giddy and I almost toppled over. Peter steadied me as I stumbled on an outcrop root on the path and I instantly tore off from his hands and with a voice full of bitterness at this betrayal of trust, I blasted off.

"I know my way, Peter! I know my direction and no man or boy can show it to me. Do I make myself clear?"

It hit him below the belt like a rock and he momentarily winced. A figure loomed before us before he could even close his wide-open mouth filled with shock. It was Mongina.

She stared at my dirt and torn dress and at Peter. The later quickly explained what had happened at least to exonerate himself from the accusing stares.

"I was afraid…" she excused herself fearfully and strutted towards us.

"All alone in that house." Deep inside me I knew here was one woman who had learned not to trust donkeys with a skirt. Peter didn't say anything again and I instinctively reckoned he was terribly frustrated.

A dry twig broke behind us and we turned to find Rodgers armed with a *simi,* sword hurtling down at us. We dashed towards home as Peter hurled items at him. Some of our cousins joined the ruckus restraining Rodgers as he dangerously brandished the shiny blade in the air. I knew they were part of this conspiracy. Where had this Satan found his feet yet we had carried him home helpless? We rushed into the compound and secured the gate behind us. He came up to the gate hit it severally and laid bare their wicked plans over me. I could learn later that in their drinking spree he and Rodgers had bet on who would be the first to lay me. Peter could have been laying his strategies when Mongina and my firmness spoiled the party.

The embarrassed Peter kept mumbling in a corner over Rodger's public fooling.

"Stupid, anybody. Dog's vomit and others." The man was so ashamed even to face the two of us. In utter shock, Mongina with a bemused glitter in her eyes, as she watched his every movement, confided to me in reference to the sword incident.

"I love him with his bowels intact."

I thought I hadn't heard her right. I knew she was married to a drunkard in the other village and had several children. She might have realized my shock when she continued to explain.

"I've a husband, yes, who is a mere pair of trousers. He drinks himself dead."

"But he is your husband!"

"Why are you shouting it? A woman needs children. A woman needs acceptance in the family and community circles. If she is fertile then isn't it her responsibility to save her marriage?" She gave me a long lecture on the family line continuity from a viewpoint of an adult. I followed her to the sheds where we milked the cows and enclosed them. Peter hovered somewhere in the background doing some errands. All this time, Mongina's eyes followed him with admiration and respect shining on them.

 The man had his own family and I wondered how he fulfilled his obligations. Why hadn't the two lovebirds met before Mongina could get into a barren and unfulfilled marriage? And what was this about sleeping with me with his women available? Mongina helped me view another panorama of a life that I hadn't imagined before. Men's behavior never ceased to amaze me. Peter had a wife and a drooling Mongina and was yearning to teach me a curriculum meant for adults, a dream I was sure his master would not condone? What did you do to a dog that turned to eat your flock? You exterminated it in the cruelest way. And what was this to do with sex that branded us as woman or man? Weren't we products of the same sex, world all over, whether acquired in love, anger, pretense, force, urge or material things? We seethed over it, yearned, boiled, cursed to have it; hoping to attain its lost idyllic and primordial rhythms in endless circles of individual fancies. Were we more fulfilled with more or less of it, frustrated, demonized or scourged by its ultimate results?

Souls kept vigil over it, worshipped it, choked on it, shrunk, cried, pained, pined, murdered over it in a mystical exhibitionist ritual enforced by fashion and cultural moguls. We labeled ourselves into classes such as prudish, hot, frigid, and nymphomaniac as we clambered the starrier ecstasy of our forefathers to fleeting explosions of primitive energies and yet Peter had said he wanted to teach me as he had been taught by someone who had been taught too. Who taught the young ones in the wild to suckle and run for their dear life? Who taught the popping synchronized movement in the act of fulfillment? Wasn't this natural, came out purely on mischance? Peter was a donkey, at least with style, since he mustered guts to ask for it, unlike some people I knew. Even donkeys would be rated.

He had asked for it without any style, feeling, reason, or dignity to bundle it to his little ego and count himself lucky and adventurous for the new conquest, massage his ego and feel great. Just that and nothing more! And for doing it, he had broken the trust that existed between the two of us, the innocence that allowed us to walk nude so long as we didn't realize our sin. And now we were naked and exposed and it was for him to carry his little sin to the grave and keep his distance. Poor Peter! Mine was a no-go zone for his ilk and type of connivance.

A week from the incident, Rodgers beat the hell out of Peter. He walked home one evening and provoked a fight and when our strong Peter went for his jugular, he coiled himself like a tiger and with a punch, a jab and a kick Peter went flying across the room with a thud and emptied his bowels. When he came back, he was nose bleeding. By time he went for his spear, Rodgers had vanished into the safe haven in the coast of Mvita. I thought he had fulfilled his ominous words that he would one day do something.

2

Sometimes I was awed by the shortness of life, a snuff of the candle, every time it became plain that Catherine only lived in our memory. She was ever present; walking with me to school, to the river; seated beside me in class; training with me some karate moves; fighting for me; conniving while crying for me at the same time, a loyal and crooked friend, an equal enemy that I could never discard. She was a being that was easily carried by her youthful energy. Could I betray her role in my life now that she was dead? No!

We had done our exams with her spirit hovering around the room and sitting on her empty desk. I didn't name my first baby after her at all. Did I fear she would become another Catherine? However, her spirit kept up with me. Was there something I had not forgiven in my heart? Could it be their trap with Felix that had ended me in trouble? But she had sincerely regretted it. When the roll goes yonder where will the proud Catherine be? *Oh God!*

In mid-February, the exam results were announced over the radio. I waited until I was sure the result was in my school before I travelled to school. Prestige had done exceptionally well. Notorious, my nickname, was a popular girl and a lucky fellow. I had vowed to make it for Catherine as had the whole class. Such an exam result had never been registered in the records of the school.

When I sauntered to the principal's office, she received me warmly over a cup of tea and regaled of how proud they were of us. So long as my result remained unknown, my blood raced and my pulse accelerated. I never knew I would be such a coward. I had scored a strong B grade though short of my dream to get into a lucrative faculty. Favour hugged me and wished me the best in life and reminded me of our earlier talk.

"This is a challenge before you. People of your disposition can make high leaps out of this. The future is bright Nerina. What you do with it matters."

She smiled and patted my back. "My office is open to you, my child."

As I stepped out of Prestige's compound, I felt that I was leaving something big behind. I had come to the place with the innocence of a child and now I was a grown up with memories and rich depository of knowledge that was hard gotten. I raised my head high and walked out of that gate taller than before. Someone had wisely observed that though learning was collective, exams and results were individualized. You took it alone and picked your own result slip and hence, each person shaped their own destiny.

A few months later, I was selected to the faculty of Environmental studies in Mvita University to pursue a course in Environmental Health. My stay at home had exposed me to the rough village life. I had come to understand how deep the loyal bonds between the likes of Mongina and Peter went. They had one set of minds to keep the whole secrets up their sleeves and whatever they knew was sparingly shared amongst those of their similar position and not any Harry, Dick or Tom.

My new university was a recent establishment and quite magnificent with several story buildings that dwarfed everything that I had known in high school. The roofs were red and the place smelled of fresh brick work, and paint. The blocks housed the faculty departments. The men's and women's hostels were separated by the computer lab and administration blocks with a neat network of cement pavements joining the giant porticos to each place. There was a beautiful work of flowers that were strategically grown and trimmed by workers who watered them using hoses from taps placed at strategic points in the expanse of the compound.

Here, the terrain was rather flat and bordered the sea where the sea breeze could be felt, especially in the evenings and mornings. The temperature switched between hot and warm but got hotter at night that we barely covered ourselves. I was given a room to share with Rita, a short girl from the Eastern highlands who had an adventurous spirit, but not as wild as Catherine. We were members of the Mt. Kenya hostel, a three storied building where we were in a room on the second floor.

Coming to the University of Mvita (UOM), you alighted off the Kiritini bus stage where a giant billboard spelt out the name and motto in golden letters: Our education, Our destiny. My eyes satiated in the new sights of the vegetation to the new dressing styles with men mostly in white fezzes, *kanzus* and sandals, and women in *buibuis,* and the accented Kiswahili that showed their religious and cultural inclinations. The rest dressed scantily in the humid weather exposing more flesh in a place acclaimed to be attractive to first arrivers, in what was called *raha*, pleasure.

I walked to the main gate where guards in blue uniforms and brown helmets manned the entry. There were students and guardians in their hundreds carrying luggage and registration forms. I followed the tiled paths to the finance and administrative registry. The place looked impressive and academic with several vehicles in the parking lot where I had to take up my studies for three and half years. I also wanted to make use of the summer classes to cover the course faster.

Life in college came with freedoms unknown to us there before. Male and female students freely interacted and slept where they wished though there were regulations and rules that had to be followed that prohibited irresponsible and careless conduct. You were your own master and you chose the life to lead, so long as you performed academically. However, the same rules were freely violated and ignored in equal measure, no wonder some boys and girls lived as husband and wife or collected women and men companions from the streets for a one-night stand. These involved exiling their roommates and if there was freedom to yearn for, it was this, unlike what the likes of Catherine had embraced and ended messing up themselves. Those who longed for this freedom earlier in life never made it here to find it in excess. They didn't find the opportunity to indulge in it. Equally, freedom had its limits. You took it in excess, and it would be your failure. There were curbs and this made the difference between discipline and indiscipline.

Some colleagues had a tendency of coming back to college in the wee hours of the night drunk and singing circumcision songs. They sang nasty things about others and themselves, indulged in sexual orgies, excreted on sinks and vomited, and uprooted police sign posts, tore down street lights. The following day, they would appear sober, clipboards and notebooks, seriously minding their academic themselves. How they managed to live these two worlds apart was a genius execution. But some got carried away and lost their direction, noble dreams by becoming total addicts of one or other thing. They would be seen picking their way in the campus or town streets, inebriated, sickly, and mad or simply vegetables who couldn't tell their circumstances. Yes, drugs victims.

There was a library with its power point presentations, slides, carrels and academic journals in the Africana section, publications. The Islands and their precincts, leisure walks, mingling with the public, the dripping sea, the waves, the sight of tourists sunbathing and sand bathing, and the weekend discos in Clubs that marked the campus life. There also were traditional dishes, historical sites, fishing wharves, canoe rides, yachting for a wee fee, sightseeing in the old town and its rich Islamic background, moorings, palm trees and coconut fruits and vendors selling roast fish and potatoes and also supplying the refreshing *maji madafu* extracted from coconut fruit.

That was Mvita town for a new comer. The abundant mangoes and orange stocks at the noisy and congested Ongea open air market. The rides in the ferries, the swimming using inflated tyre tubes such that you drifted along like flotsam when the sea got tumultuous in the evenings.
That drift with the tide, mostly shore wise, was said to allow room for a soul to communicate with his or her past and clean it of evil spirits. In hot afternoons, we swam or simply watched the inky sea, wishing to traverse into the far lands with the ripples and tides coursing in our blood and beheld the giant ships and dhows or yachts, coursing through the sea. We visited the public and private beaches where skimpily dressed tourists both local and international lazed with younger escorts.
We walked barefooted feeling the warm fluffy sand kiss our feet, sometimes smeared it on our bodies believing it would cleanse our bodies. The ambient sultry music tunes of the *chakacha, taarab, bongo,* and other local songs taking prominence from amplified earth-shaking speakers from the *makuti,* palm-roofed hotels. Everything was beautiful, attractive, promising the ease of life, but required money and more money since no pleasure was free apart from, perhaps sunbathing, swimming, and loitering.
There was something always romantic and cozy about this type of life and it would enslave you such that you forgot your real essence as a man or woman to make your own life by working hard. This was Mvita, the citadel of knowledge; Our education, Our destiny, for you.

<h1 style="text-align:center">3</h1>

I was adapting to college life, where bells and assemblies were not heard of, and our lives floated rather more smoothly. Over the weekend, I was reading a magazine lazing in bed when I heard a voice mention my name. Rita was moving out to brush her teeth.

"You have a visitor at the gate, Nerry." She mumbled mischievously and winked. Who could be calling in this new place?

I slipped into sneakers and padded down the stairs to the portico. A few other students hung about discussing animatedly. At the main parking lot, there was a long a black limousine with tinted glass. I was going to the gate when the door opened and out stepped Rodgers. We looked at each other with surprise written all over our faces. I had forgotten all about him- Saarange's young Satan. My first reaction was to walk away, but he moved faster, his arms extended in a bear hug.

Several comrades waited to see my reaction to such a high-class visitor I had received. Everything happened in a huff and he was characteristically sizing me up his usual humorous self, taking over. The last memory of him felling Peter came into the fore asking me to run.

"So, university is a fantastic transformer little, Sis," he laughed. "Jones told me and I was searching for you all over, and I've not been disappointed."

So, it was Jones. For the first time Rodgers was behaving like a responsible guardian. "Tell him that I am okay."

"Wait until I come over and my little sister will be a first-class entrepreneur." He might have seen my confusion. "I am a salesperson with Creative International. We sell everything from clothes, to gems, and even plots." He again laughed and before I would say no, he led me to the vehicle and pulled out a set of female clothing articles that were set in class. At the sight of the items, a few female friends were all over us and Rodgers, as always, saw an opportunity to make a kill. He airily explained the advantages of buying his items. "It offers you class, comfort and makes you a high-class guy." There were potential buyers already carried by his suaveness. The man could even sell you oxygen.

"Ask for anything and my little sister will tell me," He mischievously winked and patted my back and the girls were taken over and were already making inquiries where my room was, and how they would get their orders and sizes. I wanted to laugh. He winked at me as he pulled me aside.

"You aren't taking me up, girl. This is serious business and no monkey business this time." I took that to mean he was apologetic of what had happened in the village.

"You will soon be getting those beauty chemicals, underwear all imported and I am surprised you don't look…" A tall colleague was strolling to us with a silky laced blouse which she fitted over her top with little success.

"I want to have something my size like this. I'd even pay up front for three." He nodded with concern to everything, and his customers thought it was cool business trustworthiness and they bought items there and then. I was scared that the guy would take their money and vanish into thin air and leave me helpless.

"You don't want to make money, sis? The allowances are huge." Young Satan, pleaded and cajoled. Just then Rita arrived and the two bonded almost at instantly. One could think they were old friends and it behooved me how innocent women always got attracted to devils like Rodgers. Rita was by all means a simple typical village girl, untainted, pure and adventurous yearning for exploration. She was unusually effervescent when she learned that he was my cousin and what he was selling. Soon, she was showing him off like a newly acquired property and we were soon in our room where she poured him a glass of cold juice. I was so reluctant with this new found Rodgers, a part of me screaming warnings at this upcoming venture. But Rita's enthusiastic spirit told me to relax my guard and allow her to wade the waters.

We went back to the vehicle and he drove off after promising more. A few students hang about us, envying me.

"That guy is classic. Which university did he graduate from?" The ladies were drooling over him. I would have told them he was a school dropout but they were all talking excitedly about his oomph. Even the guards were all taken aback since they had never been generously tipped by a visitor. They were all talking highly of him and this brought a cold shiver to my stomach. I was afraid and expected to be called at any time by the vice chancellor, accused of conspiring with my relative to con students.

True to his words, he visited again with assorted goods. The items attracted everybody's attention, even the tutors. Soon, we set a little sales store in our room. Rita was agog with every move and since her mother had a curios shop, here was an opportunity to exercise her acquired sales skills. We partnered and we soon had a booming business. The men bought presents for their girlfriends and a few items for themselves, since the stock was mostly for females. I was seeing a lot of money that I had never done in my life without handling any. Rodgers taught us how to take care of the stock and money and told us when he could come to pick it, to avoid any mugging or theft. We fitted our room and wardrobes doors with anti-janitor devices whose codes that only Rita and I could handle.

Rodgers had materialized in my life in a different form and it was as if he was sorry of his past sins and had reformed. He now looked more mature. It earned me respect from my colleagues who had ventured from their rural homes for the first time to come read for a degree. Campus life offered so many liberties and lots of time that used well, would be good for developing a business enterprise.

Rodgers endeared himself to many of our college mates and helped them in all sorts of business, as long as there was no illegal undertaking. The girls laughed at his walking style, his V-shaped feet, as he hung back, earphones, red sneakers, bling-bling's, chains and several laces hanging from his shirt's and trousers' pockets. He would also drive different vehicles the way celebrities did. Wasn't he our celebrity and nobody any longer wanted to know his level of education? He spoke nice refined English, coast Kiswahili and Sheng. My efforts to find out what was the source of his supplies were always shrugged off. I knew it was wise not to broach the topic again and let live.

One day while replenishing our stock and coming for the money, he visited in a red Mercedes. He led us inside and ensconced in its comfortable seats was a large White man. The man warmly turned to me, taking my small hand in his, a strong cologne hanging around him.

"This is Bradley. Meet Nerry, our Campus link." The man expressed his gratitude and said he hailed from the Scandinavian countries.

"Your country is good and I have decided to live here." He chuckled and added, "*Mzuri Sana,* very good."

The man passed a special parcel to me. I blushed with embarrassment and awkwardly expressed my gratitude. I wanted to sneak into my room and find out what it was. There were more cartons of the supplies that Rodgers helped us carry into the room.

"We want to unwind over the weekend at the South Coast little, sis. It's a deserved reward for a work well done." He enthusiastically passed the message from his own boss. I managed to check my gift. It was special underwear whose edges were cloistered with beads and a flower in the middle that seemed to vibrate with the golden letters "my love." My head went dizzy with confusion. Someone saw it and wanted to buy it at once. Rita was not happy at such a preferential treatment shown me and "yet I put in as much as you." Explanation to how I had acquired it was like water off a duck's back.

Soon, our cubicle was a beehive of activity with students who were not in class milling around for the new supplies. There were more elegantly perfumed sprays, soaps, lotions, creams and clothing articles for both sexes. Rita and I had to have a timetable of operation so that we didn't miss class. We still attended class and learnt like everybody else.

On a Sunday afternoon, we found ourselves on our way to the South a coast, the booming tourist enclave. The palm-thatched hotels, the expansive wide sand beaches and the mangrove forests fleeted about as we raced in the classic chauffeured car. The sea breeze enervated us and this brought Rita's old self back. Since the discovery of Bradley's present to me, she had been silently fuming. Trying to reason with her had infuriated her the more, but the expectation for a wonderful treat lifted her spirits.

We parked by a vast hotel with white cane benches, chairs, floating houses and tunnels for sliding and tumbling, and a blend of *chakacha* and *taarab* music on the sea-front known as The Ambrosia. Tourists and other men of class hung about semi-nude girls giggling and flashing their well-lined teeth. Our guide led us to a table where we had a view of a live band with buxom women with cherubic cheeks swaying themselves to exaggerated gyrations as some two or three white men jumped to join them to a good cheer to those who cared to watch. We sat on white plastic chairs on a table of the same color under which a shiny floor reflected our faces. A waiter in white uniform reached our table and the guide gave his instructions and told us to wait as we sipped a cold juice and listened to the music.

Rodgers walked in, dressed in a woolen suit that seemed to have cost a fortune. Rita immediately hugged him and I was left alone. She took off his coat as if she wanted to tell me now it was her turn to enjoy as I cried. Mr. Bradley walked in a few moments later and it was my turn to eye Rita wickedly and remind her I had a White man with me. The food we had ordered arrived and the table was groaning under its weight. We ate in silence punctuating it with small talk, our inexperience slowing us down as we didn't want to go overboard. Bradley kept explaining to me and urging me on. I looked at his tanned skin with some splotches as if he had suffered mosquito bites, and his hairy skin. I had not seen so much hair. His eyes had shades of blue and whenever they were turned to me it was like they were picking the microscopic details of me. The wine was next, I skipped it because of religious inclinations and I was twiddling my fingers around uneasily when I heard Rita asking my companion what he did for a living. Why was she jealous of me and wanted to snatch him?

"I sell gems."

"Gems?" I asked my eyes big. He wiped his hands on a paper napkin and pulled from one of his pockets a set of magnificently stones in lapis lazuli and emerald colors. Rita's lips sucked in excitement. He picked a piece and placed it on my lap. From the corner of my eye I saw Rita swing away the past animosity coming back. I pushed the set into her lap. She suddenly turned to me her eyes saying "thank you baby, you were nearly making a mistake." I laughed and our hosts picked it up.

We moved to the backyard and strolled to where the boats and engine were floating lazily against the slight sweep of the sea waters. He looked older almost the age of Maina but there were other younger girls shepherding around some grandpa like companions in comparison. He offered to paddle me to the sea after assuring me of my safety.

"I hail from a mean coast with fords and wicked tempests and did some fishing before escaping village life." I was interested to know about him. I however didn't know how to thank him for that gift of underwear. We were two villagers of different ages and experiences. How could I broach the topic since it brought some little sweat beads to the tip of my nose? His nose was longer and sharper than mine. He was huge while I was a small thing that could be fully protected under his hold. I felt so safe in his presence that I wanted the other campus guys to come and see us and know they would no longer merely joke with me.

A breeze rippled the waters in the middle of the ocean and the boat rocked awkwardly and my heart lurched with fear. There were other boats in the sea going at different speeds. Ours was steady as he used his hairy arms to pilot us. Rita and Jeffrey had taken a motor boat that they straddled and was now splashing in the waters as she clung to the driver and Rodgers clung to her; they seemed to ride with the waves as their laughter echoed across. I was growing ease with him and I explained my roots but not the bit about being picked up by an old woman. All the same I told him about my mother's running away.

"She could be death or living even around or abroad who knows."

When the boat hit the wall of water I was not prepared and I was sure we were going under. The waters in the coast are really rough in the evenings. I lunged at him so suddenly that he almost lost the control of our floating savior. He frantically brought things in control as I shrank back to my corner the aftertaste of the whole of him smothering me lingering with embarrassment.

"Let's go back. I can't swim in case…"

He laughed and turned us around. My mind was in turmoil? Was it the gifts he was throwing at me? Was it because in him was a different class, color and status combined? Did the open jealousies from Rita egg me on for fear of losing him? Was I the first one in this expanse coast to have reached him? Wouldn't some people say that while as an educated girl I was supposed to know better than hurl myself at a little-known Whiteman because of his money? As my feet touched the dry sand there was an instant sense of catharsis. He grabbed me and carried me from the moors since the waters had eaten up the ground hitherto dry as I protested. I felt like I was dying in his hands as his hot breath smelling of garlic and his blue eyes rocked base in my soul. I was waiting for that breaking kiss as he good naturedly laughed off and freely sloshed in the waters bearing me like a sacrifice for his altar. I was truly disappointed when moment he placed me down. I fled up the steps to the hotel as he came hot on my heels.

We were like young children playing hide and seek. Inside the hotel a live band was pelting some Bongo music, strobe lights rhythmically matching to the beat in a magical spell. I had lost my way and when he saw me cornered, he started dancing in romping leaps that both annoyed and amused me. I walked to him keen at showing him how the beat was easy to dance to and jigged over. He pulled me to himself and I was lost in his wide chest for a moment and I felt the feet quake below me. He brought my face up and when I looked into his bluish eyes, I was suddenly afraid. I pulled away and went to a nearby seat and sat down. He danced from a few more minutes before he came over.

He directed me to our original place and we sat there talking about business. It was not until 8 o'clock when Rita and Rodgers strolled in, birds of the same feather, their bodies shining with the glory of nice time spent together.

We didn't stay long but had to leave with our in-charges escorting us up to the college gates. I rushed to our room and wanted to have some time to think about my actions when I found two notes addressed to me under the door. The first one was about Erastus flying back with his family from US and I was supposed to attend the welcoming party in the city. The other one was from Nixon; he was in the coast and might slip in to say hi.

The latter note shocked me to my senses. Here was the man who could resonate with me, one who knew all about me and was dying to have me and had a genuine dream of walking me down the aisle. And then here comes a Tom, Dick and Harry and I am ready to jump to bed with him. I had to be truthful to myself. What did I want from Bradley? Could it be love in its genuine and rightful sense? His money? His class and skin?

Nixon walked in a few minutes before 9 o'clock with a campus guy called Jim. The latter excused himself and left Nixon to me. He looked withdrawn. I was about to ask him about his long silence when Rita burst in bubbling with sheer excitement. I suspected she had gone to show off her new gems to guys and brag how great she was around here. She coldly greeted the spoiler. You've a *mzungu*, Whiteman and you are inviting a skinny needy fellow to top up.

"This is Nixon, my fiancé." I had not talked of him ever since I had met Rita and she showed surprise. Guys who were never talked of are insignificant. No wonder you are dragging him up after a romp with a *mzungu*.

"He is finishing his studies at Sun City University." I saw the shock in her eyes. She had assumed he was part of our campus. She shook his hand a minute longer and quickly fixed him some cocoa (we owned an electric cooker).

"You've been so lost?"

"You never replied to mine." He looked at me and Rita.

"Why don't you say something?"

"What is there to say Nix? To lie. To build some castles in the air." I could confess that I had my Achilles feet, penning letters. And especially when the guy had not declared his true feelings in a way I could perceive as bold and strong. Not now when I was busy shuttling between classes and sales. He looked at the well-furnished room with a fine taste that meant lots money. I then couldn't figure how to say I loved a guy with what I had gone through in the past a few hours. I could sound hollow and as stale as a moldy biscuit. My idea of love was reassessment, something that grew finer with time, not rushed, that was why my reaction to Bradley had embarrassed me.

"Do you fear my presence?" Rita announced and walked leaving the room to us. I felt like taking him into my hands and the yearning for true feelings of all these years get fulfilled in his arms. But he sat there causelessly.

"You look thin," he observed.

The remark scared me. "I could be dieting." I added confidently.

"I'm serious, Nerry. I want to be assured of your health, love and our future."

"I don't have to be fat for you to determine my health status. I find you offensive."

"I'm sorry. Jeffery wrote and told me he is settling in the States." Why did have to change the topic? The picture of a teary Irene quickly flashed in my mind. She had passed her exams and was planning to join a teacher's college.

"Why did you come?" the question took him aback.

"I came to tell you I love you and will always love you." I wanted to ask him to prove that he actually loved me.

"There are so many out there. Your class mates and others are pursuing better courses than what I am taking. Why should it be me?"

"Love is jealously selective. Your sparkle draws me nigh. Over the valleys and hills, it does."

"How will I ever know?" I stammered. His expression was unabashed.

"Deeds will. Give me a chance, Nerry."

"I think you're just out to fool me and laugh at my long punishment. My resoluteness not to surrender."

"What do I stand to gain? You're now mature and can read the signals and decamp."

I looked pensively to the dark future. I couldn't visualize him and myself sharing this life. Instead the image of Bradley's blue eyes threatened to suffocate me. Colored heavy kids running up and down the steps of a home.

"I know what is going ..."

I was rudely awakened to the present. Had they told him about my flirting? A quiver ran through me and I was suddenly very afraid.

"You know we are violating the rule, being in a lady's room at wrong hours." He chuckled and said I should not worry myself to death as he could move in with Jim.

I rose up and stifled a yawn.

"I don't want to disappoint you but you're going away empty handed." He rose up and blew me a quick kiss. He threw away his coat and dragged me to himself. I restrained his reaching hands with a strong no and I saw his eyes panic. Other guys violated the rules all the time accommodating their male companions. On reflection, it wasn't clear why I continued to resist Nixon's love while early in the day I had become jelly kneed before a stranger. Here was an ebullient handsome man, simple and well behaved, yet no god or angel that I loved twirling by the fingers torturously.

I saw tears blob down his eyes as wracking sobs crushed his spirit in my hands. The fact that my conceited Nixon was crying in my hands should have made me call the whole world to witness. *The proud have fallen.* Instead I felt terribly sorry for him and proud I had made a point of calming him when the pain of all these years would have swept us off our feet in a cataclysmic surge. He apologetically took a hanky out of his pocket and dried his eyes.

 I held him to me feeling his tension quietly ebbing. Was there something wrong with me? This could have been an opportunity to climax all my wants and lust in the hands of a man I suspected I had a sense of love. It was my moment of glory to have him weep in my hands and so, like a baby. Yet I had the audacity to ask him to behave and send him to his sleeping quarters. By the time he left my room we were good friends. I wished Ms. Oduor my project professor had witnessed this indignity of a brilliant chap. She always harped that men were babies who needed constant butt wiping or was it whipping? I wanted to laugh and laugh my head off.

Rita came back at 3 in the morning. When she found me alone, she began lecturing me on the wisdom of making informed choices. From the way she talked I could guess she had voted the *mzungu* guy.

"Why?" I asked her, sitting upright on the bed. She was floundering.

"I only expressed my honest feelings…"

"Which feelings when you slept with a stranger yesterday!" Her jaws dropped open while her eyes shone with guilt.

"I did what Nerry? Stop being stupid. Holding a man closely doesn't mean you slept with him. How can I do such a stupid thing with AIDS ravaging people? What to you take me for, Nerry? You've to withdraw that remark. If there was anybody dying to be laid it was you!"

I hit her smack on her face with an open hand chop and she screamed out in surprise as blood came out of her mouth. I went for her and she clung to her bed begging for mercy. She was sure I wanted to kill her. Her gesture of helplessness shocked me for I wanted her to fight back and I hit her again and again until all my frustrations petered out.

Instead it was my turn to go down on my knees and in tears of shame and guilt beg for her forgiveness.

Rita was a wonderful girl for she pulled me off my knees and I grabbed her to me and we cried. I cleaned the blood; she had bit her tongue and nothing was broken. What was this Rodgers stupidity that was threatening us apart? Wasn't our friendship bigger than any material gifts dangled before our craving eyes?

I brought out the Bradley gift and other gifts we had acquired from the men and shred them into pieces and when we were sure nothing could explode, we put them in a heap at the corner of the room and dousing them with the paraffin and burned them. The smoke rose high, struck the ceilings and came down to sting and choke us. It was as if we were two spoiled children driven by an evil spirit. It was almost morning when bleary eyed and exhausted from the dreary of the day we crept into the same bed and like a pair of Siamese twins slept snuggled to each other.

4

My journey to the city was beside to welcome Erastus home an opportune time for me to have a long intimate talk with Colista. The issue of Nixon and Bradley was eating me up and it was showing. I was certain that Bradley was showing a more than a business curiosity over me and I needed to ventilate to one whom I felt could not mislead me. Ever since our tour of her university and having proved I would work towards my dreams she had grown to become my urban consultant while Saarange called the shots in the village. At the bottom of my heart, I had learned not to trust anything in trousers.

One minute he would be reduced to tears craving miserably for attention and the next minute when he had taken your breast and sucked to his fill, he would despise you. It was the same naughty tendency exhibited by babies. They would bite the breast that fed them. They would burn the stores that had their succor. Similarly, men were multifaceted creatures only next to Lucifer in their cunning. Then what was this dynamo called love? Did it grow on trees of our fantasies and blossomed and flowered and came to fruition until its fruits grew ripe and were picked by the world? Could one touch it, preserve it and show it off, flaunt it to the envious world? Could you beat your chest around telling everybody to look at it, admire it or they would help steal it and laugh, laugh at your failure to mature and retain it to fruition? Nixon had his indescribable qualities that required I go down and painstakingly study them, for didn't we women ever curious go for the mysteries of men thinking we would learn them, muster them and tame them in our little triumphant manner. If there was a man with more mysteries it was Bradley. Yes, Nixon's baby face and effaced smiles held to me a beam of a bright future while Bradley's universalism and experience would expand my scope and world viewpoint and make me fly yonder in one great leap to sudden unmerited material comfort. I was honestly fearful.

I arrived in the city by two in the evening and it was when I learned that Erastus flight had been brought forward and so the reception would be that evening. The Maina clan was already in the city with our maternal uncles ready for the day. At around seven we drove to the airport in three vehicles to the beehive of activity of thunderous take off and touch downs as the big bellied juggernauts engorged and disgorged their passengers.

Everybody was excited led by my father, Hortenzia, Jones, Colista, Madge, Alice, a maternal uncle called Tom and an aunt going by the name of Selina who had brought Humphrey along being their protégé. He was no longer a puppy but a tall young man bouncing with youthful energy. Jelita who was expectant had her husband present as she and Saarange remained at Jones home as they didn't have the stamina to withstand the cold city night. My father had the same robust frame while Hortenzia was quite big and no longer the shrilly tiny woman she had been because she was unrivalled in eating her husband's gravy.

She hugged me like a good mother: "You have grown big, Nerina." Uncle Nyabayo who was Rodger's father wondered why I had not paid them a visit in Mvita where they lived. I wondered whether he knew what we were up to with his son and by the way we had never broached such a topic. He good naturedly gave me his house number and contacts and I made a mental note to make it an issue next time I met Rodgers.

As we stood huddled together behind the security barrier the expected flight landed. Our excitement went a notch higher as each of us tried to figure the kind of man we were welcoming. I barely remembered him and he still remained a young face among many faces. As the passengers climbed down somebody pointed him out. The lights were not really bringing the man to focus and I waited for him to come up to us. We had to wait for about half an hour as clearances had to be made by domestic and security desks.

He emerged from the ground tunnel, a man of medium carriage pushing a trolley packed with big trunks and bags. He was light skinned and hair curled into knots and we immediately recognized him. The same eyes and smile had not been lost. In tow were two kids and a blonde of white woman of an athletic frame carrying an irritated boy straddling her hip. She was dressed in a green jacket of padded shoulders with red and yellow strips over a black skirt reaching an inch below her knee. He whispered something to his companion and let go the trolley and reached to us with hugs. Efforts by Colista to get the boy off her mother so that she frees her mother to hug us were fruitless as the young fellow bawled a warning. The older boy was charmingly going around aping what his father was doing.

"She is Boke," Erastus introduced his wife using a local name which elucidated a lungful cheer from us. "Pamela Boke." She turned around and respectfully greeted us in our language. My father welcomed her to the family without hesitation. The son was introduced as Maina junior. My father was beside himself as he hitched the boy high who in turn burst into a hearty laughter. When it came to Hortenzia she enthusiastically flung herself at Erastus and I saw him look at Jones for guidance. The latter was uncommitted as he pretended not to be seeing it. Maina came to his aid and introduced her. He screwed his face and Hortenzia who automatically read the message stiffened and I knew what should have been a good family reunion was an awkward start. Maina introduced the rest of us in a way to hide the embarrassment. We couldn't surmise what kind of stories Erastus had been fed about his step mother.

We loaded the luggage into the vehicles and hopped inside. Hortenzia who had traveled together with Colista chose to travel with her husband in a different vehicle. She could be uneasy throughout the party.

I snuggled close to Pamela, we had struck off and the young boy, Lameck as he was called was cooing happily in my hands. The way to a mother's heart is the child's reaction to their surroundings. The ice between our souls thawed considerably and we were soon chatting off as old acquaintances. I silently studied the child's features the wide set mouth, the sharp lobes, the longish nose, the black silky hair, the nice blend of Afro-Caucasian features and knew this was beautiful. A wicked smile weaved through my face: a Bradley and Nerina fusion.

The homecoming party was held in one of Dad' friends expanse compound where a few tents had been fixed for the family and friends to afford us an elbow room to dance. After the formalities and a light meal, we found ourselves strolling within the compound. The men and the elderly ladies where sharing some brand and there were animated voices and guffaws that pointed which direction things were going. Lameck had fallen asleep and Pamela was freer. We moved to the verandah of the large house, the blossoming flowers in the electric light giving their colors a golden bluish hue that caught our attention for a while. The compound had lawns nestling with flower shrubbery which showed the owner's taste. There was a bench next to the verandah and Pamela dragged me to it and we curled ourselves watching the a few stars above the inky sky as her legs were curled under her.

"How do you find this place?"

"Oh lovely. So beautiful." She drawled. Our talk drifted to our career pursuits and I learned she was in the health field.

"I love working with people and learn more about them in a closer curious way." She was happy when she saw people's health restored. "Especially mothers, it makes me happy to see them healthy and back to their numerous daily chores."

"I thought you people enjoy more liberties than here where the patriarchic upbringing seems to suppress womenfolk."

She laughed her golden teeth flashing in the light. "I think the whole world is the same all over. I may say there could be some advantages and more freedom from what I have read and heard but certain things remain the same."

"What I hate about you is your extremism in everything. Your search for liberty I mean feminine liberation goes to crazy monologues. Well

the freedom to have your way to do what your body wills; I think is
dangerous whatever you call it. Can I walk naked before everybody?
No and yes. May be when I am married and before my husband. Not
in the public." My student agitation was taking over, hammering what
I though where the shortcomings of western values. All these gleaned
from books and movies of course.

I saw the circles of her eyes dilate at my outbursts. She studied the
trees swaying slowly to the cold breeze. It was a cold night. Some
dense cloud formation was gliding to some mountains in a slow pace
like a reluctant entity.

"Every society has its own intricate and unique problems. I want to
take my time and learn how things are here."

We could hear Colista and Hortenzia's laughter coming from the
direction of the house where some cooking was going on. The host
had gotten somebody who was playing a traditional music on a harp
and there rose waves after waves of excitement meant the listeners
were enjoying themselves. It appeared that Maina junior was growing
restless and the two women directed him to us. The boy at seeing his
mother ran into her lap and I thought he wanted to sleep.

"I hope we aren't interrupting anything?" Hortenzia came up and
asked curiously. Her eyes were saying: "What could a mere girl who
doesn't have a baby be sharing with you?"

We welcomed them moving to create room on the bench.

"Women are everywhere known to gossip," Pamela added and looked
at us as if to confirm it. We all laughed heartily.

"We are the chicken of the earth." Hortenzia picked the cue.
"Whenever the cocks are around," she waved her hand in the
direction of the male voices. "We swoon over. Isn't it distasteful?"

Her words instead did not arouse in me their truism but awakened a
past memory when a voice was screaming that she had been beaten by
us Jelita, Alice my mother and me.

"What have you done then big chicken to change that?" My voice
echoed in a rotten anger that even surprised me. I couldn't understand
the source of my bad temper of late.

"With the way things are, what do you expect her to do?" Colista cut
in quickly in an attempt to erase the stink from the words. Hortenzia

was also trying to adjust to the present not sure her ears were receiving the correct signals.

"I admit I didn't do it, right? It's the chicks with the young and warm blood that can do it now. It's your kind that can make every woman's dream true if you only hold the right reins and rightly so and set for the gallop. But what are you doing when the mother hens have gone to roost? Clucking for mischievous cockerels?" Her eyes had a shine, something close to mischief and the way her lips curled up in mockery, it was an expose of our dark past.

"Yeah, I now understand. The chick came clucking for the real cock and you know what, in that single master stroke our whole Maina family was devastated. My mother hen disappeared and ever since I've failed to have another hen to replace her and give me direction. What much do you expect me to do?" Why did she have to imagine I was seeing all sorts of boyfriends? Hortenzia's face ran with emotions from shock, pain, anger to choking. The mask had been peeled.

"What did you say, little girl? I am your mother and yet you can't give me even an iota of respect." Her breath came out in strenuous gasps.

"My mother, ha ha ha. Tell it to the birds!" I think, Hortenzia ever since I was young had been used to chastising me. Her crooked fingers reached out aiming at my face. The boil of the years had ripened and facing me was a fellow woman, one I had been suspecting of so many things in my life and yet she wanted to assert her authority over me in the same old way. This wasn't an Alice and Jelita affair and I wanted to establish my status in a simple way that would earn me her respect. I parried the errant fingers and at the same time drove an upward chop aimed at her chin. The contact resonated with the anger bottled in me as she honked in bewilderment.

She tumbled forward, asserting her senior status, sinking her teeth to my left arm and we all fell into the ground in a flailing heap of limbs. The teeth really penetrated my flesh from the pain that shot to my whole system and I rolled in another tumble to free my arm as I pulled my knees to my chest. I kept pounding at her with my elbow, at one point, my head as Colista who had failed to separate us screamed for help. Several feet ran in our direction and somehow, we were on our feet for a moment. Hortenzia was sure footed as my injured arm hang painfully beside me almost dislocated. I swung up as if to kick her and she blocked the blow and I lashed out with my better hand but she had stepped aside and I reeled past her and her fingers clutched together slammed unto my side like a hammer taking the breath out of me and I staggered into the ground.

It dawned on me I was up to an able opponent only for her to dive at me blindly. I leaned sideways and bent my knee and then rolled. She came rushing and, in that instant, I hit her hard and she went careening to the men who stood there watching us in bemused amusement. She would have hit the ground hadn't our host prevented her. Colista pulled my hand behind me. More blood oozed from the fresh wound in my arm and in my blind rage I could only see the dim figures of our family and friends as Hortenzia rent the air with unprintables. All the time, I hadn't uttered a word. Pamela was beside me, checking my arm and advising us what to do.

"A lot of anger Nerina inside you. What is the problem?" she managed to word her concern. I simply nodded my head too embarrassed to say a thing. Hortenzia had been silenced and I would make out Maina's agitated self-walking about as he clicked in murderous embarrassment. He came towering over us, Hortenzia beside him and asked I follow them aside.

"How dare you disgrace me before our host? Washing our family linen in public, isn't it? I don't understand how two mature women can do it and yet you attend the church and worship services every weekend!"

He turned to face me, his jaws moving without words for a moment.

"You have read books and expanded your horizons, haven't you? Yet you're capable of fanning a raw and stupid assumption that your step mother had a hand in the disappearance of your mother. There is a law about being innocent until proven guilty. What happened to that modicum of reasonable behaviour or have things changed?"

He turned to Hortenzia who was raked in sobs maybe by the damning message from god Maina. His ranting hadn't hit anything in my soul? Wasn't this the same man who had deflowered me and now what moral authority did he possess, leave alone condemn my acts? I loathed his holier-than-thou attitude and wanted to tell him off. I looked at the curious crowd standing and wondering in a distance.

Apart from Alice the rest were in the dark about my mishap? Jelita and Saarange were away in Jones' his home. Hortenzia might have not believed a word of that incident. I didn't want to cause more scenes on Erastus' homecoming.

"You embarrass your position, degrade it. As my number two you equally degrade your motherhood to the same level of these children." I feared he would ask us to go down and before everybody else cane us, the way he used to do it those old days. I wasn't prepared for such embarrassment and I prayed the ground to open up and swallow my shamed face. Instead, he held our shoulders and led us further from the curious faces. I was sure Hortenzia was praying for the same as she had calmed. He questioned us on how it had started and our excuses really sounded silly even in our ears.

"You've really messed up everybody and I want to see the two of you going back there as friends. I'm sure that is what your faith teaches you."

The old man was really serious and could not brook any rubbish.

"People say things but not all is true. Do you know how costly it has been to stay away from my family because of …?" His voice broke off and I think that was a new territory he didn't know how to handle. My mind was again wandering in the past realm when I heard him say this after sucking on his breath like an actor adept at his lines and real tears blobbed from his eyes.

"And when my family finds a unifying factor in Erastus, the devil threatens to tear us apart in a form of you." He coughed and brought up his fist to his mouth to smother what I thought was a war cry.

"I'm hundred percent certain the boys are with me. Now you two decide one thing. Either you come with me as a family or if you find another better option walk out on me now!" The last word was pronounced with a damning finality as his feet stamped the ground. An old hyena never lost its style, only its agility.

"The choice is yours. One, a wife and a companion, and the other, a daughter, a segment of my flesh. Walk out now!"

This was not time to rationalize about my origins and this man's past shortcomings. I was positive we had messed Erastus and Pamela's party and the horror of whether they would ever forgive me was so horrifying. The two of us stood there condemned by our irrational actions, the way a sinner stands before the maker in his convicted sunken form by their transgression. We turned to each other the pain of my arm more intolerable as some of the blood had stained my clothes. This was my blood and it was oozing out, being spilt for no course. An attack of dizziness threatened me but I held out my right hand. Hortenzia was waiting and her eyes somehow rested on her offending tooth marks.

And she drew me to herself crying in piteous shame. Someone started a clap, it was Pamela and everyone took it up; so they had been watching. The picture of Erastus clapping too showed that my sins had been forgiven. Hortenzia took my hurt hand and asked for water and washed it with a salt solution with the help of Pamela. The later found some drug and bandage in her fold and she treated the wound.

That night the partying took a merrier form, the eating and drinking and open dancing as if a grand message of forgiveness of the prodigal son had been accomplished. The persons missing were Luciana, Saarange and Jelita but in our hearts we did everything for them. My father was jollier, a master of intrigue, still the firm head of the family in control. Our host, a play mate and school mate openly dared him and remembered how when the jiggers were threatening to tear their feet apart, they had decided to burn those parts off.

"I can never stand straight even presently. *Yaa*, play mate, come here and try it."

The two men stood side by side and took of their shoes and socks. To our amusement their toes crooked sideways and we really loved the show.

"God has been good to us. We're able to celebrate the successes of our children." They agreed in a celebrant mood, recounting some of their childhood escapades including stealing fruit, sleeping with animals, on dry skins, inside sacks; walking long distances to school on empty stomachs etcetera etcetera. We laughed our bellies sore.

Before we retired to bed, I took the advantage of the bonhomie atmosphere and presented my conundrum to Colista. I had thought she had forgotten about it until we traveled to her home where some of us had to sleep. She made some earnest remarks based on the five Cs namely commitment, confidence, comfort, convenience and choice.

I took a quick summation of the two guys their strengths and demerits on lifetime setup. Somehow Nixon scored high points in terms of a period of unhurried courtship.

"But I don't feel anything particularly strong for him inside me."

"Then you don't know that the fire that bakes is not normally the hottest." Colista quipped, philosophically.

I went to sleep dreaming of blue eyes, gems and surly waters.

5

I am not an avid reader of newspapers besides reading the horoscopes and the cartoons on what love is. That morning, however, my eyes were attracted to the Daily Star headline. "A White con arrested," the racist slant quite obvious.

"Where did that one happen?" I asked Jones who was partially covered by the paper he held against his face.

"Just down the coast, Mvita," he said shoving another paper towards me. This was the Morning Chronicle. The lead story was about the arrest of a white man who shuttled between Southern Africa and our country for businesses that ranged from cosmetics, gems, ranching, and IT accessories. He was caught with others not in court in possession of *mandrax* and heroin drugs worth over 350 million shillings. The consignment meant for the upcountry market was discovered inside his personal vehicle KRS 290 Prado concealed inside packets of women cosmetics and lotions. This had happened following a tip off that had made the man to be under police surveillance for some time.

The culprit was to be arraigned in court as from Tuesday after comprehensive investigations would have been over. 'The police are also pursuing potential links to some local universities which are said to be the lucrative market for this type of business. A source claims that most students in Mvita University provide the major market for the business and most of them have lost the essence of being in such a citadel of knowledge. Police have positive leads that they are following in their investigation. "The drugs are killing the bright future of our youths," the District commissioner in charge of security in Mvita region commented pointing at examples of youths who are raving mad, others in rehabilitation homes.'

Deep inside, I saw my little haven toppling around me. I would connect the little dots and my heart lurched and my legs seemed to have been cut under me. I was saved from collapsing by a quick action of sinking into a nearby seat. I looked around to see whether anyone had observed my unusual behavior. My hands literally shook and I felt totally sick.

 I knew the vehicle registration and I knew the gentleman in question and according to the report I was part of the cartel supplying drugs in college. Was there a mistake in this? Were we selling drugs, unsuspectingly, to students which meant the police were crawling all over the place to arrest us? I was flabbergasted to say the least.

I went back to the paper but it remained one grey patch mocking my eyes. I had never dealt with the police before for I dreaded them and the nearest it had come this close was when one tried to stop during my rape ordeal and mom had disappeared. Then I saw them comb the whole compound taking their good time which I could say was perfunctorily for we neither talked nor shared anything with them.

Perhaps, I have to mention that the police were generally viewed as arrogant distant sadists who lived to terrorize everybody for the tipping that they relished from people who didn't want to sleep in their cold cells. At the sight of a policeman or a uniformed person, the villagers would literary vanish into the thin air!

I wrapped my hands close to my tummy and bent over and breathed more deeply, allowing fresh oxygen to flow into my head. I stayed in that position for what seemed a whole century and was startled by a question poised to me by Madge who had been hovering close to me. She might have read the paper.

"What did you say, honey?" I wanted to get it right, hoping I hadn't imagined it.

"You see, auntie, I was wondering whether at university you don't abuse drugs like say bhang?" The good girl now in standard four in one of the prestigious city academies cheerfully made it known. Oh ignorance. Even a good number of people believed that university students smoked something and that was why we were ever rowdy, noisy, stubborn and very brave as to pelt the police with a few stones on various claims to do with violations of our rights. Once a matatu tout who had found himself in the uncharacteristic end of the "comrades", as we called ourselves, had argued that he would only blame the bhang that 'we smoked and that remained in our heads for decades even into employment.'

It was time to reflect about the recent hectic activities such as riding in classic limousines, visits to 5 star hotels, the free spending bordering extravagance, the flurry of selling the very items mentioned in the paper, the creation of a dream, this Bradley, a businessman extraordinary and gemstone juggler, handsome, good at spinning spellbound stories on his childhood and army career; a creation of a dream that embraced marriage overtones and now crushed by the very paper in front of me.

Then, what were we selling to the students in campus? Was it drugs expertly concealed in the articles of cloth? That meant the students were part of the orchestrated conspiracy and would this explain the fast sales? I remembered the warning signs when Rodgers had visited on the first day. Was Rita part of this conspiracy now threatening to engulf me? What will my proud relatives say of me if I got nabbed by the police dragnet along the mastermind, con, drug peddler, lover and husband to be? Would they find reason to forgive me, on the understanding that I was merely chasing every girl's dream? The dream to have a financially stable future. And what of this star-crossed Rodgers who spelt trouble to me every time we encountered? I was devastated and swore under my breath never to have any engagement with him. I was simply fed up with this guy!

"Madge, I've never smoked anything like that...!"

I ran my fingers through her neat plaits and admired the texture of her black hair. "Someone said you fought grandma?" Jones' third born wondered so aloud that it embarrassed me. This swept away the bit of ground remaining under my feet. Some two or three adults laughed as Jones tried to explain that the fight had nothing to do with bhang smoking. Colista bundled the kids out of the room on the excuse of helping her to clean the cars but that didn't pacify the turmoil in my mind. Perhaps, what I needed was time to reason with these little minds and bring things into perspective.

Was I unknowingly smoking some bhang? What of my violent disposition of late? Was it all steeped in attitude or was I actually helping Rodgers sell drugs and somehow getting the effects of their content from mere handling? I needed urgently to travel to Mvita whatever the situation and put the record straight with the faceless police.

This was another time Rodgers was embroiling me in shit. Good God, up to when would Rodgers keep getting the better of me? The time to conclusively and concretely settle things between the two of us was now and not later. That evening, despite Erastus wishes that I accompany them up country, I painfully extricated myself from them and caught the night bus to the coast.

6

A slip of paper with the university logo and the president's insignia was brought to me by a messenger. The more I examined it the more I was wowed and intrigued. Rita could have seen the physical effect the note had on me before snatching it away. She cooed naughtily and reminded me that the president's car was waiting outside the Female hostels' parking.

"If I were you, I'll go," she egged me on.

My arrival at the coast had left me wearied to the bone and left me with stiff swollen feet and the usual journey blues. When I arrived inside the campus nothing unusual seemed to be going on. Rita was deep asleep after a night long partying in some popular entertainment spot with her new catch; Rodgers of course. The moment she saw me she lifted a tired hand in a sort of a wave and babbled how the sales had improved greatly and she was wondering whether we would ever manage this business here or we needed to locate to some other place. Here was a girl bubbling with great news about her future and a hint to me that she was in the dark.

"I've you seen the papers, baby?"

 She waved at me dismissively and turned over arching her body naughtily and began to snore. Was I being paranoid over nothing? Was someone deliberately hiding something from these campus inhabitants, what I had seen clearly from the other side, or my imagination was playing tricks with me? That meant the only answer to my questions was Rodgers and I wondered why I hadn't thought of it and saved myself the journey. If Rita had been with him then that meant he was somewhere sleeping.

I looked for his number and went to the college booth and dialed him. The call was going through but there was nobody on the other end to pick it. After several attempts I gave up. Back in the room Rita had gotten up and was in the washrooms sluicing. I was still apprehensive and sick with worry. It was as if I was the only one swimming against the tide, a turbulent bark in a calm sea. When Rita walked over and excitedly regaled me with her adventures I completely calmed and wanted to know more. And now the note from the professor!

I was literally trembling and from those stories I had heard of Professor. He was one crazy randy fellow with weird sexual cravings and trysts with "wild" college girls that would satisfy his bloated ego. Why I had featured in this man's radar in a college peopled with all sorts of women, more than two thousands of us was a matter of hard conjecture. Rita was at handy bubbling with excitement, preening all over, choosing for me some creamy dress that gave me room to swing and spring into action in case I needed that.

Why a sixty-some old geezer would fancy me was still a riddle of some sort. I wasn't such an academic person, the tough hard-nut thing that made the professors refer to their notes every time s/he cracked up. The man had airs of importance over him, a giant in his own right, a wiseacre and brilliant debater, professor emeritus who greeted everyone around who cared with the back of his fist.

When we spilled out of the room a few cars were parked around, perhaps of a few men who had come to pick their girlfriends for the long weekend. We sashayed to the green Prado at the park with blinking tail lights and the door was thrown open for us. As we snuggled to its velvety seats a few boys cat called and put their thumbs up in the air. There was a rumor doing rounds that a students' *kamukunji*, student's informal meeting, was going to be held at the graduation court to spell out the next plan of action following the recent adverse reportage on the papers of the university. The chauffer with an oversize cape that sat on his head like a piece of overused tissue said nothing as he revved and drove to the gate and into the busy street.

The sheen of blinking electric lights like collapsed stars marked the lane dotted with uneven dark trees along the edges as we penetrated the posh estate of the rich and top government functionaries. As the chauffeured vehicle's gentle engine hummed, I had this feeling that we were continuously climbing into a different class quarters away from our humble abodes.

At the gate of the one-story house with red roof and white walls, the vehicle swung towards a black metal gate. A peep of the horn and a gateman in a green uniform opened and did more saluting and foot stamping for full effect. As the gate clicked behind us, I turned to the quiet Rita squeezing her warm hand as if I was telling her, we are all together in this now. She looked up at me and smiled. We climbed down. The chauffer glanced up at us as if to signal the directions and pulled off the cape. It was the president himself staring at us with a wicked glitter in his eyes and as he waited for the message to sink into our shocked faces, he gave us a welcome and a smile. He was tall and dark with a bald strip that seemed to divide his head into equal segments at the middle both ends with coarse stubble of grey that remained permanently unkempt. He spotted a pointed beard that gave his face an elongated wise appearance. Add to that his tinted glasses and his renowned humor that would enthrall his listeners for hours.

There were rumors that the man was a magician who could turn himself into any animal and eavesdrop to the student's strike plans and avert the whole thing at the eleventh minute reaching out to ring leaders. No wonder Mvita University had never experienced a tough strike that was the order of the day that bedeviled other universities. He was also an ex-army sniper who could blow your brains at the slightest provocation. It was things like this personal involvement at picking us from the campus that mystified the man's profile.

"Girls, you're dressed to kill, eh?" he muttered and punctuated it with a hearty laughter and slammed his fist into the palm of his hand. His hands opened as he gave each of us a peck and an embrace.

"What a timing professor!" Rita who had recovered her glib tongue added.

As he guided us through a trellised path to a double door at the end an arched high porch and wide stairs, he walked briskly.

"I am not back to youthful exploits, darlings, though who said an old cat cannot drink milk." Another hearty laughter that was contagious as he good naturedly held us like a grandparent around his grandchildren. We found ourselves laughing along as we got into a neatly arranged expanse lounge spread in pink and walls that exuded a gauzy ambience of white. There was a home theatre, some hi-fi system and a 40 inch flat TV saddling glassy trolley, table and some cabinet at the corner, another glass book cabinet with domes whose backs held their titles.

There was an exotic display of a collections artifacts, mementos and framed drawings from all over the world on window sills and the wall. A couple of terracotta plant pots, and grotesque statues were mounted on strategic points as if this was some kind of shrine. The silence was about to creep back as we were still in the dark over reason for this expensive ride when he switched on the music, some oriental brassy thing that vibrated in low waves all over the room. One particular painting in green with a stump like apparition captured my attention.

"That one is from a community in Thailand, a celebration of their rain God." He shuffled across and came with tumblers and a green bottle.

"Girls, some wine for you. It will leave your Christian roots intact," he offered perhaps anticipating refusal. Rita took a sip and rolled her a tongue.

"This is juice…" she laughed. I took mine with unusual enthusiasm. The man for some time harangued us on his favorite subject to do with human development and economies and how ours was to ever remain a subsistence economy, whose driving motto was, "eat and eat for tomorrow you never know what tidings the weather might bear."

We were lost in that fluid world of academic intercourse and our tumblers kept emptying that fast. After some refills, the man stood up, did some jig that left us in stitches. He suddenly turned around and facing us squarely said conspiratorially.

"Those boys, I mean the journalists, are at it again. How do you print such a damning report without even a mere gesture of verifying from me and expect the world to sit down and play poker with you? Sometimes, I feel I should resign my position and invite the know it all to run the university. This is not high school or some village polytechnic but a universal bastion of knowledge where everything you say is supported by authoritative facts." We were slowly catching the drift of his conversation.

"What was the agenda of today's *kamukunji*? During our college days, our meetings were driven by ideologies. Today's student can strike over the tear on his underwear." He laughed derisively until we pitied ourselves.

"They will discuss the drugs. Demand an apology from the papers. Tempers will rise after the demagoguery. They will spill into the streets and pelt vehicles of innocent motorists rushing to their home havens after a stressful hard day. The police with their batons, tear gas and guns will intervene. Some arrests, rape, injuries or deaths will occur. The place will be closed indefinitely, a fine to replace destroyed property. Some expulsions or suspensions will be definite before another wave of protest the following year. That is a typical modern university life for you!"

We were awed by the ominous listing of the series of events likely to materialize in case the *kamukunji* went haywire.

"Why don't you do something too…to stop it, professor?" I asked in shock.

"Save the innocent ones normally caught in the crossfire." Rita wondered.

The man laughed as if he enjoyed our agony.

"What can I stop? The *kamukunji*? The strike? The police? The government? The paper? The expulsion? Things should be allowed to run the gamut. You can't stop fate."

"Young girls beaten and raped…" Rita aid exasperatedly.

"It's the lot of society that we have to bear. Look here, this is a university where students are free to express their ideas. Hot facts, in hot young minds from hot principles of life need airing: ventilation. If I dare stop that the hot resentment would grow up into a volcano and when it will explode, it will sweep me along. As for the papers let them be responsible."

An eerie mood hung around us as if we were privy to some conspiracy about to spill all over with cataclysmic and devastating effects. The man took out his characteristic pipe and stuffed it into its mouth. At no time had I ever seen the contraption emit smoke.

"Girls, now tell me what your role in this drugs saga is?"

Our mouths dropped open. We gasped for more air. I had had that sickening feeling that something rotten was in this business fronted by

Rodgers and his friends but my love for the upkeep money had blinded my reasoning. Now it had come down to this. It was the night of long swords.

7

"That's preposterous professor!" Rita muttered as anger rushed through her neck veins bulging them for a moment. "We don't do or sell drugs, professor… And if you want to solve your problem through us then you're barking up the wrong tree."

Rita eyed the man for a long time as none of us spoke. My knees grew jelly with each passing minute. Was my intuition proving to be true? I was more afraid because Rita was not aware of Bradley's arrest but I decided to play it cool so us to assuage my troubled soul and gather knowledge.

"Unless you tell us what makes you think we are involved professor? It will be hard to…" I offered miserably.

The aftertaste of the drink in my mouth had grown dry and sour. Rita's shining eyes turned to me, wild and in shock and then slowly nodded as if to confirm a point.

"You bring me memories of a past, Maina… a girl I married but now back to her country in Egypt for my failure to make our marriage work. I was a bookworm; no time for her. We have two daughters' professionals in their right, one an engineering consultant with Symphony International in New York and the second born a doctor pursuing her Masters in her field at Cardiff. They were given a chance to pursue their dreams through responsible parentage, community support and appropriate mentorship. No drug trafficking. No drug peddling. No running around in flash-cars with moneyed hair brains. Am I losing you?"

A feeling of disgust rose in me like a swollen dam threatening to break its banks. I looked at the man's bald head, wisps of hair sneaking around his ears, nostrils, his pointed chin, the blackened fingers curled around the pipe like claws. What I had been doing was now being viewed as some form of money chasing, laundering or something nasty and I had not known it. When I picked the train, I spelt out clearly my role in selling of clothes and costumes to fellow students. The money was modest and kept me going. It was my entrepreneurship spirit to do something to cover for my upkeep than becoming a beggar.

"If selling those items is the equivalent of drug peddling then I am lost for words?"

He eyed me like a rare breed of gecko shoved into the experimental table.

"That is how you have helped sell the drugs to the group's customers in the campus!" there was conviction in his tone.

I gawped like a saint finding himself in the gates of hell. Rita my counterpart stood up as mental and body seizures of unimaginable magnitudes gripped us. I felt as if I was locked in a restrained cage where I was finding difficult to breathe. I unbuttoned the top of my dress. Rita came and sat beside me tears in her eyes. The man had broken us with a swift but gentle blow.

He sat there for a while like a hawk examining its prey from behind his lenses. There was a glitter of glee in those humorous eyes.

"Let's go back and organize our thoughts," I moaned.

"C'mmon! You haven't known the decision of the University over you yet."

"You're not going to convene a senate meeting right away? Yet, won't it be communicated to us?" I was one desperate diver gulping the last dose of oxygen.

"I mean the best you face is an expulsion. Do you've the revised edition of our rules and regulations?"

"That amounts to blackmail, professor. You abduct us from college and you bring us to your house and you threaten us with expulsion," Rita thundered as she stood up and headed for the door.

"Don't be silly girl. Your friend Maina is not in hasty because she knows her brother, sorry cousin is involved." That stopped Rita on her feet. How many times had she colored my world with her little dreams with Rodgers? She involuntarily gasped.

"We are going back, professor. If expulsion is the best remedy so be it, so long as the evidence will indict us." I said as I moved towards Rita.

"Look here, girls. We don't produce half-baked students from our institution. An appearance before the senate to defend yourself will be the best opportunity to examine your arguments. By the time the police and courts come in you wouldn't know what has hit you. You will at least go wherever you will in the world with full knowledge what it means to face a full senate, to go through the guillotine of the best brains in the world. They will grill, interrogate, roast, and barbecue you, oh dear…" he laughed wickedly before he waved us back to the seats.

"Professor, do you have any iota of respect for anything female, their opinion?" I asked as I held the door's handle.

He threw his hands into the air as a sign of giving up on us.

"They have stoned the vehicles already. The police are swarming around the compound ready to pounce in. I should exercise caution."

We looked at each other.

"I suggest you wait for…"

The sound of a vehicle driving into the compound held his attention for a moment. He took off his glasses rubbed them and placed them back his behavior thoroughly changed. "Sit down, at least…."

The door wash shoved open and there stood a tall dark woman with wavy hair, golden earrings and chains on her neck and in a grey body-hugging bodice above blue jeans. She swiped off her dark glasses and at the sight of us huddled in a corner, brushed a dismissing hand and charged in like a rhino. We were transfixed like marionettes waiting for the worst as professor sat perched at the edge of his seat his silence making things worse.

"You're feasting on my …" Her eyes turned out, burning in anger, bursting on us like a ghoul.

She cast a wicked glance at us and dropped her clothes on us. Nudity glared before us, her smooth tapering long legs, and the seat of her knickers disappearing into her endowed butt. Her trousers formed a rugged ring about her feet out of which she hopped. She unfastened her brassieres flipped them over and let the balls of her breasts flap about her chest and bending over like under the influence of a damned spirit tugged at her panties, arcing it over her freed feet and flipped it to some safe part of the room.

She dragged the limp professor's hand and let it to her pleasure points and yanked him flop flop, half dragging him, pulled at him as if she feared he might vanish. The man staggered, coughed and when they were about to vanish through some door, she slapped him until he seemed to about to topple over. His coat was pulled over and we stood there more petrified than offended by every bit of action, unmoving and unblinking.

"Lick it! Yeah! There, baby. Lick it! Like that, got it right!? My! My!" All these over groans of pleasure and…….

Time refused to race as if it had revolted against our expectations. Time left us like stranded statues, but unhampered from listening to the wild on goings on the other side, punishing our imagination in a way we found offending until Rita came out of the spell and discovered her true human senses and turned up the volume of the radio. The two of us foolishly hang where we were figuring our escape route when the woman came out now in a light evening dress and without any ceremony addressed us.

"I am driving you back!" The words were acerbic, we doubted our ears had picked them correctly. She opened the door and we walked out to the dark and cold night as she stomped around spoiling for a fight and we followed speechlessly.

She opened the door to a brand-new sports car and signaled we get in. Once the gate opened, we shot out of the compound up the elevation unto the road like a rocket as if we were customers for her murderous rage. An oncoming vehicle barely missed us as there was a screech of brakes and swerving but our driver only snorted and raced along the windy lane oblivious of the other motorists.

"You're beaten this time…" she snorted wickedly. "I reached him first. He is my territory. I found him intact… we have two kids. And I don't want any nosing around for I am nasty. I've killed before…" The car raced along every jolting turn coinciding with the message she wanted to deliver. She didn't even hesitate to join the highway for there were several screeches as she cursed and drove on as if those were irritant flies flirting with her busy schedule of life.

"I wonder where some people look when driving. Idiots! I even wonder where modern hot pants look when they cling to an old geezer and follow him home for academic favors. Shit! Sex for degrees. If you get admitted to college then you should read. I didn't go to university but I've enough sense to carry my head higher than…"

"Stop!" the words came from me.

The car screeched to a halt in the middle of the road. "Woman we don't need any of your dressing down. Your know-it-all attitude is despicable. Look here, you don't know why we were where we were. We don't need any academic favors, not from anybody, not even professor. In fact, what you need is some spanking to stop that foul mouth…and if I were you, I'll drive with some little sense, not like rat fleeing fire." My courage was a shocker to even me.

The woman turned around over the hooting of vehicles whose lamplights cast shadows of death around us as they careened down as if they were wont to send us to the other side of the great divide. Before us she seemed like an ogre that went full circle of transfiguration. Her breath coming out in short breaks. She drove the vehicle to the side of the road and pulled something from her jacket and shoved it into my hands.

"Then, go ahead and shoot me to the head to make it over, lady!" In my hands was a handgun, cold and deadly looking, I gasped at the fact I was holding something like this for the first time. I looked at it and spat in disdain in her direction.

"Rita get hold of this and let me teach this idiot some manners on how to treat people with respect.' I pushed the tool into Rita's surprised hands.

I was actually getting up when Rita's hand restrained me. The woman laughed.

"I am Jemima. Who are you by the way?"

"Rita and Nerina." I gave her the gun. This was when we heard the noises of running feet and stones flying all over and vehicles speeding all around us, others making dangerous U-turns. The campus strike had reached us.

8

Jemima did not wait for a second warning before she like a mad safari rally driver made U-turn before the oncoming racing cars. In the darkness, the headlamps of these cars made them appear like ghostly apparitions, descending upon us and about to grind us to smithereens. Amidst the skidding wheels and screeching brakes and a volley of curses, Jemima sped in the direction of the town Centre. We were leaving the campus and its noise far away when we stopped her.

"We're going back," I shouted as she pulled over.

"Not in this *thing,* ladies. You walk…" though her attitude had thawed she still remained cold like a bullet.

We stepped down into the cold night which was frequently lighted by vehicle headlamps. The traffic had been reduced into a trickle and the noise of the riot still carried over here by the gentle night breeze which meant we were not far from the compound. The ocean's waves splashed a few kilometers away adding some enervating sea humidity in the air. Whoever drove along this route could be some reveler crawling back to their family after a drinking binge with friends. Word about marauding students would have gone around and anybody sober could not be too suicidal.

Jemima mumbled some good luck to us as she drove ahead into town. Like lost twins we took each other's hands and retraced our steps along the lonely patch of the road raw fear alive in us. The darkly shapes of the hedges, shrubs and thickets around us took shapes of living beings shooting our adrenaline running in our system in gallons. It was a long walk.

Then the voices shouting "*Nenda fisi,* go away hyenas!" a derogatory reference to the police who were hovering about the compound in order to maintain order came over. We didn't want to walk straight and fall victims to their dragnet for those faceless fellows could work on us, arrest us and connect us squarely with the game our colleagues were playing yonder.

Just before the main gate, there was a broken fence were student revelers occasionally sneaked through into college to avoid run-ins with the gatemen on restricted hours. We started searching for this *panya route,* short-cut, not sure the police could have infiltrated it. We found it effortlessly and crept through but inched forward after a taxing studying of our surroundings. These efforts paid well because fifteen meters away there was a dark shape of a vehicle that we guessed was the police land rover. Some persons hang around it while others lurked in the shadows. The noise within the campus had petered out, though some pockets of protest could be heard in some different sections close to the road.

We made sure we avoided the route near the vehicle and moved in the opposite direction towards the farm. Our hearts drummed in our ribcages as our movements were now reduced to zero. Once away from the view of the vehicle we walked more briskly through some grove into the farm, the shadows of its structure more ghoulish and scarier. The lights from the hostels blinked invitingly at us forming a series of oval orange shapes. The farm's lights seemed to be off. Spotlights from colleagues who moved in indeterminate circles as they protested could be spotted momentarily.

We breathed a sigh of relief when our Mt. Kenya hostel came to view a darkly silhouette only a few yards from the farm. We were turning a corner when two figures melted from the pitch darkness blocking our path, their black forms and sudden appearance causing us to stop dead on our tracks with loud gasps just stifling a scream. At that infinitesimal moment I am sure my heart was tempted to miss a beat, and roll through my open mouth. A cold and eerie voice snapped like a crack of a gunshot solidifying everything around us like we had just began a prelude to a bad dream.

"Don't utter a word or we can shoot!" In the hook of their arms and outlines we couldn't attempt anything stupid although our colleagues were a few paces away. Comrade power was a strange thing that could have shielded us if we knew in advance what was going to happen. The student invincibility that gave us airs of bravado within that circle of comrades because society had a debt to pay to us for becoming clever hot heads after several years of toiling and moiling to pass all those nasty exams and punishing incidents! Students could walk into an eatery, order a meal and walk away without paying a penny, asking the management to send the bill to the institution's president. This only worked when we were united in evil, giving us the impunity that would over years desert you when you heard the nasty music "you're all alone, buddy."

"Who're you?" Rita asked fearfully.

"The police." How come we had been this stupid? The other guy suppressed what could have been a diabolical attempt at some gaiety. We definitely guessed these guys were not policemen.

"Shove it, girls!" A steel hand clamped on my elbow and propelled me forward as something cold and hard plodded my back. Rita was suffering the same fate. Our captors shepherded us into the woods in the direction of the farm. I was sure they were not up for any good.

Rape and mutilation, the words played terrifying images with my mind and I was petrified, I couldn't find my voice for some time.

"Where are you taking us? What have we done?" I asked for I had read somewhere that if you knew how to talk this would give your life.

"We want to know where the money is. Where are the drugs?"

This was the second time same evening the issue on drugs was coming up. Was this a set up involving even our professor?

"What are you talking about?" I wondered feverishly.

"The Rodgers and Bradley triangle babes," The sandy voice of Mr. Rasp muttered. "Stop pretending you know nothing for that route will be swum in a pond of tears and at best blood."

The voice had a real threat that lingered for some time long after it had kept quiet. What was this angle of drugs that was not adding up? We only sold clothes items? Had we innocently been acting as conduit to some drug cartel without our knowledge? Something reeked of a sham, a con game and how we were the answer I couldn't figure. Was somebody out to sacrifice us so that when we were not in the picture, he would have the money all to himself? Was the kingpin Rodgers or Bradley?

 What of the paper that had reported the whole stuff and the link with the rich in this coastal strip with motley of private villas, jacuzzis, yachts for the holidaying members of the royal families with the devastating effects of these drugs on the youth of the country, some reduced to vegetables? The poor and rich unsuspecting young men who wanted life in the fast lane could always be netted in the numerous clogs of using the drugs at one time or another as quick fixes and the flashy lifestyle was captivating.

Who didn't love money, the easy cash and somehow, we had been hooked into the folly without our knowledge? Was somebody using us as fall guys, some guinea pigs? I feared for us and at no moment had all dreams about my future come tumbling down as now. I reflected about my ravaged past but still noted that some people cared about me in a nice well-meaning way. Even Maina and Hortenzia would love to see me succeed but not ending buried in some unmarked hole in this coastal city.

I tried to remember where Rodgers, my star-crossed cousin could be holed or enjoying himself when I was in the hands of goons. Why did he always spell trouble for me? Was there anything positive from the interaction with this man and yet when we had not done anything threatening or wicked or illegal to anybody we were victims of his evil web?

"Where are you taking us?" Rita asked in a sour voice. Tears rolled down my eyes to imagine that she was possibly here because of me. The man behind me emitted some weird laughter like the howling of a hyena and plodded my back painfully to punctuate his act of mirth.

"Are we about the place, Cobra?" his colleague inquired. "Just one turn left." He said in his strange voice. There was something venomously deadly about the character to deserve such a name and it added another round of shivering to my body.   He took out a pen light and swung it out in a signaling arc. There was a hoot on the other end of the darkness. Our captors pushed us in the direction.

I would smell animal dung from the nearby sheds and those characteristic sighs that foretold of human presence. I guessed this was roughly two kilometers away from the comfort of my bed.

A door was cautiously pushed open and we were roughly thrust into a semi dark room. A rickety table was propped against a wall on which a candle's flame danced weakly casting grotesque shadows about the room. Several men slouched in the shadows while at the central post strapped in a half-naked posture with blood welts all over his body was a figure.   This was obviously a victim of torture. As I adjusted my eyes in the darkness the miserable man occasionally groaning with pain turned around. I recognized his face: Rodgers.

"My goodness, cousin..."   And despite the pain in my heart of all he had done me, I rushed forward as if to support him and somebody let out a sinister guffaw. There was bloody and broken skin in several places of his body and red stains of blood on his clothes.

"Whose cousin? Stay out of this mad girl?" his voice had certain vehemence. I guessed why somebody had laughed. I had betrayed his cover.

"Oh!" I opened my mouth in surprise hurt by the snub but also to excuse myself of the mistaken identity I had met before Rita would throw herself in front of the train.

A door at the other end opened followed by a sweep of cold sea breeze. A tall strong woman floated in, a sneer on her face her eyes fixed on us. A strong perfume filled the room. She studied us in silence us the men around appeared to have disappeared in fear.

"I am Queen!" her mouth had a strong set of teeth. Her skin was as if artificially fragile like the one of a new born baby. The dress hugging her body shone as if made of glass. Her eyes still had that unnerving and neutralizing effect, something sticky like a melting sugar lozenge.

"What we want is the truth my girls. The money?" She pointed at Rodgers. "The fool refused to tell us where you were."

"What money queen? Put us in the picture?" Rita asked in a whisper. Like her I believed what was happening was simply a bad dream. Which money was Rodgers supposed to be hiding? Was it possible he had stuffed it somewhere in our rooms?

My daytime reverie was brought into an end when the woman stepped forward and in a quick sweep of her hand landed an uppercut that knocked the breath out of the unsuspecting Rita hurling her across the room where one of the captors elbowed her back. I didn't wait to see what happened to her for something like a tsunami snapped inside me and my hands went for the aggressor's body. There was aloud ripping sound as her silk dress gave way, as my hands searched for her jugular. All I felt was to choke her to death with my hands. Nobody touched my body for no reason and stayed intact. The last thing I heard was her surprise scream before something heavy thumped the side of my head and I slithered to the ground a dying scream rising in my lips.

"Leave them...!" I heard Rodgers plead weakly. "They are innocent."

My head throbbed and I felt fazed. A sharp object landed on my temple. I swung my head away, tried to coil away. It was the woman trembling with anger kicking me with her pointed heels.

"Dogs spew," her voice rung in the room. I registered her figure hovering above me and was tempted to lunge upwards where it hurt most and die with her but something held me back. Perhaps this was not the time for heroics. To my horror she flashed a mean blade and I expected it anytime to be plunged into my body. Then it occurred to me she would go for my face carve it into disfigurement so that no man would ever look at me twice.

"Don't!" Rodgers who could have read her intention hollered in the dark with a strengthen that frighten even the animals. A man in red tweeds hammered his face with a fist between his eyes to silence him. Another man fatty like frog sauntered in and queen's blade vanished.

"No more nonsense, fools! What we want is information. Don't litter this place with a mess you won't be able to clean." His eyes devoured us greedily as he walked around us.

"Put them in the store." He ordered.

We were unceremoniously half carried and dragged in the fashion of local butchers carrying flesh and dumped in a dark smelly room stuffed with farm implements. Rita and I held unto each like lost children and silently sobbed our frustrations into the dark. Rodger's attempt to proclaim our innocence as the new comer, Mr. Toady ordered him to shut up still reached us. There was silence, something that was more frightening and dragging sounds across the other side before everything went dead. For Rodgers I was sure this was the end. The bugger, at least had tried to save us may be because of the tender feelings he had for Rita. We decided to wait for our imminent end.

9

We sat there in the dark and dump place our smell senses swamped by animal urine and dung. The fact that we were in the hands of vicious and dangerous killers was in no doubt. There was a throbbing pain next to my right ear. I ran my fingers through it and there was a nasty bump, clotted blood and pain. Rita's presence and warmth as we snuggled together made me have the presence of mind.

The possibility of escape was out unless God worked a miracle for us. We decided to pray. It gave me time to reflect on the events of the few last month's living in the fast lane, the partying in big hotels, Bradley's arrest, and today's remarks by the university president, Jemima's behavior and the strike and our capture.

How did we fit in the conundrum? Was it that some organization's members were in a bid to grab the business from Rodgers now that Bradley was out of the equation? Was it actually money that Rodgers had stowed away and if so where was it? Were there members settling certain scores? Or was it supposed to be some smoke screen to allow the re-organization of the syndicate? How did our college president get to know that we were part of this outfit and who else knew we were here and how would we be traced and rescued? I had to do something. Pray, yes and do something.

I stood up but Rita who had not stopped crying held her hand to restrain me. I whispered I was checking whether the door was secure. What if we fastened it from the inside? Perhaps, our captors would fail to eliminate us and the farm hands would find us in the morning. What if the latter were also part of the group? The door was firm and had nothing to secure it from inside. I fumbled around; I found an old pan, a jug, boots, a stick, some hoes and rickety wheel barrow with some sack's animal feed. I moved along and when I stepped on something tender and soft, I nearly screamed. I used my hands to feel around. It was a body. I was shocked and literally trembled. It was still warm and I yanked Rita to help me resuscitate whoever it was. In the darkness assisted by some star light we discovered it was a man, who had been terribly beaten and left for death. These heighten our sense of insecurity.

The man's pulse was steady and when we managed to raise his head. There was a bruise in his head where something heavy had been applied while his hands were secured by an elastic band behind him. Rita came to life and did all she could to give him comfort. Apart from the man's groans and occasional bats flapping against the roof the silence around was ghostly.

Suddenly, it occurred to me that the man in our hands would be familiar with the place in case he was the watchman or the farm hand. He had the key to our escape for he knew the territory. His movements had become frantic and we had no more assistance to offer than sharing his pain in our confusion. His effort to talk or sit straight   were rewarded by cries that impregnated the darkness with painful suspense probably restricted by the injury that we thought caused some internal bleeding.

Then we heard it. A low moaning voice from the other side coming at intervals like a whine of a dog in terrible pain. Would that be Rodgers? I thought he was still alive but in danger of death. We once more tried the door, still firm. Rita had assumed sudden fresh energy.

We traversed around the small room looking for the window, but then remembered it could be a common store without one.

"Man wake up…" that was Rita's voice, loving and calculated. "The police… we want to help you. We are the police." I had heard this word sickeningly many times this night.

The man mumbled something and my ears strained to get it. I urged Rita to say something.

"He is saying something like the …. yeah, the roof."

We both looked up at the same time. The thing was a bit elevated from where we stood. But there was a breeze that kept coming into the room which explained then there was another opening. I asked Rita to carry me on her shoulders to hitch me up so that I check out. Her attempts were futile because I was heavier while she was shorter. My attempt to lift her would have ended in a worse condition for I lost my balance and as she fell, she lunged out at the wall and found a metal ladder that went up the roof. She was still overly shaken even when her feet landed on the floor. It took us time to recover from the shock of what would have happened had she hit the wall. I gathered my courage and pushed the wheel barrow from the way and snaked up the ladder.

I struggled up slowly and laboriously, my head aching as the cold air coming from out there increased. It was until my head knocked on a cover that opened upwards when I released a sigh of relief. The cold night and the starry sky were a joy to behold; the outlines of tall trees surrounding the place, and the scattered lights from distant premises. The roof was sloppy and made of rotting tiles. I hung up there my one foot on the roof as I adjusted to the darkness. Rita crept up beside me, the hatchet enough to accommodate the two of us. We drank in the sounds of the night cautiously wondering if this was the freedom we had prayed for. We drew our plan of action and this had to be fast.

A few headlamps of vehicles on the highway and lights of the city buildings could be seen much better. Even the university hostels were visible through the clamp of trees, especially the Mount Kenya hostel, on a high-rise ground in the campus.

I crawled out of the hole into the roof, with lots of difficulties, holding unto the delicate tiles of the slanting roof, up to the timber apex, the old tiles creaking and cutting into my skin, slowly and painstakingly.

From somewhere a bird chirped fearfully and some groans were lifted across from the other building, mixed with animal sighs and the incessant chorus of thousands of insects doing their characteristic symphony.

A tile came off the roof and I almost toppled down to the ground. I felt dizzy for some time but I lay flat and held on my eyes closed for some time. Then the night was shattered by gun fire from the direction of the campus. All this time on the roof there had been no comrade shouts which meant that the riots had subdued.

"What was that?" Rita who was coming out to the roof wanted to confirm our worst fears. Had a student been shot?

"Do you think it will be the police?"

I was trembling and didn't know what to say. Had the vehicle stoning degenerated to this? Wasn't it exactly as spelled out in the professor's script a few moments ago? I crept towards the edge of the roof shielded by a clump of trees. At the end of it, the ground was dimly lit and I couldn't tell how deep it was.

Suddenly, there were crushes in the direction of the highway near the main gate and running feet towards the farm houses. I kept my head low and signaled Rita to do so. In the cleared patches of the open field two men materialized panting and scaled a low fence and walked directly into the house. Then another figure came along moving rather slowly like he had a problem with his body, next a woman who had introduced herself as queen clearly standing because of that shiny dress of hers I had torn up carrying a rifle, moving like a cat and peering into the darkness as she cautiously approached the place. The mistake one could make was to do something to that advance party of two and run out to escape. You would be her fodder.

A door was slammed under us with some force.

"Where are they?" the same raspy voice of Cobra asked irritably.

"Inside the store."

"Get them quick. The police could be here soon. First gate the vehicle ready. What are you gaping at?" Queen gave instructions to the man. I couldn't see where their vehicle was parked.

A shuffle of running feet. Sounds of a door slot being handled and then a door being swung open.

"Come out your heads above your heads!" a voice thundered just below us. A big lump choked my throat.

"Where are they?" queen's voice entered the fray.

"They are … nobody is inside. Oh?"

"You let them escape you fool…"

"Get back… I've been here and nobody went out. They could be somewhere."

"Get the farm hand. He could know."

There were frantic movements below us as our captors combed the interiors. I turned back and crawled towards a tree whose branches could properly conceal me. Rita was not far away from me as we made a slow progress on the uneven rough roof smelling of old wood and rotten leaves.

A movement on the other side of the compound caught my attention by the time I was almost launching myself on a firmer branch of the tree. A figure dressed in dark was making certain runs thicket to thicket all alone as they do in movies. The figure crouched behind a bush screen and listened for a while.

Then a low drone of an engine filled my ears. From the east of the compound a silhouette of a low flying helicopter materialized its signal lights flickering like a monster's eyes. Then a sudden beam of searchlights opened on the compound lighting everything that you could pick an ant creeping on the ground. In panic, I plunged into the welcoming branches of the tree, missed something to hold unto and for a few seconds I was suspended in the air before I fell I don't know how, head first through whipping and snapping twigs, crushing through them and hitting my head against some part of the tree as I tried to control my fall. The helicopter blasted overhead its engine rattling the whole building with its deafening sound smothering any effect caused by my recklessness. The pain on my head, face, hands was terrible as I landed on the forked part of the tree, breathless. I reached out with fingers a part that hurt more and felt the wetness: blood. I climbed back up the tree to the level to check on Rita. The helicopter's engine was dying to the other end. Was this the police or the gangsters?

Rita was reaching the tree too when on the roof behind her the hatch came up and a man's head popped out like a nightly apparition. I moved to the branch that extended to the roof so that I could pull her over. She might have read my horror of us getting discovered for she moved forward too soon making me loss my footing as I tugged her and for the second time I lunged into the air through the tree to the ground, Rita on top of me. Her head hit the stem of the tree with a sickening thud that she slipped into unconsciousness. I felt like I had dislodged my legs but in the grass around the tree I had the mind to crouch and pull Rita to a safer place. The man on the roof shouted some instructions and there was running around in search for us. The men were bearing directly on us when the figure I had seen in black hurled a stick to the other end that it hit the corner of the house on the other side. The men turned and made towards the place in leaping runs. A warning shot was fired in the air before a voice from a police megaphone hollered a command.

"Listen very carefully. The hide out is surrounded and our snipers would take on any one moving in any other direction apart from to the front of the house. Move now and at once. You have less than five minutes to follow the instructions. Make no mistake. Hands above your head. Now move!"

10

How could I leave Rita here and move to the required section? I felt her body, listened to her gentle breathing and wiped the trickle of blood on her nostril. She had perhaps suffered a concussion.

I decided to have the police help me. It had been one night of hell and my tired mind was not properly functioning. I crawled on my stomach so that I'll cautiously creep in the open when I was all too sure.

A hand clamped on the neck of my blouse from behind and tugged me gentle to a sitting position.

"Relax, Nerry." I suppressed a cry but facing me was Jemima. She was the figure dressed in black that had been hurtling from bush to bush. My mind was full of questions when by the wave of hand, she compelled me to wait and maintain silence. From her position she waved at the figures in black and balaclava helmets carrying heavy arms waiting.

The helicopter engine was growing in intensity meaning it was coming back. The police had mounted a search light on one of the trees and the place was well lit, at least to give room to the surrendering criminals. When I explained to Jemima that we needed to save the casualties the farm hand, Rodgers and Rita she explained that this could not be possible until the enemy lurking in the shadows had been overcome.

"It's dangerous to stick your head out there. Ever heard of friendly fire…"

As if to confirm her fears the first casualty was the light that was hit by a bullet plunging the place into darkness once more. Several figures melted in the darkness and Jemima signaled that I keep my head low as I raced after her to the place somewhere in the front. The firing continued for long everywhere as if the target was to cause panic. We were getting into the front when a man lunged at me. In the panic Jemima fired and the bullet missed the man and the attacker vanished into the bush. We crawled into the building's corridor, Jemima diving from wall to wall as she covered me.

We found him leaning against the wall his face messed up, his limbs hanging loosely about him. He looked benumbed and when I called him by name he looked up as if he wanted to register something, process it before reacting.

"Where are they?"

"Who coz?"

"The police. They may have run away, cowards."

"Let's move. They are everywhere."

"They, they …" he burst out into tears.

"Fool, let's move. Quickly." All this time Jemima squatted cautiously her gun ready.

"I've to revenge," he cried vaguely as I dragged him on his legs. I didn't know why I was risking my life for him at all. Was it blood or love or mercy or all of them combined? Rodgers, this young Satan, had always wronged me and others, always exploiting our weakness of being too trustful. I tugged him keeping our heads low.

"The police are shit…" he kept muttering vaguely. He was weakened and might have lost a lot of blood.

Just as we were getting out of the building Queen materialized before us like an apparition a heavy gun pointed at us.

"Let him go!" it was an order and I obeyed her.

"Boy, come with me," he called on Rodgers. "You don't belong here and by the way we are also going with the cop."

I saw Jemima move her hands almost unobtrusively.

"Don't be silly, Jemima." Queen warned her. "Keep them up where I can see them."

"You know me?"

"Who doesn't know, Professor Matesi's hot pants?" She snorted wickedly. She eyed me with murderous glitter perhaps following our earlier encounter.

"As for you heroine, I'll put this one on your head and end your miserable life."

"Nooo!" it came from Jemima.

Rodgers dived at her deflecting her aim and throwing her off balance with an energy we had not imagined he possessed. It was enough to make us dive for cover in the bushes around. Queen fumbled to her feet quite fast and gave him a tough swap on his head like you do a naughty goat and yanking him like a broken doll, he used him as cover, daring Jemima to shoot as she headed for the helicopter a few meters away.

Somebody might have let loose the animals and in fear they were also racing in the battle field, with terrified cries as if they were mocking our human folly of killing one another. I had lost Jemima and I was edging away from the stampede when a vicious hand clamped around my neck.

"I got you babe," the words were raspy, losing any romantic timbre, if ever there was one. I froze on my tracks.

He turned me round and the delight in his eyes was horrifying. He thumped me with a fist as if he had used a club. I shook my head, to make it clear as he continued wrestling me to the ground. I freed my hand and lunged them to his stomach, dug up my knees to his groin. He brought the butt of the gun on my head severally as I cried in pain and using me as a human shield directed me to the helicopter.

The grip around my neck was choking. I grasped for breath. "I'll have you to myself girl. And then carve your meat into pieces for ravens to partake what remains of you," he gloated devilry as he dragged me to the machine about to take off.

"Women are all stinky mess. I swear you do more stinking than anything I've ever touched. By Jove, I've never been hit by…"
He continued to shake me like a damp rug as his grip tightened around my neck, constricting my throat, choking me, starving me of saliva and breath. I made incomprehensible sounds. It was as if the demon in him did not give him time to reason. The guns had gone silent in the semi-darkness as a signal. Then the unexpected happened when Jemima walked out her hands in the air.
"Leave that girl alone. I'll give myself to you so long as you don't hurt her."
Jemima dropped her jeans and peeled off her top before us. This was the second time she was doing the same act and I wondered what her line of work entailed. My assailant sucked his lips, studying the poignant naked flesh before him in the darkness. What drove this woman to this craziness? I wondered in confusion. Why did she want to save me after that ugly first encounter?
"I have the experience that can take you to the clouds unlike that messy, baby…" she laughed nicely. Her voice was like honey drips.
"Jezebel, away now! Don't move!" his words were curdling, benumbing every joint of mine.
"It is my choice, Jemima. I love them young and inexperienced. Blame me for my bad manners. I never saw care from a woman anytime of my childhood. Why should I care what I pick? Now tell the police to get a car ready for us. You are going to drive us out of here naked as you are, very dramatic, eh?" Ha ha ha. His voice yowled into the dark enjoying every moment of the new prospect.
A vehicle engine started. The helicopter was off with his occupants, its blades sending whooshing sweeps of wind at us. This was a night of all nightmares for me.
I expected the so-called snipers to take my captor but nothing was forthcoming. Jemima let the way her naked flesh in the cold night involuntarily sending shivers up my body. Why did she give herself for me? We were closing on the police car and the policeman who had driven it to the directed point came out with his hands up. A muffled shot rang out latching on the roof of the vehicle. Cobra panicked and swung his gun on Jemima who was bending over to get inside and I hit him with my elbow deflecting his aim. A burst of fire from his gun

screeched, ricocheting along the ground and into the bush barely missing Jemima who was already inside the vehicle.

 I dived to the ground dragging him with me at the same time kicking his shanks. He yelped and let go off me to recover his balance and sweeping his gun in wild circles as shots rang everywhere. I rolled away as somebody cried and fell on me wetting me with what I thought was blood. The shooting had stopped as fast as it had begun. When I found myself loose, I turned over and still lifting himself on his elbow a wicked grin on his face was Cobra. He rose a little before the last volley brought him tottering, displaying him down on me, blood and juices as his fingers that seemed to have found me clawed and dug into my body as his screams and mine enjoined in a macabre embrace. The last thing I felt were his slackening fingers as life ebbed out of him and I for the fear of death lost consciousness.

11

I woke up to the therapeutic smells of sulfanilamide and laudanum. My body was dull as if it had undergone numerous pricking and panel beating. I was very weak. There were voices whispering around and my groggy mind was trying to come to terms with the situation. I decided to let go and slipped into a sound sleep.

I saw Mama Luciana come in with a basin of water to wash my hands. She poured the water on my dirt hands and gave me a towel to dry them. Then she opened a cover of the plate and inside were pieces of sweet potatoes. I picked one with a fork and when I took a bite the fork pierced my lips like a sharp knife, drawing blood. I cried with pain as blood dripped unto the floor creating dark clear stains. I hurled the fork away with the piece of food and tried to stem the bleeding and I was afraid it was really bad and I felt dizzy to imagine losing so much of it.

I rushed out crying for help but it was Mongina who walked in surprise in her eyes with the same water. She held me down trying to calm me and using water and salt solution cleaned the wound. The water turned out into a brown mess. I raised my eyes back and traced my journey and saw the trail of blood stains weaving a pattern on the floor like a thread that started from some point and ended a few steps to where I was being treated. The solution intensified the throbbing pain. I wanted to ask her where mom had gone only to see Rodgers on the other side laughing his head off. I called to mom and was really afraid. I woke up with a start and found someone peering down on me.

"Where is mum?" I asked in a panic.

The face looked familiar. It was Nixon. A smile creased his mouth as he watched me in excited silence and placed his hand on my face.

'What are you doing here?"

"I came for you."

"Where is this? Where is Jemima?" I was retracing the last few moments of horror.

A drawling voice answered that the place was hospital. It was Pamela. Next to her was Erastus, and Jemima, Jelita and Alice, the loyalty of Maina's family that never failed to confound me. Every time there was a tragedy or a function involving a family member, they trooped to give moral support. Even though the family patriarch had been somehow dislodged, the love for one another had never faded. I was not sure if they could ever discover that I was an alien to them. Would their matchless love ever survive? To them I was always the little sister they had come to love and accommodate and I never doubted their sincerity.

"Thank you for saving my life." I couldn't be any more grateful. Jemima buzzed over me saying in fact I am the one who had saved hers. I recalled those moments with a taste of bitterness.

"It was the Daily Star headline" Erastus proudly put in. "A brave girl saves a police officer"

"You're a police woman?"

She gave a broad smile before adding quietly, "*Wira ni wira,* any work is as good." She pushed a package which was a flower set in a polished ebony structure with the inscription, "Wishing you a quick recovery." The sight was breathtaking. My hands quivered slightly as my eyes watered.

"Where is Rita?" I suddenly remembered I had left her in some thicket.

"She had to be operated on and is recuperating well." Nixon explained. He looked like there was something he was hiding from me. It could be something to do with Rodgers. He might have seen my curiosity when he pushed into my hands a small red box. Inside was a golden ring set in a white background.

As I hesitate not understanding the implication Jemima was haranguing me with the details. Time seemed to stand still between the two of us.

"The gang had escaped with Rodgers and we are yet to trace them. I think this was a botched-up mission. The police standing there with the best snipers not shooting at that helicopter or any of the gang members. I believe it was an inside job involving some of our bosses. I hate to remember I was making a fool of myself in the whole thing when nobody was really serious."

Nixon was in self-doubt. He gathered the courage slowly as his lips quivered and then flipped his tongue over his lower lip. And what he could not do when the two of us were all alone as if in competition with time, he did it in the presence of Maina's family. On a bended knee, he gripped my hand in his as if comparing them.

"You were once dead and now you are alive. Honey, will you marry me?"

The words hit me as a bullet couldn't have done. The room had suddenly fallen into a pin drop silence. It was as if everyone was waiting for my answer.

Nixon was a likeable handsome man. Many a time he had stood by me, his humble background not denying him the opportunity to treat me with dignity. I wasn't marrying money for he hadn't any. I had tried that with the likes of Bradley-Rodgers with devastating results. What I needed were loving hands, somebody to live with our dream. Yes, somebody to walk with and make our own money if that was a prerequisite for real genuine love.

Before I could utter the answer, he slipped the ring into my hands. Pamela clapped in triumph and a few other claps followed. My tears burst out like a river as he embraced me showering me with endless kisses. Nixon could have extended the ring down the length of the finger were it not that Mr. Maina appeared on the scene arguing with a nurse.

"You are tiring my patient..." The livid nurse burst into the private room complaining.

"She is my daughter!" he thundered angrily.

Nixon turned to face the new arrivals. The man walked brusquely and without even looking around placed his hands on my forehead. I felt like choking for since that Erastus party incident I had never interacted with him that close. I would forever loathe that touch that had robbed me my innocence and believed his were always crocodile tears.

"Nerry, you are lucky and beloved. I couldn't sleep an iota since I saw the newspaper. Get well my daughter." Large tears blobbed out of his eyes and he shook with emotion.

Hadn't he sacrificed me as something picked in the roadside when he had said "No I am very normal, babe. I- I love you and nobody will ever take you from me. No Man. No god. Not even Satan." And offered me like a sacrifice to the gods of lust as he sung drunken praises at me, to his ingenuity and prized catch, a move his evil mind had schemed step by step.

Nixon stood there like a school boy examining his fingers and I wanted to spite the old man by offering myself to him. Yes, at least another mortal would yank me from his hands openly and before our clan. I waved him over and propped myself up in bed and placed the finger strategically.

"My true love and sweetheart, I will marry you." Nixon slipped the ring its whole length and jigged pleasantly and hugged me. I thought he would next get his coat off and swing it in the air the way he used to do it during sports. The claps once again took over and I saw Maina's face cloud with embarrassment as he cringed away. A man made of blood and flesh had snatched me from him. Openly and publicly, before his own eyes and family.

 Then, Jemima let out a war cry.

"Mr. Maina, Nerina is your daughter? My good God, tell me I am not dreaming." The man turned around as if struck by a rattle snake. I saw his hands tremble and in an obtrusive cold voice muttered.

"You're here. What did we use to call you?'

"Jemima, Maina," her voice mocked. "The one the newspaper said was saved by your brave daughter!"

"A police woman?" It was a mere statement as if to confirm his doubts. He greeted the other members around the room. I was getting drowsy and when sweet sleep stole me. I was happy Mama Luciana had visited me in a different form: a wedding ring.

12

The wedding arrangements picked up in earnest and Nixon who working with an NGO found himself time to organize things at his end. There was the bride price to pay, some substantial amount which I didn't have control over since the old men decided on the figure with considerations of my academic achievements, *aka* earning potential though the system smacked of abuse like you were some kind of commodity being sold, an out dated carry over from our primordial past. But honestly, from the bottom of their hearts no woman couldn't appreciate having her parents receive some token for their effort to make her who or what she was. One's sees nothing that was so torturous in life, as precarious and risky as abandoning your childhood home, kith and kin, climate and shifting your alliance to a completely alien environment with only hope as your guiding star.

This dislocation, this change of homes, for better or worse needed to be integrally approved by society. Wasn't it outrageous to uproot yourself from my brothers and sisters, our childhood joys, common experiences, honing on the same adze, forgotten, deserted, ignored on mere excuse of love? Was love this thing that made people breathe as if they had a cloth article shoved down their throats? Was this a dream that made the world glide along? Who could deny the constant sourness of this feeling that made you forget moments; the thing that made everything assume a purple color taste, begat ripe fruits? And provide survival of the world on the lubricating oil of love like an old squatted woman cuddling every child at the cradle and bosom, even with threat of disownment, still extending its gracious hands to gather one to some warmth.

And civilization at all times might have been propped up on the pretext of this feeling fueling ambitions to strife and bloodletting to brutality; bestiality, oppression, etcetera and the covenants of bridging the chasms in society; to soar, to grow, to develop and teem. Even the marooned by either, disability, disease, status, class came out of their burrows to serenade its smooth rhythms; to even it out with enemies; to traverse the face of earth; to toil and moil; to scheme and manipulate just to satisfy every inamorata's need. Whence love shortens distances, shortens life spans? And without incident the beloved anchored on appreciation, approval, admiration, rare qualities that ensured this feeling warranted longevity.

True love that always drew the penultimate boundary between the ugly and the beautiful; the old and the new the black and the white; the educated and the illiterate in cascades of music. Love felt in the water and wind, taste of food, hobbies, aromas of oils and flowers. This total feeling of fulfillment that often walked on our skins with an aura of togetherness and oneness' and in comfort seeking to thrive forever!

My latest encounter with the gangsters had left me a national heroine of some kind and you could bet the press was hovering around to catch the newest bits about their recent catch. Rita had healed well and had gained her robust past despite the dark hue of the missing Rodgers. He was yet to be accounted for and we couldn't be sure whether he was alive or death. There were so many intrigues on the drug case now that Bradley had been released for lack of evidence. (It was being whispered that his rich donor country had demanded it be done all they would withdraw their support for numerous programmes in our poor nation).

Talk of a richer neighbor who called the shots even when he had stolen your chicken. He walked home smiling while you were left locked in the chief's cell for character assassination! The whole thing smelt a rat and as Jemima had once put it; it was as if the police were under instructions not to shoot! It was a cover up and may be one day the good elements with the heart to put things straight would have their day. As for my heroism there was the juicy part bordering on the impossible when you could hear people saying that Nerina, they didn't know my face, had at the flick of a wrist deflected the bullet from hitting the police woman.

"You don't know it, *Bwana*, man. I saw it with my naked eyes how she stopped the guns firing with her smile. Then got hold of the chief gangster with her two hands and tore him into pieces. Do you understand that woman has the strength of a tigress?" I let them enjoy themselves.

And the tigress was marrying the tiger? The papers crooned of an assuming charming beauty that had recently foiled… blah blah. What were their sources for news? We flung ourselves into the business of formalizing our marriage, the way a thirsty throat yearns for cold water. The longing (I had not known it existed until I said, yes) and we were engrossed to reach the finale. I am sure had one come to suggest we postpone it for a day we would murder him or her. Perhaps, I was worried of another woman snatching him from the mid-step of our D-day, some calculating femme fatale, leaving me holding unto the feathers as our people locally put it.

I wanted to hear his sonorous voice, they all had a thorn on their voice boxes on such a day, declare he had left all other skirts for me. The longing blinded me from those other realities of marriage like inquisitive and officious in-laws, the throes of child bearing, the endless school fees and medical bills, the pain of betrayal, the agony and fears of widowhood. I swear I had not foreseen this side of the coin. I only wanted to see the butterfly like maids flapping their wings of angelic innocence, nimbly marching up the church aisle, in step with the brass music, in some intricate pattern that gave their male counterparts reason to detest the flamboyance. But then who wanted their wedding cheap, too cheap? I wanted mine; yes, women seemed to cuddle the price of such an affair. It was judged on the price tag of Nerina's wedding and not the bridegroom's.

I had ten girls doing the marching for me, some from my home and colleagues from college, Rita among them. Rita and I had cleared our studies and looked forward to our graduation before the tarmacking for jobs. But the fact that Luciana was absent, Hortenzia could always be mom, whatever I thought of her. What a dampener! I wished Luciana was there to share with me tears of joy, unexplained longings and worries and assuage me that my womanhood was not to let the world down.

At least, the other family members were present. Who couldn't honor notorious Nerina with their presence because we had chosen a neutral place to have it? Saarange aged but sharp in mind wanted to wrestle the boy who was stealing her apple of the eye, remember I was her child, her Nyabisio. Mr. Maina keeping his distance because I had been snatched from his megalomaniac power to hold me tied to his devilish ego as a sacrifice of his own phallic totem. I later learned there were irreconcilable differences between him and Jemima that had to do with when she grew around our local market as a young girl and she didn't miss to flaunt it to whoever cared to listen. The man looked pitiable in his aloof stance as if he wasn't part of this. He was the one who delivered me into the hands of Nixon before the vows and his speech encouraged us to give love a chance; the way he did in our home, uh?

My brothers and sisters my cousins and friends, then the press, some things we didn't proclaim. The rot in our home, the evil played on us because it could be fodder to the public to fuel the rumor engines and besmirch us. Had we lived the cruel past enough to forget its nastiness? Were we merely pretending to have done so? Peter and Mongina whose company I had come to prize whenever I was at home, and in all this fanfare, their love, an expression of their departure that cried and cried to remembrance. I couldn't explain it all. A past was being left behind me.

To think of the ultimate prize; the joy of getting your heart's desire, the tears wouldn't march the heart's loss. Nixon… was it possible to think, to pretend that the keyboard's chords, soaring in melody and motley of voices, cymbals, brass, saxophones, and singers' sweet voices bring no grand memories tumbling into mind? Somewhere there were cordons of crowds, my fellow villagers and yours; Nixon, on the sidewalks come to witness the big occasion; waving their hands sore with excitement in the wind; smile-lit faces as we moved shoulder to shoulder in a gait uncommon. Then the bits of paper, confetti, showering on us like many blessings of rain; carpeting our path and the sonorous voice of the pastor leading the ceremony.

My trembling hands slicing the cake, shoving it into your mouth; to those of the inner circle around us, and the thunderous claps and ululations from the congregation registering their approval on my skill to feed you and them. Those are the words of testimony before all the sundry; words being bitten by us, one by one as if we feared to make pronunciation mistakes; words that bore both the promise and hope of success, our success.

The choirs' delivering encouraging hopeful messages, fervent and energetic as ever; though marriage could be a thorny path; stressing the need to walk with Jesus. Then the presents we flippantly received as if our minds were fixed in another world, the thanks, the shaking of the hands until your shoulder and wrist were fatigued. My father, Mr. Maina's gift of a double bed, artistically designed, a thing to jump onto and procreate an offspring of grandchildren; and other gifts from friends, relatives pushed into sacks and plastic drums for easy carrying. The delicate moments of speeches from either party of appreciation, advice and the like: "if she breaks the radio, just tell her sorry, darling, it was such an old thing, we gonna buy a better one!" So simplistic and theoretical. Oh, theatrical.

I can remember the glorious faces of Pamela, Colista, Alice, Jelita, all my sisters, Erastus' drawling; Jones yapping to those who cared to listen, and the lanky Humphrey dwarfing everybody. I wonder what the boy was eating for he was like had not stopped growing; my father twirling his hat exposing the shiny pate now threatening a fringe of grey hair by the ears. Nixon's father with humorous eyes, making a few jigs in pleasant excitement; and oh goodness journalists attracted to the wedding of the officer saving heroine. News is hard to come by in this country and now they are falling all over the place and whodunit?

It was quite a panorama of my youthful moments and explains reason behind my inconsolable tears in my present state. Sister Favour had found my ear and in her confident musical voice whispered "BRAVO!" as she handed me a big envelope. Some thousands of shillings to buy swaddling clothes. Babies! How ambitious? And a clock inscribed "keep time to great heights." I couldn't help but thank her a thousand times.

There was Irene, cute and chic with Jeffrey's son, now a young guy in town. Jeffrey had sent his appreciations and she was planning to join him abroad; talk of love flames that never die. Then Madam Jane, laughing and motivating like a mother that I had always missed; Big Head, dangling the keys of his newest car, a Porsche, preening with success, his broad shoulders having diminished the bigness of his head.

Peter our loyal servant and donkey, grinning ear to ear his eyes avoiding to meet mine. He who had thought he had lessons to teach me! Mongina? Where was she? Saarange, my grandma bent like a bow with a big staff (who supplies this nimble soul with such apparatus) to propel her around, driveling with joy. Had she wedded, in her traditional way and now grown supple? But the trill of her voice and her sharp eye sight and then daring Nixon for a wrestling match, her tears of joy a sign she welcomed our accomplishment. Who was missing, Catherine? Rodgers? The list was long…

The gifts, a houseful of furniture from wall units to plastic utensils all needed a truck to carry. As we approached our new home the people demanded to walk us the remainder of the journey. The people mobbing and singing around us. The village's energetic women with big bums wanting to give a swing that could have send me flying in a scattered heap; dancing until dust clouds rose, singing themselves hoarse and dry. The procession snaked up the hilly and gullied paths as we moved to our new home. Nerina, the daughter of Maina, notorious, Nyabisio, fortune, had been married.

Young children pushing forward, wanting to touch even the hem of my train so that they would have a story to share long after. Ah time, the great criminal, how come this was just yesterday when you carried us from a murky swamp to rosy beds and back to the same murky as if the irresistible tide of the sea smiting the beach is fore ever restless? The village welcomed me with grandeur, everyone came, a-running and I was enthroned inside that grass thatched house that Nixon had put up.

People didn't want to leave us alone so that we rest. After my mother-in-law had received the bouquet that was symbolic of her formal reception as a member of the family, I was sneaked to my house to change into something light. I loved the fresh smell of clay and cow dung done on the walls. There was something primordial and hedonistic, original about this place like in all thatch huts. The visible patches of clay had been plastered with some white chalk so smoothly done and newspapers and magazines neatly stuck on other areas. Outside there was yap-yap, eating and drinking, for during a wedding was time to raise your generosity a notch high. You can't miss a drunken chorus even if your family hasn't supplied beer!

Then with time people retired to various places and we gathered each other into full-blown embraces, and like twins stayed staring, reading the map of the route to our long-deserved waiting. There was nothing lustrous than that, nothing glorifying than that one moment to crown everything that mattered in our lives.

"Nixon, darling," I muttered and tried to stifle a sob rising in me. My heart fluttered like many wings of birds in sudden flight. Why was I crying instead of being happy?

"Weep not my love," he responded his tender hand brushing away the tears.

I remember this one detached behavior with fleeting thoughts of another moment when Felix and Daddy had come calling. Nasty experiences in other people's hands. What if Nixon discovered my uncouthness? Was this the price to pay? There was no pain but endless pleasure. "I love you," he repeated as his hands unrestrained went all the way seeking, setting engines of love on fire, my body heating and I repeated the words as I sought his soul so that we were threatening to grow into one big wave riding on other waves, everything else forgotten. His lustful voice sung some tune, full treasures, freely and willingly thrust into the trusted and right hands, to be fingered, enjoyed, as a full fruit, in surrender of trust. We rode the celestial mists, the long dammed well of love, that something yearned wrongly, breaking. And almost instantly, almost wishfully, I desired honor for Nixon's image to be cut inside me, because the real Nixon had sounded the right chords of a song inside me.

I lay there cuddling him as he slept from a work well done listening to the sounds of the night that rode into my ears. He was surely done, snoring and as I peered into the alien darkness. How can one sleep in a new home like a fool? I resisted a wild feeling to wake him up and ask him how he found me and whether I was worth his dreams or below average. But I only laid my hand cross his hairy chest possessively and murmured and drinking the musk of sweat and muscle. "For life and death." A ring of laughter ripped the night from somewhere away, not an eavesdropper, though, and I smiled at myself wondering whether it was only on wedding nights when lifelong spouses found themselves.

"Be happy," I again addressed the darkness and sleep stole me away. Like me, a few women would claim conception on that first time.

These are the fond memories, enshrined in the core of my dream that accompanied our settling down, as we sought to get used to new rhythms of a new life, frictions and yawning gaps, as expectations sometimes failed us, both erotic and physical. We went visiting places, friends and relatives and a good number came home. They were welcoming us to this new pedestal of life, in the church and community and with enthusiasm we shared food and tea.

13

Nixon's flight abroad for further studies was supposed to be a blessing for our family. We had prayed and wished for this opportunity and when it came, we embraced it fully and thanked our God for it. At times he could turn to me with doubts about our family whether we would remain faithful to our marriage vows but I urged him on.

"I'll be there waiting for you, darling. Go out there and learn everything. Don't hesitate so long as it's for the good of our children. Keep the faith burning! Will you be faithful, Nix?" Like all men he was elusive with the answer as he mumbled something incoherent. I didn't want to be a stumbling block to my husband's academic advancement so I wished him well.

Before he left, we cried in each other's arms, our nights full of yearning and doubts but the future was a path hidden from us therefore ours was to trudge on hope for the best. We would sleep in each other's arms as if we feared we would disappear from each other's lives. And when he left the tears were so many so we led them flow. Our children joined the crying band but we put a brave front for their sake. The relatives were only happy to see Nixon successfully vanish into the clouds.

"I'll come, Nerry, for you and I promise it will be paradise." Nixon's promise kept ringing in my mind and got me moving around as if nothing was amiss, as if I could open our house and find him waiting. And as if this was what they were waiting for usual tensions began between me and my mother in-law. It's like she wanted everything to be provided for her within her own terms ranging from household things even the ones she hadn't enjoyed while her son was around.

I tried my best to assuage her god of materialism for a little while but I proved with the little money I couldn't manage with the little family I was raising. Her first reaction was when she started bad mouthing me together with my sisters-in-law generating one rumor after the other even on my moral standing.

"A woman who wears trousers is a whore," they would say that when I was not very far and laugh derisively. I thought it would go away and concentrating on my job and bringing up our kids. I could say Nixon supported us with the money that came from his industry abroad, despite the difficult economic times, he would spare time to do menial jobs where he earned pittance. And this was what he sent home with instructions on what could be done.

He wanted me to put up a house for his parents. I called on them and explained everything to them. My father in-law was excited over the whole issue and looked forward to it.

"This is the moment to make people know educating a child is fruitful," he quipped.

"Over my dead body," my mother in-law cut in her eyes blazing. "A wicked woman cannot put a house in this compound as if we are crippled. We can build our house when God gives us ability to do so. I don't want to hear that subject in this compound again. As for you Nerina go ahead, sleep around with every man and say Nixon has sent you money…"

It hurt me so badly that I stood my grounds and gave them a piece of my mind.

"I can't stand that rubbish. I know what you think of me but I need my respect, dignity as a daughter in-law. If you think my efforts are unwanted then I had better declare that you don't expect anything from me because my money is immoral. I work and earn a salary."

One of my brother in-laws hit out at me and there was chaos. My children joined in screaming and the villagers ran in to find out what the problem was.

"We can't have this prostitute destroying our good family name," Truscilla Nixon's late brother's wife lashed out, broadcasting everything to those who cared to listen.

I called Nixon and explained the happenings and that day I moved out of the compound to a new premise I leased with my family. I didn't want to have anything to do with jealous conniving relatives who wanted to hold me back.

I think since I came to this family I was seen as an intruder. They had felt neglected, playing second fiddle while me as a stranger I had financial control over them. They had forgotten that I hadn't come here a desperate being because my education could afford me employment or enable me put food on the table. They expected me to beg, to crawl to them and pay obeisance to them, as they lorded over me. I would milk their measly cows, pluck their unproductive tea and beg for droppings from their kingly table.

But I came in and upset the cart and I was never to be forgiven. Cooking something decent, out of the ordinary was courting for trouble. It began with my sister in-laws, then school going babies who wanted all that their brother bestowed on me as his wife and then was taken up by the women such as Truscilla married to the homestead at the goading of my mother in-law. My father in-law, I had never seen a thoroughly hen-pecked man, sat there like a stooge not questioning the logic of what was going on in his home and blatantly before his eyes. The envious poison was coming out to be something corrosive.

Nixon advised me to play it cool and give it time. The languor had grown into crazy magnitudes and it would take something drastic to cure it. But nothing changed her, instead my mother in-law was a vicious hardened enemy. On the day I was at the airport to welcome Nixon home she was determined to have her revenge.

All the time I sent word that I was going to fetch Nixon home she kept mum. At least I had asked him to send them own money to their account but to have her dressed as a scarecrow was sending a message of some shivers.

I knew in her wardrobe there were the best and modern dresses but she wanted to send a different message. *Your wife doesn't care how I appear before you so she is below you?* I was supposed to roast but I hoped sincerely, Nixon would understand and absolve me from the blame. But he was her own blood and I was the stranger strung only by threads of love to him and now kept apart by distance, I couldn't confidently say Nixon was the same old love flame. Even my efforts to pay school and college fees for my in-laws were not acknowledged by a vain and vengeful mother. And they were all in support of her, the notion that whatever never went well in their life, I was the evil force behind it.

I had tried to lead them across the river without rubbing off their motherly daub, influence, call it whatever with a disastrous result. They had all been poisoned by her to the point my own children could wonder loudly whether they were dad's kin. But I had my own vision that couldn't be darkened by wicked shadows of damnation and redundancy. I was a woman, yes, but a woman had to try too, at least to keep afloat.

When I hugged Nixon to my bosom the longing and the bottled anger and anxieties burst out in a river of tears. I choked in his manly smell; the unique bodily signature assigned to him and felt my body stir from deep inside in demons of desire. I felt like opening up for him just right there so that we could ride wave over wave of desire as I gave my all to him. My body trembled and a weakness overcame me as I held to him.

But there were others to be attended to, the relatives, the mother in-law and they stole him from me and wanted to have a share of him. I felt cheated as he hang there for eternity taking every form of their messages, yapping and yes, the rubbish they had about me. Nixon's mother's sweeping movements of hands showed the vehemence of her soul and message. She kept her voice in a steady low monotony of a misfiring combustion engine.

As we snaked off the airport into the flower lined Mvita road, with tourist hotels and condos of red tiles and coupled with terraces of potted flowers and white spiral stairs on the outside I had this heart-rending premonition like an evil cloud that I had lost Nixon forever. Lost the promise he had gone to bring for his family. Was it because of the relatives' interference or the life abroad? What had happened to our promises, our parting shots of faithfulness? Our hitherto love inscribed on the rocks whether buttressed by waves and the sea of life ravages was wont to hold strong forever. Was it one big false dream or a mere mirage?

14

The cold seat of the lavatory embraces me like the hands of death. The pain is overwhelming. I push. There is some trickling. A languid and sour smell. The pain follows quickly, spreading like a globule of oil soaking on a plain paper. Nothing is ever enough to wash my pain away.

A deep-seated guilt envelopes me. What did I say in the flurry of things that was out of place? Stupid! Was I a victim of the unknown or another lamb whose fate had to end this way?

My insides are churning. Will they come out if I just pushed harder? A throb of pain. How come I didn't shatter any bone? I feel disjointed.

The rhythm rides in my ears. It is like a wave, a sweep of water bashing my eardrums faster and faster. Every crash, a painful crash, growing in intensity as I scream, push, frail out and coil away. My mouth is wobbling for a word, a sentence, in taut suffocating motions livid with fear and shock.

A door clashes. Another one. My senses are now alerted. He is in the bathroom. The water running probably on his body. The pricking on his skin will enliven him again. Refreshed, he will remember the receptacle. He will go a hunting his senses his own compass! But he is washing! Did he find me wanting, dirt and a bore, a memory to be discarded? Hell had no customer like a rejected woman!

Whenever our feet get muddy, we hunt for the doormat? We damp our dirt on its face without care. Clean and free and lighter we walk in.

In fact, opening and closing doors would always scare me. There could be sounds of running or pounding feet. Slaps and kicks followed by more slaps. A fall. And the abuse. No! No!

A trickling into the basin. Spasmodic reactions as my taut muscles twitch fearfully. I close my eyes. I want to scream. I want to die. I want to vanish into the thin air and never be found again.

Over my closed eyes I can see the grinning faces. Their laughter. Memories of a past I have been trying to bury.

"She has had it."

"She was looking for it."

Oh, good God, why should it be always her? Is there always something wrong with the woman who surrenders her soul, her body to the man of her love? Society's logic always oversimplifies our intentions in the court of the suspect. It brutalizes and dehumanizes even genuine feelings.

I stand up on my trembling legs and ran my hand over my stomach. Might be something ruptured could be sticking out. I feel that something has been ruptured but I can't tell what it is. I feel like a broken pot. I grope with my fingers. The rim. Something could be torn. The gadget to be secured is the inner self. It is my being that should survive beyond adversity. Oh, guilt!

"No, Nixon."

The shreds of my cry fall upon me. I twist my mouth in a wry smile. Over the years I had been waiting for this occasion.

Forgive me if I appear to lose you by marrying quite two different incidents like this. It's because of my state of mind. After staying away from him and the vicious campaign against me that I was seeing other men meant to snatch him from me; I was one angry woman and also hungry. I welcomed him home with the waiting of the years, the way it falls heavily after a long gathering of clouds laden with water.

I shed my tears, my fears, my setbacks, my pain, surrendered all to him in a bid to have him back, to own him, to still love him in the name of a faithful companion. I found him equal to the task thirsty and hungry and I shook everything from him, sucked him dry, his marrows and even blood. What could help me retain him in my bosom if not this unprecedented performance? But then I found myself dreading everything.

"This was out of ordinary performance. A practiced hand she was. She had been learning all these in the hands of other men. So, what my mom and Truscilla had been telling me was true? Nerina is a whore?"

Would that be how I lost him? In fact, with his coming back our love life started going down the drain in a gradual slow motion that we saw but didn't have a power or a trick up our sleeves to save it. I tried all the tricks in the book but it needed more than this. An honest sharing to dislodge the stain of suspicion deeply implanted at the back of his mind. Like Saarange once wondered what had they done to him?

Could a wife completely steal a son from a mother who had borne him for nine months in her womb, suckled and wiped his butt by true and earnest love? Weren't our scandalous words more dangerous and poisonous that reason vanished wholly from even the intelligent? We lived a friendly love affair and it made me question the logic of having Nixon go abroad to study only to lose our flame.

I am not saying I was an angel. What of our characteristic feminine stupidity, the pouting, the nagging, the refusal to apologize even when I had stooped too low for him and his demanding that I should apologize or else even when my view point was absolutely different from his? Why did men want us to see things in their way? Why could they be bothered with our little female silliness and instead just bear with us and convert us gradually to their apex of masculinity if they so wished and believed their level was better than ours?

"Could it have been any better?"

I think I want to laugh. What I need now is a thorough wash! I open the taps.

15

Perhaps I should stop whining and tell my story like a real story free of anger. I am one angry woman, I've to admit it and if you see the fits thrusting out of my tone understand it is a normal-natural reaction of a woman given a raw deal by life.

****

I've shed all tears I had to shed such that I need not go that path anymore. A thing always rises in my throat threatening to choke me, a wicked spirit full of demons, rancor and bitterness, as freshly as ever. I don't expect your pity. I don't expect your pretense showering me in false light with your get-well messages. I have come to learn the base human lies, the make-her-feel-good stuff that is filled with the honest talk in the corridors away from my ears, "We don't think she will ever walk." That is the truth you should come over and share with me, but when you come up and outwardly lie "Oh Nerry, you look smart today. At this pace you will walk soon. Get well." Oh, friends and relatives, how you bore me stiff!

****

Things are a bit whirly here. Today I placed my left foot on the floor. It had no feelings though. Have I confided to you that my legs collapse below me like old dolls that we stuff under the bed away from the visitors' sight? Like a baby learning its first steps I was propped into the wheel chair. Thanks to my niece, she has been beside me supporting me. I sometimes wonder whether I am taking advantage of her. She finished her high school and she is waiting to join college but the toll on her time and humanity all for my own good. How would I ever pay the debt?

I worked my hand to pain trying to rotate the wheel to move forward. I need to learn something about braking if I don't want to break my nose next time. The thing whirling along the corridor is quite heavy. They whirl, screech, and refuse to cooperate until I adjust something. Silly me, you don't apply the brake and push, simple logic but who prepared me for these silly moments. With the noises here add to the wheel chair, mine is becoming one big whirly world.

****

Which woman doesn't treasure certain unfoldings in life with a sense of foreboding? The day I arrived in my husband's home I was such a treasure. I was some queen in everybody's eyes. A beauty and a graduate were rare tags in the village, from those whispers being traded around by the curious gathering. I gathered everyone wanted to see and hear me talk, trill like they do it around and they would soon discover I was just a local woman with local moorings. I was equally treasured by the host who took it upon themselves to introduce me to visiting villagers and others whenever the opportunity presented itself.

I was the idol, the soft-gentle species to be protected, yeah, at those first moments whenever I wanted to do anything I would be pushed aside as someone did it for me. I never fetched; the water was down some valley, a trickling thing that necessitated queuing for order. The *posho* mill was a no-go zone for me, the *shamba*, farm, but they owned me always taking me along to the market and carrying the entire luggage and in church and everywhere ready to declare ownership. And those who did my introduction, I felt they put up some airs, some quality to their voice to show how their status had been elevated by this graduate and beauty.

And I was down to earth, doing the common things with the village lot of women and without complaining. Yeah, there were a lot of traps like finding out whether I could cook ugali for the sizable family. There was always a quality that makes my people's ugali unique, fired and fine from proper boiling of the initial flour mixture; the smooth fine mixing which calls for dexterity and the final proper waiting and allowing the heat to simmer it properly as you keep turning it over.

Even the experts sometimes make mistakes and the connoisseur, usually the family head can declare the whole thing a disaster and not many girls can pass this test unless you were brought in the homestead of Maina and learned it in the hands of Saarange.

I even plucked the tea, the right way and balanced the basket on my head to the tea buying center where we waited endlessly for the reluctant clerks to arrive to weigh and buy it. I've never seen a reluctant lot, uncaring lot like these staff who are assured of earning their salary and steal some of your tea by popping those things up with the knee and write less kilos for the unsuspecting villagers.

****

Today the world celebrated the women's day. Women's day? What is there to be celebrated for womenfolk condemned to be shackled by religion, culture, poverty, disease, war, hunger and man. Man, the immediate *god* over woman, from time immemorial because of the cable dangling in his fork. This cable somehow has to connect the plug and light, oh, heat the future...

Instead, man god or god man, for nothing special but sheer desire to have a punch bag, has found a place to release own frustrations and failures in his clueless life. It could be your sister, wife, daughter, and competitor? They hate competition, they want it easy until the woman comes into the picture and the madness starts.

I propped myself on bed and decided to browse the internet. The atrocities perpetrated on womenfolk are simply mind-boggling. They read like Solomon Mines tale... Betty was battered to a coma by her husband for not having his meal ready, a meal he had not worked for. She succumbed to the injuries. Lucy was butchered by her husband in full view of her children and her body stuffed into a sack. The relatives used to her cries never intervened to the familiar song. A woman's cry. It's us who always cry a tune, a soprano, an alto or any other advanced note, in this equation. They say even those who discipline their male companions cry all the same. Has nature conspired to reduce us to lachrymose beings?

A man comes home and finds his wife has cooked lunch using a portion meant for supper. He goes berserk and taking up a machete butchers his dear family, hacking them to pieces. Aren't their cries for mercy enough to arouse a calcified heart? What happened to love, human dignity, understanding, and communication? Are we all living an illusion called love and once peeled off, the real raw and palpitating anger remains like a monster bent at destroying our own? Are we living a dream whose night is not yet done?

There is pain on my side and I can't continue browsing. My head aches and my neck is stiff. I won't capture everything. Do I need a microphone; some application to register my thoughts for I can't type everything, the flow of my thoughts overwhelms my speed of typing. I am determined to spend the last drop of my blood so long as the world knows this. Will they listen? Will they change their bloated egos for the sake of humanity, nay, womanhood? Smothered by culture, religion, favors, advantages would they stop strangulating, stifling womankind on fake excuses of being ignored, being disobeyed? My foot, let me laugh, what's disobedience when your dear wife is questioning your silly conclusions, helping you to reason straight… She wants to prop you up, shape, update you and make you king. Why brother are you afraid to reason? Think… stop being lazy. Who told you that those who ill talk your wife or husband have the best interests of your life?

****

Whenever a woman looks back there is a price she admires most if she has paid it. The price of bringing forth another life is such a great joy. We dared count our chicks before they were hatched because we had bought the diapers, some unisex clothes and other baby nursing assortments. When it came, a baby girl, we called her Vega. What a joy Vega was to us –a young couple gifted with cadences that soared into the walls of the heart, plastering us with hope? At no time I had clearly visualized that the round mass growing heavier and bigger in front of me would materialize intro flesh and blood; it was simply a miracle! The skin of my tummy looked stretched to the extent it had a lighter color than usual.

There was the blackish line down and up the navel, growing larger with progressing time. The fetus made those jolting movements, most of which brought me to a paralyzing cold sweat. We counted the months, the weeks, the days and the hours. But it came suddenly with the lower back ache throbbing and incessant. I hadn't been able to go church that morning and by 11 o'clock I couldn't bear it anymore. I asked my sister in-law who was with me to accompany me to hospital. We had carried a few particulars.

Our journey to the hospital was the slowest ever as the available matatu crawled along in its process of picking and dropping passengers in their usual lackadaisical pace I feared that the baby would pop out on the way. By the time I was ushered into the decent maternity hospital the pain was intolerable, apparently knifing into my spinal cord, sharp and acute I coiled over. The travel would have acerbated it but a bit comforting because at each bout of pain I kept wriggling my bottom against the seat to calm the pain far better than the walk from the gate to the reception. My sister-in-law held my hand as I walked along with blurred vision, my hand rubbing against the pain, the way one brushes away marauding safari ants from her body.

After the admission there was the long wait and rounds of forced drills around and about the corridors, the longest minutes of life, compounded with pain and anxiety. I might have sung all the songs that I knew when the pain became unbearable. Human beings, more so women possess a unique capacity to bear pain beyond which sanity flees. When this miscalculation of time ended, I was unceremoniously pushed onto the divan. I tried to push oh God tried until the pain shattered my back, and in the name of *Yesu Kristus,* I screamed and screamed as a new side pain nicked me in the name of scissors and then a fleeting lull; filled by the cry of the newborn. The fresh pain smarted terribly and someone was piercing the torn ends until I screamed and ordered them to stop and apply some anesthesia. A woman has to be bloodied by the bloody experts in the name of birth.

What a callous sense of entitlement by some health workers during this polished end of improved medication!

I survived the maternal ordeal in which others die or are maimed forever. Mothers have to be stained in their own folly of love in the name of continuity. Let the blood flow and let the pain reign for we are accomplishing the greatest feat for humanity. I was luckier because someone listened to my request and they sedated me so as to mend my 'broken walls'.

The first thing I asked when done was the baby be placed in my hands and as I saw her chubby hairy body, glistening hair matted to her skull and closed fingers wriggling causelessly and saw that every of her limb was sound, I thanked my God for it. Tears of joy spilled from my eyes and I fell into a long deep sleep. The chubby limbs, the cooing, the doodling, the cries during the first three months on earth accompanied with restless twists and turns due to stomach gas and acid reactions and more acute during the wet season would be my treasure forever.

****

Wasn't I treated like a queen going from the look in their excited talk "How lovely? How lithe! How queenly! when I landed in your home Nixon?" Everyone wanted to reach out and touch me, see me, hear me talk. It was a combination of a village's expectation on a beloved son and the kind of girl who had stolen his heart and confused his mind. At least I wasn't older than him, too short all too tall than him so that they would have demonized me, berated me for snatching what didn't belong to me.

People are not anybody's friends, not anybody's spokesperson but they express their joys and frustrations in the same breath. Whether it hurts or builds, it is least of their concern as long as they exercise their freedom of speech. What happens if their son overhears their negative comments on his bride? Are the villagers an integral part of the bridegroom's perfect marriage? What then is their role? My first moments of glory made me their idol, received by soft gentle welcome speeches of those who mattered in the circle. I was even spoiled by the quality of food cooked to impress me. I was a welcome guest, then, but now….

****

The rhythmic whirl of overhead fans and bleep-bleep of machines has become an enslaving music to my ears, something loathsome, and something that reminds me of my mortality, vulnerability. Who can deny the fact that a few months I was fit and walking around with my two feet? How could I've foreseen this turn of events so fast and drastic that I am now at the mercy of others to perform what I could do all myself just because of love gone sour?

Grrr grrr grrr grrr, the wheels whirl in the same monotonous rhythm, an unchanging even beat of the machine until my ears smart with pain. I have become a good listener all these months confined to bed. Yes, shackled to helplessness that creeps all over my body to my feeling-less feet and hands, until I do doubt whether all this is part of me. I can tell between the sound of opening and closing doors even far away the long drab white corridors, even other surrounding rooms. From these sounds, I know an angry bang, a friendly dab, a reconciliatory tone, all human emotions carried in the air to my hearing like they are punishment for not heeding to them when I was on my feet.

To be where I never imagined before means I've everybody to blame, both imaginary and real enemies for the pain, the realization, the truth! Have I ever poured the same vitriol on myself? Have I seen how I was responsible for this affliction? Nope. I was an innocent woman going along in her usual intrigues of survival when a rabid husband turned the tables on me. Were there tell-tale signs to this slide or things merely happened spontaneously? When did it begin to rain? Does a normal human being just turn into a raging murderous being as if a switched-on machine? Was I too much swamped in love, in an illusion I didn't see it coming? That's for you dear reader to judge. I may have blamed others except myself for my woes. I am only mortal and full of weaknesses. My only request is that you learn to treat any woman with respect. That's all.

16

I remember that scene more vividly, always replaying in my mind as if it happened today. Jemima had just whispered to steady my hopes when she came to my hospital bed. I had just undergone the first operation and been sedated from the excruciating pain tearing me apart. It was three days from Nixon's attack.

"We will make it girl."

Jemima was sharing in my pain as before, inviting me to be joint partners in the challenge ahead. Then my frail father, Mr. Maina, at least my foster father and one who broke my innocence, wasted by disease had visited. Who couldn't recommend his loyalty to me, ever turning up in my pain and joy?

"Bull of Auckland—it has caught up with you at long last, eh!?" Jemima's voice sounded glad while referring to his positive HIV-Aids status. Maybe something in his present form brought back certain memories of her past.

Had Mr. Maina, taken advantage of this woman the same way he had done to me? Which soul forgives and forgets that betrayal? I am a woman like all others and I swear my capacity to remember certain things is natural.

"What?" Mr. Maina swung around. Could his anger conceal his sins? During my wedding the two had almost come to blows and here they were spoiling for the same battle, and Jemima had sworn to shoot him next time. The root of their bad blood still a mystery.

Several necks turned to them. Jemima had never told me why she always attacked the man. Maina's stick rose to strike out but a vicious cough ravaged him. He had to steady his fall by the same stick as he wheezed breathlessly.

"You can't even see that you are finished. That girl you once gave a lift, and 'the things girls desire most when at the threshold of adulthood' is here. You hooked her to *mbeca*, money, impregnated and threw her out!"

The sick man raised a weak hand in protest.

Time stood still for a moment.

"You wanted *her* to abort, didn't you? She kept the baby and gave birth; the rest is history."

The man straightened out as if awakened from a bad dream.

"Where did the child go?"

"Silly! The child, I gave it to your wife. RTS- return to sender."

"Oh, God. Oh, God!" The next thing I heard was a falling stick and a thud followed by rushing feet.

In dread, I thought Jemima had finally fulfilled her last threat and raised my head. My body responded with unnerving pain but what was happening around me was cataclysmic.

 The man was sprawled on the floor, a mess, as several family members and nurses went for his aid.

I swear I hadn't heard the shot if there was one. Instead, something like a fresh blow rose inside my brain, building up until I began gasping for air.

I remembered what Saarange had once told me in my time of great mental turmoil. "A baby wrapped in newspapers…. I called you Nyabisio, fortune…"

That child Jemima gave birth too was me. Jemima, the hot panted wife of Prof Matesi, the police woman extraordinaire, the one who had saved my life… O, the one whose life I had saved too. The woman who attended my family occasions… The woman I had grown to be friends with, in spite of our shortcomings, was my biological mother! The awkward girl who didn't know what to do with a baby was my mother… And I was the baby Saarange had picked up and given to Mama Luciana to bring up. That meant Mr. Maina was also my biological father!

"Oh my! Oh my!" Jemima's hands were all over my body as she hugged me and cried out.

It was a cry of pain, bottled up frustration and betrayal. It was a whine of deep shame nursed over the years, felt deep in the heart. Probably, a cry of both triumph and shame. An interesting show of emotions.

I fainted with the overwhelming mental and physical pain. When I woke up Mr. Maina was miserably coiled in a corner, his eyes red with crying. Jemima walked around agitated, her eyes are so red, her fingers opening and closing.

My biological mum? No. My mum would always be the gentle Luciana and not this wild apple!

Was Jemima, really wild? What if I had become pregnant of Mr. Maina? What would I've done with the baby in my confusion and innocence? Wouldn't I've left the baby in the similar circumstances as Jemima did me? Wouldn't have the first mistakes earlier in life hardened me like this Jemima?

Mr. Maina, shuffled to my bed and pleaded for forgiveness… He bent on his knees, his weak body summing all his energy to appease his damned soul. He wished he died. His apologies were not for abandoning my mother… It went deeper than what those present knew… The blood stains forced on me by a man who treacherously disregarded my trust in him as a father! Death could be a sweeter respite in certain circumstances.

But I had my children to live for. My doting family who had never left my side whenever tragedy struck. Yes, whenever life decided to stain my path with blood. Loyal Saarange, Jelita, Alice, Colista, Jones and a new ally in Pamela…

Vega, I quaked to know out there the Mr. Hyenas, Mr. Mainas could be waiting in their sleek ties and suits, beaming smiles and guiding hands. *Donkeys*, like Peter, Rodgers, Cobra and the bigger crowd of sickening men, ready to draw blood and stain the paths of her nimble feet, of the green girl...to satiated their broken egos.

It breaks my heart to know it… But you've to walk the path. I can't swallow you back to my womb… You've to swim your broken path. Be confident. Be keen. Be steady. Face the ghosts and let your voice be heard. Many fear feminine voices raised against injustice. They gang against such voices. But be woman. There are so many virtues being yourself.

Two weeks to the incident at hospital and the revelations about my origins, I received an unexpected call from Jemima. The fatigue and shock associated with this occasion had not cleared from my confused mind. The physical pain and reality of my deformed future were scaring wounds. The news that I was her and Maina's child were not the big shock either.

What shattered me was that all this time she had wanted to run from her past act of abandoning her child and not curious to know what could have happened to me. She had run from her past until it had accidentally caught up with her under strange circumstances.

Why hadn't she brought up the topic when she had met Maina just before my wedding and waited this long? Did she fear to learn what had become of the child abandoned at the roadside to the mercy of the elements? Or maybe she never believed the child survived and wanted old scars to remain buried. What if in an attempt to find out she would discover I had been a meal for the dogs? Some things were better left buried. But some skeletons always broke out of the closet, in a strange manner demanding for justice?

Why did I have to be that child, now bed ridden, stained by own biological father and a dear husband? A child deserted by both biological and adoptive mothers? Why was my fate intertwined to this end, like something wrong had crossed my star of life?

These were endless questions I had to square out with, my mind subjected to vindictive trauma? Was there reason and purpose to live for if everything seemed star-crossed? Was there any appropriate reason for looking forward to tomorrow now that I was crippled by a person I dearly loved?

"How are you girl?" she always called me that.

"I am at your home where I want to learn how it had been to grow up around." At first, I laughed off the whole matter. Was she terribly guilty about her past? Was she catching up with a past she had deliberately knocked out of her chapter of life?

"Well, well, I wish you a lot of luck. Have you met Peter and Mongina? They are lovely angels?" I laughed encouragingly but my enthusiasm had gone and I was now nursing a different enemy. The recovery to normalcy and lack of appetite every instant I saw food. Not so for those who wanted to lay to rest their past ghosts.

"The place looks out of place but cool. I'll tell you after I've had it all, baby." She said this as if she knew my hesitant mind could never give her the answer she wanted. I wished her more luck and in fact forgot all about it.

It was about four days later when she made a spirited call and from her voice it was like something wrong was in the offing.

"What is it lady?" I asked laughing.

"I don't think it would be right to talk over the phone. I need to meet you at the hospital and explain things." I didn't press the issue. I had come to know Jemima well and I was to her a new daughter like she was a new mother to me.

She walked in one evening as it was raining, her hair covered in a black nylon paper bag and her coat drenched with the rain. After the pleasantries had been exchanged, she rushed into the topic. The way she held me and made me nuzzle into her bosom like a baby was sign something unpleasant was coming up. I bemusedly thought she would ask me to suckle the breasts I had foregone as a child but her face showed serious concern.

"We have found her."

 The news was confusing and my body language might have communicated the message.

"We found Luciana's body buried under the bricks that have been in the compound for the last twenty-five years."

I suppressed a cry. I didn't know whether to cry or be happy with the news on my long lost 'mother". I'd always been used with seeing Luciana alive, coming to cuddle me in her arms. Not dead? Why didn't I cry like I thought I should if I ever found Luciana? She could always be the missing mother in the core of my heart.

Jemima had visited our home to check on how it had been to bring me up. She wanted to pay tribute to a woman who had taken me up in a way to reconcile with her ugly past, the guilt of throwing away a child, to calm those daunting demons.

Peter and Mongina had welcomed her. They had met her and they knew who she was to me. And there was that soft spot they had for me. They took her around as she relived her missing gap in my life.

She wanted to see it all, to walk the same path my adoptive mother had done. She moved in and about "the palace", drinking in the sights and sounds and wondered why could a woman leave all this and simply disappear. She came to the bedroom and asked if they could open it. The two looked at each other uneasily but they didn't want to spoil the party for Nerina's mother- the gal whose company they had enjoyed more than any of Maina's children.

They somehow found the keys. The room was stale with dust and cobwebs choking the window grills, the corners and some screen of un-tampered dusty hang everywhere you touched. She drew the curtains and opened the windows to allow in the light and oxygen.

And the two elements gushed in style. This was where Luciana had lived and planned how to bring up her family. This was the bed she had conceived in love and nursed her children. This was where her 'co-wife' she mischievously thought had done everything worth a woman her mettle.

The wardrobe, two walls covered on the top and with some lines and hooks for clothes now out of disuse. The safe, a cupboard on the wall, housing some contraption that was used to lock money away. She wanted to drink the same oxygen as her, to listen to her small yearnings, to relive her wholesome experience. She felt Luciana's presence, a voice talking to her, telling her how it had been. It was when Mongina who seemed so uneasy and stuck in one place started to protest, to sway her hands in wild agitation.

"Go away, Luciana. You can't accuse me of that Luciana. I've been faithful to you *mama*. It can't be! Nooooo!"

Jemima was paralyzed with shock when Peter rushed in and without ceremony held her.

"You didn't take your medicine, baby."

She pretended not to see it. Came in to assist but down in her heart she had witnessed something. She would love a repeat of the same when she would come with a video man. She down played everything and took it as a normal occurrence. The truth was about to be spilled and in a big way.

Two days later she was back with a cameraman and equipped to capture everything in film. Mongina who lived in an adjacent room was a bit uncooperative but they pretended to be fitting some new curtains which she was to help them fix. They got in and busied themselves on the work. As it had happened before, Mongina was stuck on the same spot and the whole drama as before began to unfold in their view. The argument with an unseen Luciana and then the pleading.

The cameraman went to work. She was hypnotized to the spot, blathering like someone possessed. She was going for her note book in the car, when she found Peter in the corridor with fresh leaves and animal dung and earth concoctions that he had sprinkled around the corridor. The first reaction was one of alarm, his mouth wide open as he thought of an excuse.

"I am helping her by Jove. I am innocent."

"What is it Peter? Helping who?"

His mouth hang open for some time, his jaws locking and unlocking.

"I didn't do it." He was trying to conceal the twigs behind him rather unsuccessfully, the smelly stuff dripping into his shoes and floor.

"I swear to God."

Jemima screwed up her face in a glare and took out her gun.

"Yeah, I know everything. Spill it."

The man fell on his knees. And confessed what he knew of Luciana's disappearance.

It had been a normal day and he heard the two women carrying out a heated argument and he came in to peep. It was something to do with money. He decided this was women's affair and spirited away only to hear a sudden loud cry that chilled his blood. He tiptoed back and sure enough lying on the floor was Luciana with a broken skull beside a round stone used for grinding.

Mongina's crying and helplessly wriggling her hands as she stood there like a naughty child that had broken a glass container. She regretted what had transpired. She had in a rage hit out at her mistress killing her instantly. He rushed forward trying to save her, resuscitate her but it was futile. He then realized to his horror he had touched the body. Wasn't there a popular believe that dying eyes captured images of the assailants? And the police would be dusting for finger prints. Who could believe he had no hand in killing her? Mongina's shock had reached another level. She was hysterical and saying she would say he had helped her kill her. There were wads of hundred bills beside the woman that Mongina picked.

He had to do something. He quickly rushed to the store and came across a tarpaulin that was now used for spreading grain and wrapping up the body together they bore it to an open hole dug next to the bricks and laid it inside. They arranged the bricks neatly on the top and rearranged the whole heap careful not to show any disturbance. Luckily nobody found them.

Then he remembered the money. What if they made it look like Luciana had ran away? This would account for the lost money and stop anybody looking within the homestead and discover their little secret. He asked Mongina to move fast, put on some of Luciana's dress get into a vehicle with a bag like somebody in a hurry and pretend to be on her way to Mvita. She did all this to the booking office and when she was sure some people had seen her clothes and heard of a woman traveling that direction she got into the ladies and changed into her normal clothes and traveled back home. Luckily again she was back home in time before they sent word to Maina that it looked like Luciana had ran away.

The man bought that and made a follow up and he confirmed that a woman of a given description had inquired of travel arrangements and could have left with some bus. With the body out of sight and the impression of running away created, the rest was to mourn Luciana. They really mourned her like everybody else. The police could have failed to piece the facts together because of the travel theory and the sorrowful state in the home enhanced by the devastating show by the faithful servants and her family. They glossed over it and expected things to sort themselves out in a family where the two wives always fought like big cats.

The two would have enjoyed the sudden fortune showered on them, money they wouldn't have earned in this home in a decade as combined salary. But Mongina began to hallucinate as her guilt conscience haunted her and she would cry endlessly in the cool of the night and almost gave herself in for the act. He was told by a friend that there was a guy who could treat them to withstand the guilt and chase away the ghosts and they fell into this.

A similar amount of the money that they had taken from Luciana and more from the sale of an assortment of property went that route. The medicine man new a juicy prey when he saw one. He prepared his proper protective concoctions and it might have worked for them all these years and kept them safe until this Mvita woman with a more powerful magic, as they reasoned, had come around and spoiled their party. Peter had been trying to calm the ghosts and the magical influence of Jemima when she had caught him red handed. Their goose was cooked.

"I am finished mama, Nerina. This woman has finished me and stolen me from my children and family. O God, where will I leave my children?" That was how Peter wept blaming Mongina for everything.

The once weepy Mongina did not react and was very calm throughout the ordeal. Had she been masking her true character in the guise of being servile and humble? Was Peter really what he seemed to be, a humble spineless worker or there was more of them hidden in that cover of obeisance? It shocked everybody including the Mainas.

I could still remember that day we came home and found her devastated by the news of Luciana's disappearance. Had all that been acting? Not a single soul would have laid a finger of accusation on the two humble souls of Maina's clan!

The police and the villagers dug up Luciana and with specialized tests it was indeed her. An honorable woman sent to her earlier unmarked grave in a witless act of anger and buried with the conspiracy of her servants. The Maina family was there to witness the ugly scene in tears except me. Nobody wanted to tell me because they wanted me to heal first. Had they started to view me as an outsider? But I was their father's blood? They wanted me to worry about other things; my health.

The two 'lover birds', there was always something about them that I linked to romance. Or had it been a relationship of convenience, aimed at concealing the truth from the world? They were apprehended and became key witness to the inquest conducted by the State. Their conspiracy smacked of bizarre rites to commit each other to absolute secrecy. They were slapped with five counts of manslaughter, perjury etc.

Mongina was now behaving like a crazy woman but Peter was so remorseful and kept pleading he had behaved silly to save her skin. Was it an act of love? Whoever thought guys like Peter were simply stupid because they worked in the farm was silly. The donkey was an intelligent animal in spite of its beast of burden role, more intelligent than the horse and that is science for you. He had fooled everyone else with an unfathomable shroud of humility and secrecy that the police and our family could have second guessed forever.

"The donkey?" I burst out and Jemima curiously eyed me. I explained how I'd once tagged him so and she really laughed.

"This was one clever donkey, Nerry. Not the farting, wallowing, braying, jumpy and ugly skinned beast we all know." By the time she left she was still amused by this donkey idea of mine.

The discovery was an additional laurel to Jemima and would earn her a promotion. Perhaps, she was simply one lucky woman and I couldn't ask her to begrudge what she knew better to do. I also learned never to underrate any person for they could be the key to some mystery.

We hugged and the serious tears spilled for Mama Luciana. Jemima had paid back her debt to her in a special way. She was interred in an unparalleled ceremony in the village outside the 'palace' in what was a grand gathering that individuals and government functionaries attended. And Jeffrey who had visited me in hospital had come for the ceremony and not to see me as he had said. Irene was with him in the USA and they were doing great.

I sat there long after she had left trying to piece the pieces together. Life was so mysterious and served you with the unexpected twists and turnings. Rodgers was yet to be seen with rumors that he was living in the Seychelles with Queen. Maina was done, his body growing weaker each day (was it Saarange's curse or taking too many risks than it was necessary?) while Hortenzia had grown hysterical with the knowledge she had been infected by the man she had snatched from another woman.

I had always believed that she was involved in Luciana's disappearance following her reaction on the same when we were helplessly crying. Still the image of the mourning Mongina was indelible, her misery at the unfolding and yet she was the mastermind behind it! Saarange was getting slowed by age and never moved beyond her homestead, tending to her vegetable garden, chicken and goats in her mumbling slow way as her sight was also failing.

And wonders never ceased. Madam Jane had told me that Mobisa had resigned from teaching because of poor health. His legs had lost their strength and he was bed ridden and could only use a wheel chair to move around. What had befallen him too? Life never failed to confound.

17

The vehicle came up close to the newly ramped verandah. The family house was under construction when Nixon attacked me with proceeds of our combined loan. It was a big thing with wide doors, an expanse living room, five bedrooms and three rooms on the top sitting on a walled compound with a simple space for playing and raising a garden. The plot was next to the tarmacked road of the town we had chosen for our home. While in hospital and with Nixon on the run my loving family had carried on with the construction and when they brought me here I was crying with joy.

The family trooped out from the other vehicles and formed a ring around mine and when the chair was unfolded, Pamela, Vega and my niece helped me get down to the seat. The spectators among them our new neighbors who had learned about me from the media clapped in approval. I placed my legs on the appropriate foot rests and they pushed the chair towards the door as I waved and beamed at them. This was a home I had dreamed of walking into with my two feet but now…The whirling bore me into the intestines of my home with my children running ahead to wait by the doorway in a circle and the moment I reached the doorway they burst into ululations and broke into a song.

"Happy birth day, dear mama." I was crushed by the beautiful and young lilting voices and as they steered me into the lounge balloons came floating towards me, light of different colors blinked on and off strategically in the room in harmony with bells that chimed. This was creative and as Pamela could have said it *"beautofool."* A terraced cake and plenty of candles were casting their simple flames of violet against the cream wall and the lettering on iced sugar with the orange, green and blue hues was splendid.

This was some coup since somebody had known my day of birth and I hadn't been told. I couldn't remember when I had celebrated such an occasion for what was there to celebrate in the roadside with the insects and ravages of weather. This was Jemima's hand at work. How could she celebrate that one act of stupidity of abandoning her bundle of *pain*, discovered in adulthood? Wasn't this a propitiatory act of shame coming this late in life?

The children were bubbling with excitement because they were acting at the bidding of their grandma, one who recognized them, one who wanted to spoil them after finding her long lost daughter.

Jemima had once even brought her husband and children to visit me at hospital. I could always call him Professor and it was never lost to me that his single act of sneaking us to his home had done more to me; had found the other part of me and given me a husband and at the same time lost him for me; found me a mother and helped me come out strong… There was so much I owed Prof and wished him great times and my 'brothers' also, the two charming *boys* now in high school.

It even worried me mom was still working as a police woman, and loved her work so much even with the imminent dangers. I had been pestering her to ask for earlier retirement and when she cracked Luciana's disappearance riddle, her desire was to scale more heights of her career with more gusto. I wondered why bother if this was what she enjoyed doing.

I negotiated my chair to the cake and blew out the candles to the celebrating cheers. Vega passed me a shiny knife and they guided my hand in carving it into neat pieces. Thunderous claps followed the act.

 That was how I was welcomed to my home in a wheel chair and I didn't have to pity my bad fate. Unlike Luciana, wasn't I still alive and could do a few things for my children? Life at home was falling more into step, thanks it was on holiday when my children were at home. They wanted to spoil me and I was getting accustomed to the rhythms of this life.

Two weeks later there was a knock at the door over the gaggle of cutlery and my children's voices as they ate their lunch; this was a neat family get together. They all had stories to tell, craze and amusing exploits in their schools. Omare could imitate every voice and walking mannerism of almost everybody around and I was afraid he could turn out to be one terrific actor. All this time was like they had never wanted to bring out the topic on their father. I thought this wasn't healthy and didn't know the best way of doing it either. One thing very clear was their father had done a terrible thing and apart from first hand witnessing the papers had had a field day:

A UNIVERSITY DON BATTERS WIFE.

A humble one rap that was almost hesitant sounded on the door. Omare dashed to find out and pulled it open. Standing there in an overcoat and a woolen hat pulled down his face was a man. Some gesture told me it was Nixon. He had been on the run from the police all this time.

I saw the boy turn around to us his face covered with horror and speechless as if someone had put a gun to his back. His siblings might have taken in the message as they formed a protective ring around me. And before us as Omare paved way, Nixon inched in, a haggard figure, unshaven and forlorn, his eyes blood shot and instantly fell to his knees. Who had done the same, -er, Peter before Jemima; a new fad, the guilty falling before women?

"Please forgive me for all that. I can't tell what happened. I don't know why I had to do it. Kindly, please forgive me. You are my family. Nerina, save me. Vega darling, Gym, Omare don't think I am mad. I've learned my lesson and I am to blame for all this."

He should have gone on and on wasn't it for the single act of Vega that equally shocked me. This girl was growing headstrong like her grandmother. She by passed her father and looked up to us all and said in words that didn't hide her animosity.

"Well, we have heard you dad. Get up and take a seat. But this is pay time and I've to call an arbitrator. Mom, tell me whether it's wrong if I do it and then I'll never stay in this home again with that sound of the wheel reminding me you're a cripple."

I winched at the way she said the last word. She eyed us and her face had the hard features of inside agitation. She dialed the cell phone and lifted it to her ear. It was on loud speaker mode. It was something she had planned well.

"Hello eagle, one, two, three, can I raise you?"

On the other end a voice laughed and jokingly answered.

"Well, what can I do you sweetie."

"The donkey is back. Read eagle, one, two, and three. The donkey is back." There was a cough at the other end. Was Vega becoming a cop like her grandma?

"Are you serious?"

"More serious than ever before."

"Help is coming pronto. Try to be calm and don't do anything rash, sweetie."

We all sat there as a family, speechless. A donkey? My little secret with Jemima was now unfolding before us, Vega being the key player. How could you call your parent to his face a donkey whatever his crime? Was this the defining factor for the new generation?

We didn't have to wait long before a vehicle drove into the compound and a dozen of policemen with guns at ready bounded inside. The silent Nixon rose and extended his hands to them. And as they let him away in handcuffs, he riveted his eyes on all of us, tears in big blobs gushing out of him. We heard the vehicle drive away and the ring of the phone startled us to our senses. Vega picked it.

"Thank you, sweetie. The donkey has been captured."

"Give your mom the phone."

I took the phone and failed to talk. "I know how you are feeling but rally the courage of your children. I am catching a flight so as to be with you baby." Jemima spoke so sweetly.

The four of us held hands and cried ourselves dry. We had never known how to deal with such a scenario.

"You know what mom; even if the enemy could be laughing at us, we know one thing. We are ready to face our nightmares squarely and have them solved. Nobody is going to hide from the reality." The surprise words came from Omare.

We looked up at him. I smiled and hugged him.

"That is true son. We are one goddamn close-knit family and we have to stay as one. Okay?" They nodded and piled out to the various parts of the home. Cleaning, cooking and washing. Grocery purchases were going to be done. I wheeled myself to the store. I had to sort the food out for them.